AF440174

In the Golden Mountains

Ashwini Shenoy

Published by "The Great Indian Book Tour"
Imprint : **Holistic Publishing**
www.tgibt.com
106/91, Ashok marg, Vijay path
Mansarover, Jaipur, Rajasthan-302020
Phone : +91-72400-68114
email : prashant@tgibt.com

Title : **In the Golden Mountains**

Author : **Ashwini Shenoy**

Copyright © **Ashwini Shenoy** 2024
All rights reserved

First published in 2024
First Edition 2024

ISBN : 978-93-93262-92-9

All rights reserved worldwide. No part of this publication Maybe reproduced, stored in or introduced into a retrieval system, or transmitted, in any form, or by any means (electronic, mechanical, photocopying, recording or otherwise), without the prior written permission of the Publisher. Any person who commits an unauthorized act in relation to this publication can be liable to criminal prosecution and civil claims for damages.

DISCLAIMER: This is a work of fiction. Names, characters, places and incidents are either the product of the author's imagination or are used fictitiously. Any resemblance to any actual person, living or dead, events or locales is entirely coincidental. The opinions expressed in this book do not purport to reflect the views of the Publisher.

CONTENTS

ABOUT THE AUTHOR

Ashwini Shenoy is an Indian Author and Freelance Blogger. In October 2019, Ashwini made her debut in the literary world with her novel, "Shikhandini – Warrior Princess of the Mahabharata," published by Leadstart Publishers. This extraordinary tale garnered critical acclaim from readers and book lovers worldwide, showcasing her talent for weaving together history, mythology, and strong female and transgender protagonists. Shikhandini was featured in many prestigious newspapers like The New Indian Express, The Hans and News Today, Chennai. Shikhandini's Tamil translation rights were sold in 2024.

Following the success of her debut, Ashwini released her second novel, "Gift of Life," in 2021, once again published by Leadstart. This heartfelt story captivated her readers, establishing her as a beloved author among readers who eagerly anticipate her future works.

In 2022, Ashwini embarked on a new creative endeavor by teaming up with Leadstart and Spotify India to launch her very own podcast, "Word by Word with Ashwini Shenoy." This podcast serves as a valuable resource for aspiring writers and seasoned authors alike, providing practical guidance and insights to improve their creative writing skills. In addition to her prowess as a novelist, Ashwini is a freelance blogger. Her popular blog covers a diverse range of topics, reflecting her versatility as a writer.

Ashwini penned her first story at the age of eight and has continued to explore and experiment across genres, drawing inspiration from an eclectic array of sources. Her unique talent lies in bringing underrated yet pivotal characters, whether real or fictional, into the limelight, inspiring readers with their captivating stories.

CONTACT:

E: ashwini.shenoy.m@gmail.com

I: ashwinishenoym

W: www.ashwinishenoy.com

INTRODUCTION

In December 2022, after a lifetime of believing I lacked the stamina or energy for a winter trek, I found myself in the enchanting village of Ranachatti, Uttarkashi, trekking up the lesser-known peak of Dinnala Bugiyal in the Garhwal Mountain Ranges. This transformative experience was all thanks to my adventurous husband, Karthik. The trek was not just a test of endurance; it was an exhilarating journey into the heart of nature.

In the serene embrace of the mountains, sipping ice-cold water from the Yamuna, savoring simple home-grown vegetables cooked over a firewood flame, and immersing myself in the soulful strains of Pahari folksongs, the idea for 'In the Golden Mountains' was born.

My primary source of inspiration was our trek guide, Aditya, a remarkable young man of twenty-one who had journeyed thousands of kilometers from his hometown to make Ranachatti his home. Aditya's passion for the mountains led him to add this hidden gem to Google Maps, unveiling its beauty to the world.

The characters in this book—Gitanjali, Rakesh, Gattu, and Girvesh— are lovingly inspired by the incredible family I stayed with during my time in Ranachatti. The house in the story is a heartfelt reconstruction of the cozy abode where I enjoyed hot rotis, piping hot rajma curry, and sweet Gur Chai in Gitanjali's kitchen, while listening to captivating tales of mountain life from Rakesh. Even Harper, the Himalayan sheepdog, is based on a furry friend we befriended in Ranachatti.

The experiences of the city dwellers in this story, as they reach the summit, are drawn from my own unforgettable nights spent sleeping under a canopy of stars and waking up to the golden peaks of Saptarishi, Bandarpunch, and Bali Pass.

This novel is my humble attempt to introduce Ranachatti to the world, often seen merely as a pitstop on the way to the famous Yamunotri yatra. It is also my heartfelt pursuit to preserve and share the precious memories of this magical place.

'In the Golden Mountains' is more than a story; it is a love letter to Ranachatti, a village that forever altered my perception of adventure and tranquility. I invite you to join me on this journey, to explore its hidden treasures,
and to fall in love with the Golden Mountains as I did.

PROLOGUE

The air was thick with anticipation as I stood on the edge of the cliff, the cold breeze sending a shudder through me. Abhay's voice echoed from below, his excitement contagious. My eyes were fixed on him, his joy radiating like the morning sunshine that made the Dawki shimmer, but my stomach churned with nerves.

"Just jump, Kshama! I'm here. I won't let you drown," he reassured, floating effortlessly in the icy water. The river stretched endlessly behind him, its crystal-clear surface hiding the depth beneath.

Taking a deep breath, I clutched my life jacket and closed my eyes, feeling the weight of the moment. A silent prayer escaped my lips as I propelled myself off the cliff. In the following seconds, I saw the water change from glittering to blue to darkness.

The world fell silent, and for a moment, it seemed as if time had stopped.

The impact with the water was swift and disorienting. Panic gripped me, and the freezing cold embraced my entire being. My heart raced, and the world beneath the surface blurred into darkness. Was this the end? Had my heart given up?

Then, a deafening roar filled my ears as I resurfaced. Everyone who had dived after me was now around me, shrieking and laughing in excitement. But my heart was hammering in my chest as my legs desperately searched for stable ground. I was at the mercy of the water. The cold had numbed my legs. My eyes refused to open.

Then, I felt someone firmly grasping my hand. A voice urged me to open my eyes, but I kept them closed. As I moved with his help, groping for the rocks with my free hand, I sensed the shore getting closer. With my body now only a few feet in the water, the cold clung to my skin, but my heart was no longer pounding in my ears.

I sat down on a rock and slowly opened my eyes, hoping to see Abhay's mischievous grin at my baseless fear. Reality crashed down on me – the man who had rescued me wasn't Abhay but a kind stranger. He waved at me and then went back into the water.

Panic surged as my eyes darted around, desperately searching for Abhay's familiar face. With each passing minute and the decreasing number of divers, a sinking realization gripped me – Abhay was nowhere to be found. He had left.

The fear of once again losing someone I deeply loved clawed at my chest, and the icy water beneath seemed warmer than the dread that enveloped me.

PART 1

CHAPTER 1

Present Day, Ranachatti, Uttarakhand

Kshama woke to the subtle warmth of the rising sun on her face, which felt like a blessing on such a chilly winter morning. She contemplated getting out of bed, whose warmth seduced her to linger a bit longer. She picked up her cellphone from the bedside table and groaned at the calendar. It was Saturday – the day she ran her errands, cleaned the house, bathed Harper, and accompanied Gitanjali to the grocery store or Amruta to the Barkot market.

In the evening, as the temperature dropped and the sun hid behind the mountains, Kshama sat down to work on her latest travel post that would go live the next morning. For a few years now, this had been Kshama's life – organized, scheduled, and monotonous – a stark contrast to the spontaneous and adventurous life she had lived not very long ago.

But today, Kshama would have to set aside all her errands and make her way to the Apna Travels office in Dehradun to meet Prajwal, the owner of the travel agency. The six-hour journey to the once scenic but now bustling city felt both physically and mentally exhausting. For as long as she could remember, Dehradun had always held a bittersweet significance for her. It served as a reminder of the first time she had taken the route from Dehradun to Ranachatti seventeen years ago, armed with little money, a bag containing all her worldly possessions and a million memories. Dehradun was a place that evoked a foolish yet undeniable sense of hope every time she visited. After all, it was where she had found the purpose of her life. It was where she had learned to love again. It was where Abhay lived.

Kshama was now thirty-four, twice the age she was when she had first moved to Ranachatti. She had lived in the little Pahari village for half her life and all of her adult life. Sometimes Kshama worried if in a few years, she would lose her childhood memories and the people who were a part of it. Their faces were already a blur.

On special days like her brother's birthday or parents' anniversary, Kshama attempted to resurrect their faces, the warmth of her childhood home, and the idyllic village she had grown up in, through art. She was not an artist, and her amateur sketches consistently fell short of encapsulating the true essence of her lost past. Seventeen years was a long time. Enough to forget things and forgive people especially when you had nothing to remember them by – no pictures or heirlooms. Not even a lingering scent or a faded letter.

Kshama had half a mind to cancel the meeting with Prajwal and sleep in. But Amruta had said it was important and insisted that Kshama accompany her. Also, it had been months since she last visited Brij Vatika. Maybe her absence had softened Abhay a little, she foolishly hoped.

Wrapping a thick shawl around her shoulders, Kshama walked to the living room and found Harper eagerly waiting for his breakfast. She patted his head and entered the kitchen. Harper followed her, wagging his tail and sitting down at the threshold of the kitchen. Kshama poured food into his bowl and placed it at the regular spot by the side of the main door. Harper gobbled up the food quickly.

Kshama's cottage, Saanidhya, was a modest duplex with two bedrooms, a living room, a kitchen, and a verandah. It featured a sloping roof to withstand heavy snowfall during winters, and sturdy wooden beams supported the structure. The open space around the house served as a playground for Harper during the summer, and the apple trees, presently bare, added rustic beauty to the place. The house, not unlike others in the neighborhood, was crafted with locally sourced materials, particularly wood from the forests above, showcasing a harmonious blend with its natural surroundings.

In this regard, Ranachatti had not changed much in the last seventeen years. It was still a rustic little village isolated from the rest of the world by large mountains and dense forests. But now it had cellphones, television, and the internet which in many ways was both a boon and a curse.

After freshening up, Kshama made a cup of *Gur Chai*[1] and stood by the window watching the snow-capped mountains that glistened golden in the morning light –a sight she could never get tired of. Kshama took pride that her room had the best view in the whole of Ranachatti. She had planned it to be that way when she had decided to move out of Amruta's house and create her own haven. The house was at the very top of the village, a little speck of pleasant blue against the winter-clad forests. But her favorite part was waking up to the mountains. In a world that was changing so fast, these mountains were her constant.

Kshama walked to her study with Harper by her side. She sat at her desk facing the window and turned on her laptop. Harper plopped down at his usual spot next to her chair and quickly dozed off. She smiled at his drooping face, the flappy skin that covered his eyes, and the sagging belly – a harsh reminder that he was getting old and that she must cherish the moments she had left with him.

Kshama shook the thought away as she remembered she had to finish the article for her blog before leaving for Dehradun. Opening a fresh document on her laptop, Kshama wondered what she could write about. Her four-year-old blog was simply named The Indie Traveller, something she had started when she no longer had the desire or will to travel. It had begun as a journal to record her travel expeditions of the past decade and a half, hoping to reignite the travel spirit in her. Slowly, her reader base, drawn to her writing style and storytelling, began to subscribe in hundreds and then thousands. Newspapers and magazines began requesting articles for their travel sections, and before she knew it, Kshama had become a travel writer with readers from around the world.

As she began typing, Kshama found herself describing the scene outside

____

[1]: Sweet milkless tea infused with jaggery

her window. There was something about Uttarkashi winters and the serenity that settled after the Yamunotri *yatra*[2] season ended. She made sure not to mention Ranachatti and its lesser-known peaks in her articles. It was her private haven that she wasn't quite ready to share with the world.

Kshama let the words fill the blank screen with love, warmth, and joy. Occasionally, she looked at the wood-carved world map on the wall. Little red flags were sprinkled around, showcasing the countries she had visited. The map gave her affirmation on days she felt unmotivated. It kept her sane from self-sabotaging thoughts. Sometimes, it even filled her with pride. At seventeen, even in her wildest dreams, Kshama would never have dared to envision a life where she had traversed more countries than her own age.

It was during mornings like these, as Kshama sat at her writing desk, that she found herself pondering the path she had chosen. What if the disaster had never struck? What if, in the aftermath, she had chosen to return to her hometown instead of forging a new beginning in Ranachatti? Where might she be now? Would she have ventured beyond the borders of her quaint village? To these questions, Kshama had no definitive answers, except for one. Given the opportunity, would she choose differently? Not a chance.

For the Pahari people who scaled mountains as part of their daily routine, the six-hour journey by road to Dehradun was a cakewalk. But for Kshama, who had first travelled this route carrying loss, pain, anxiety, and a tinge of hope, this journey always felt emotionally exhausting. Despite her reluctance towards the journey and the memories it brought along, Kshama had taken this route hundreds of times in the last seventeen years. The roughly 200km stretch that one had to make in a jeep, usually crammed with double the capacity, was the only way Ranachatti connected to the rest of the world.

An hour after passing through Barkot, Amruta fell asleep, her head resting on Kshama's shoulder. Kshama smiled and wondered what her life would

---

[2]: A spiritual pilgrimage

have been like had she never found Amruta. Amruta's carefree and no-non-sense attitude had kept Kshama sane during the worst days of her life. Amruta had shared everything with Kshama – her family, her home, even her clothes at one point in time - a girl she had barely known when they first met.

Despite the bittersweet memories the route brought along, Kshama always found herself mesmerized by the view. The road, adorned with serpentine twists and turns, revealed panoramic vistas at every bend. Lush valleys below stretched out like emerald carpets, dotted with tiny settlements that clung to the slopes, seeking solace in the embrace of the mountains.

Kshama watched the translucent Yamuna below maneuvering around gigantic snowcapped mountains, its surface glistening in the mid-morning light. As she listened to Jaunsari and Kumaoni songs that a little boy sitting in the front was playing on the Bolero's music system, her mind travelled back to the time she was first introduced to the native languages. *Kingari ka Jhala Ghughuti, Pangari ka Dala Ghughuti…*

The first time Kshama had heard her co-passengers talk in the language, she had found it foreign. Today, the folk songs that had accompanied her on hundreds of similar journeys had become the welcome sound to her home.

When the jeep dropped them at Dehradun, Kshama shook her head in disappointment. Dehradun now was very different from when Kshama had first visited it more than a decade ago. Back then, it had resembled Ruskin Bond's Dehra that she had grown up reading about. It was the master storyteller's vivid descriptions of Dehra's mountains, valleys, and forests, that had played cupid in Kshama's love affair with the mountains long before she had seen them for the very first time. Today's Dehradun resembled Delhi in many ways, struggling to keep its charm and elegance while people turned everything green into gray in the name of development. Every time Kshama spent a day in Dehradun she longed to run back to unchanging Ranachatti and recover in her lap.

Squeezed between a cheap motel and an old grocery store in Paltan Bazaar, Prajwal Rana's travel agency, Apna Travels with its clean, artistic welcome sign stood out like the proverbial sore thumb. Kshama had first visited the agency fourteen years ago accompanied by Amruta who had wished to get out of her house and away from Gitanjali, her nagging mother, for a few weeks.

Amruta, then twenty-two, was considered old enough to get married. But she wished to work and find financial stability first – a strange concept in Ranachatti then and now. Back then, every day their wooden house had echoed with words of anger, frustration, and misunderstanding between Amruta and Gitanjali. During the winter break that year, Gitanjali decided Amruta would spend a few weeks with her paternal grandmother who lived with her younger son, Prajwal in Dehradun. She hoped that Grandmother Yamuna Devi would draw some sense into her naïve daughter and educate her on the importance of marriage in a woman's life. Grandmother Yamuna Devi did educate Amruta. Just not the way Gitanjali had imagined.

When Amruta requested Kshama to join her, she had first hesitated, wondering if Prajwal and his mother would be okay with her intrusion. Amruta had finally managed to convince Kshama when she hinted at a work opportunity at Prajwal's agency. Kshama who had by then lived in Ranachatti for three years doing odd jobs jumped at the prospect of finding something stable and interesting.

Soon, Amruta and Kshama joined him at the agency. At first, they observed, then helped him maintain ledgers and accounts. Amruta who had just begun exploring the world of web designing offered to create a website for Apna Travels which Prajwal gratefully accepted. After spending two months at the agency and understanding how the travel agency worked, Kshama who had always dreamed of traveling, found her calling. When she expressed her desire to work with him, Prajwal who was short of staff at the moment, decided to give her a chance. Amruta on the other hand, inspired by her grandmother's romantic tales, had found her calling in Rishi, Prajwal's neighbor. Apna Travels did not get its website that year.

Prajwal Rana was a man of ambition. He had dedicated his entire life to Apna Travels and taking care of his ailing mother. He had remained unmarried for the sake of both. A simple man of the mountains who one day, at only twenty-four, decided to leave timeless Ranachatti and the mountain life, to find something more adventurous and exciting. After living in several states of North India and Nepal, working for different travel groups and agencies, Prajwal decided to open Apna Travels which would offer affordable, and customized tour packages across North India.

For six months, Prajwal was kind enough to let Kshama accompany him on every trip across North India and realizing her potential trained her. Amruta declined the offer. As the business boomed, Prajwal decided to try his luck conducting package tours in South India known for its rich cultural heritage, stunning natural beauty, vibrant festivals, and delicious cuisines. Kshama's fluency in Kannada and English helped greatly in this regard.

Kshama's storytelling ability attracted tourists who seemed to enroll for the tours more willingly. Kshama read extensively in advance before visiting any new place. Upon reaching the place she mesmerized the tourists with the less-known facts and tales related to the place. Within a year, Kshama who was only twenty three had developed the confidence to independently conduct tours across the country. Amruta and Rishi had married by then and moved to Delhi where he had secured a job. With Amruta gone, Kshama found it easier to stay away from Ranachatti.

Presently, walking into the agency, Kshama and Amruta were welcomed by Prajwal's boisterous laugh. He hugged them both and offered them piping hot tea as they made themselves comfortable on the chairs across him.

"What did you want to talk about, *Chachu*[3]?" Amruta asked.

"I want you girls to know that despite the pandemic situation, our agency seems to be stabilizing. The number of travellers have been increasing slowly and data suggests that in the coming months they will multiply by many folds."

"People are tired of being cooped up in their houses for months," Kshama added. Prajwal nodded in agreement.

---

[3] : Paternal uncle

"We need to make the best use of these coming months. Try to attract as many tourists as possible. I could look into digital ads and sponsored posts," Amruta offered.

"I can help design new posters. We could post them on my blog and newsletters as well," Kshama added.

"And that is why I want my best girls to be by my side this season." Prajwal grinned as Amruta and Kshama began discussing their marketing and promotion plans.

"But there is something new I wish to try this time," Prajwal interrupted their spirited discussion. The girls waited for him to elaborate.

"Adventure trekking packages in the Himalayas."

"But those are already a rage," Amruta dismissed her uncle's comment, "Kedarkantha, Gulabi kantha and other peaks will be overflowing by the end of the year."

"Yes, that is why I think it is time we bring Dinnala Bugiyal on the map," Prajwal replied, "Kedarkantha and the other treks in the region have become very mainstream and commercialized. Trekkers are on a constant lookout for new places with difficult, less travelled trails. They don't want the entire trek to be planned out for them. They want to be surprised. They want to wander and explore. They want to remember the journey when they return home."

Kshama had thought about this before when the winterwear shops in Barkot had started putting up posters of organized treks to Kedarkantha, Bali Pass, and many others along the Garhwal mountain ranges in Uttarkashi. But she had decided against broaching this idea to Prajwal who she knew would push her into pursuing it.

Kshama had firsthand seen how less-known places in the hilly or rural regions had transformed for the worst when tourists began swarming in large numbers. The majority of these travellers were irresponsible and thoughtlessly littered and damaged these places. It is for this reason, Kshama had never introduced Ranachatti or Dinnala, the mountain peak above the village, in her blog or travel newsletter. There was also an irrational fear that if

Ranachatti – the starting point of Dinnala Bugiyal trek – opened up to the rest of the country, someday someone from her past would find her and her biggest nightmare would turn real.

"Dinnala might be a good option to start with this season. What do you say, Kshama?" Prajwal asked.

"I'm not so sure, Chachu," Kshama replied.

"Why?" Amruta asked Kshama.

"Ranachatti is home. It is our escape. Our constant in this ever-changing world. I don't want Ranachatti to become what Dehradun or Mussoorie has become," Kshama replied.

Kshama knew how naïve she sounded. Especially to Prajwal to whom this was about keeping his business running amidst high competition. She also knew the consequences of her decision. The upside was these trekkers, often city-dwellers exhilarated from close encounters with nature, paid the localities well in return for their hospitality. Could she deprive her villagers of this? Especially the women who were struggling to make ends meet in the off-season. Not to forget what the government would do to uplift these places once they were on the map. The last two years had been rough on the resilient villagers whose income had dropped drastically due to the pandemic.

The downside was that within a few years, Ranachatti and its peaks would no longer be unchartered territory and the trekkers would go looking for another unexplored place, leaving behind a trail of litter, tarnishing the once pristine environment.

"I understand Kshama. And I respect your thoughtfulness about Ranach-atti and its environment. But you must understand, Beta, if not you, someone else will. If not now, definitely in a few years," Prajwal replied.

"And not everyone thinks of the environment as you do. If you do it right, you might be able to protect Ranachatti and its forests while bringing in the business to help our people. You know better than me that they need this income during the off-season. With the increasing expenses in every area, Ranachatti and its people can't afford to remain the same," Prajwal added when he noticed Kshama was unconvinced.

"Okay… you think about it. If you feel this is unnecessary I will drop it completely. No hard feelings. But if you think you can give it a shot, I will let you decide everything. You can choose what places to expose, what route to take and what to keep hidden of your beloved Ranachatti. In fact, you could lead the trek. It is high time, you got back."

Kshama knew that Prajwal was trying to hit two targets with one arrow. He wanted Kshama to lead this trek not just to expand his business or bring Ranachatti into limelight but to also help her restart her life. It had been six years since Kshama had last led any trips. Without Abhay, travel meant nothing to her. Instead she had helped Prajwal with planning, budgeting and promoting trips and working on her travel articles. Kshama now wondered if it was really time to let go of the past and start afresh once again. It had been difficult the first time but now it felt impossible. Every time she thought of moving on, the void in her chest expanded, reminding her of its presence.

"I think Prajwal Chachu has a point. If we don't grab this opportunity someone else will and that someone may not think about Ranachatti and its people as much as you do," Amruta said as they left the Apna Travels office.

"I understand, Amruta. I don't want to lose the opportunity either. I owe it to Chachu. He has done so much for me."

"Don't worry, now. Let's go back tomorrow and think about it. I'm sure we will figure a way out," Amruta said grabbing Kshama's hand as they rushed across the street just in time for the traffic signal to turn green. Behind them a cloud of smoke and dust rose from the ground and settled on every surface.

"Shall we grab lunch at our favourite place? I'm dying to eat their *Chole Bature[4],*" Amruta suggested, smacking her lips.

---

[4]: A popular North Indian dish consisting of spicy chickpea curry (chole) served with deep-fried bread (bhature)

"I was thinking of…" Kshama hesitated. Amruta looked at Kshama's expression – a mixture of hope, pain and vulnerability.

"I think you should go. You'll regret it otherwise," Amruta said, "I'll wait for you at home."

Kshama smiled at Amruta gratefully. Amruta stopped a taxi and Kshama gave the driver directions to Rajpur Road. As the taxi neared her destination, Kshama's heart drummed in her chest and her palms began to sweat even in the chilly weather. Kshama had experienced more than her fair share of grief and loss but the fear of rejection she felt every time she travelled to Rajpur Road made her feel small and helpless.

The taxi dropped Kshama outside one of the many luxurious villas in the area. Surrounded by a manicured garden, cared for by a dozen workers, and run by a warm-hearted matriarch, Sumitra, the Brij Vatika Villa that was once the pride of the town, was now deemed cursed among the neighbours. Earlier, people of the town pointed at the house and explained its grandeur to outsiders whenever they passed by. Now they merely give a sympathetic look before rushing past it. Sumitra, once known for her exquisite taste in jewelry and sarees, her lifestyle, and her talent for running several successful businesses, had now resigned to become the primary caretaker of her only son, Abhay.

Taking a deep breath, Kshama walked to the front door and knocked. The house help let her into the living room. Everything was exactly as it had always been. Bright, squeaky clean, not a thing out of place. She sat down on the plush sofa waiting for Sumitra. This had once been Kshama's monthly ritual – spending an evening with Sumitra talking about food and travel.

"Kshama?" Sumitra's voice cut through the silence in the room. She walked with a warm yet half-hearted smile towards Kshama.

"Hello, Aunty," Kshama smiled. Sumitra embraced her. The duo sat in silence for several minutes. There was so much to talk about yet nothing enough to make their situation any better.

"I must admit I was almost relieved not seeing you here these last few months," Sumitra began. Kshama looked away.

"How is he doing now?" Kshama asked hopefully.

"He is the same, Kshama. Still not ready to see you," Sumitra's words stung but Kshama knew how much it was killing the old woman to say it.

"I'm sorry, Aunty. I did not mean to intrude," Kshama blinked back her tears, "I tried to stop myself. I really did. But it is not as easy for me to end this relationship as it is for him. I just can't give up so easily."

"I understand, Kshama. But you must also understand my situation. I can't force him to change his mind. Neither can I see you like this – looking for hope where there is none." Kshama had had this same conversation with Sumitra so many times in the past that she could now easily guess what Sumitra was going to say next.

"Abhay and I," Sumitra's voice came out hoarse this time, "I am grateful for your presence in our life, Kshama. I really am. But I can't let you ruin your life like this. You need to let go."

"Aunty…"

"No, Kshama. This cannot keep going. I let you do this for so many years against Abhay's wish. It's time you stop," Kshama was taken aback by the finality in Sumitra's words.

"I can't do that," Kshama replied, gathering the last bits of her self-esteem.

"He is never going to accept you, Kshama. You know him well enough to understand that. He is too proud," Sumitra said rising from the sofa. Kshama too stood up, wiping her tears.

"Kshama it pains me to tell you this. Abhay has asked me not to let you into our house again. He does not want to see you anymore. And I hope you will find enough kindness in you to not put me in this spot again. You must stop coming here," with that Sumitra walked to her room. The house help stood beside Kshama waiting to escort her out of the house.

As Kshama walked out of the house, realization dawned upon her. It was the end. She would never see Abhay again. She had lost the man who had healed her broken heart and taught her to love again.

He does not want to see you anymore. Sumitra's words ringed in her ears.

CHAPTER 2

Dehradun, 2013.

Co-organizing?" Kshama asked as she watched the burnt ashes drop from the *Agarbatti*[5] holder onto the wooden plank where Goddess Lakshmi and Lord Ganesh sat side by side. The strong fragrance of sandalwood circulating in the ill-ventilated room made her giddy. Outside a truck sped by, honking loudly leaving a trail of thick black smoke in its wait. Dehra was changing.

"Yes. He is a traveller and a business man. He has spent many years travelling to many countries, building contacts and understanding how tourism works differently there. Now that he is back in India, he wishes to invest in our agency. If things go well, he wants us to open a branch in Mussoorie," Prajwal replied as he stirred his afternoon tea. "He has a lot of plans and honestly, his enthusiasm is infectious. I think it will be good for our business, Kshama. But first, he wants to experience firsthand how we conduct our tours and what the customers feel about us."

"So, he is going to audit us," Kshama asked sitting down in front of him.

"Well… I guess you can say that. But he is a good friend. I promise you both will get along well."

"Chachu, you know I like to do things my own way. I don't want someone,

---

[5]: Aromatic incense sticks

especially a stranger, to interfere in my work."

Kshama watched Prajwal take a deep breath. She had worked hard to establish herself in this predominantly male profession. She was the only woman in and around Dehradun who organized and guided group tours across the country on her own. While there were a few well-known female tour guides, organizers, and travel agency founders in Delhi, in Dehradun, she was the pioneer. Over the past five years, she had gone above and beyond to help her customers, building a name for herself and for Apna Travels. It was only natural that she now felt apprehensive about a man joining her and potentially taking over.

"I understand Kshama. But Abhay's mother, Sumitra is a dear friend who took a big risk with her money when she decided to invest in this agency while it was still in its infant stage many years ago. She trusted me when my own family did not. Now when her son has come to me with a similar pro-posal, I cannot deny it. I hope you understand my situation."

Kshama thought about it for a long moment. Sumitra was to Prajwal what he was to Kshama. Had Prajwal not placed his trust in her years ago when she was a naïve, young girl, Kshama did not know where she would have been today. There were not enough ways to repay him. What he was asking of her was a very small favour, and had it been any other boss, it would have been an order.

"Okay, Chachu. I will let him tag along. I'm sorry, I did not understand your dilemma before," Kshama smiled. Prajwal nodded in appreciation.

"It's going to be just this one trip though, right?" Kshama asked as she stood up to make her way out.

"Well…" Prajwal began but trailed as he watched a tall figure appear be-hind the transparent door.

"I hope not…" the door opened and a voice boomed. Kshama turned around to see a tall man dressed in a black crewneck sweater and blue jeans – both doing a poor job of hiding his athletic body. The man appeared to be around her age or slightly younger.

"There he is," Prajwal stood up and embraced the man.

"Kshama, I want you to meet Abhay. My close friend, Sumitra's son and your travel partner for the upcoming second-innings trip." Abhay and Kshama shook hands and exchanged pleasantries.

"Second innings?" Abhay asked raising his eyebrows, "I thought it was a honeymoon tour to Goa." He winked at Kshama earning a glare. His gaze shifted to Prajwal who shook his head in warning.

"Sorry," Abhay cleared his throat.

"It's a group of retired bank officers with their families. It's a five day trip to Goa, mostly the North and we will explore heritage sites and temples," Kshama smiled widely, "Still interested in joining?"

"Of course! I have always wanted to see Goa beyond the beaches and booze. I think it is a wonderful idea. Do you have the itinerary yet?" Abhay asked while Kshama tried to ignore the hint of an accent in his speech that sounded fake.

"Kshama is still working on it. But the places she has chosen and the events planned are unique and perfect for the group," Prajwal replied.

"Great! I too have some places in mind. We can work on the itinerary together," Abhay said making himself comfortable in Prajwal's office. Kshama narrowed her eyes at Prajwal who promptly looked away.

In the coming weeks, Kshama and Abhay met several times at Prajwal's office to discuss and finalize their plan, working on the granular day-to-day details and the finances involved. Much to Kshama's dismay, Prajwal had briefed Abhay about how the last two senior citizen trips had received negative or, at best, neutral feedback. This was a significant concern for Prajwal, as he feared the negative feedback would jeopardize Apna Travels' opportunity to serve the annual sponsored trips for employees of many banks and government organizations.

This time, in particular, was important because a senior retired officer of a Nationalized bank was joining the trip. His feedback was valuable in deciding if his ex-colleagues and juniors would also opt for Apna Travels package tour for their trips.

After every meetup, Kshama returned home feeling exhausted. Abhay challenged her every decision and had an alternative to her every suggestion. Sometimes she wondered if he did it just to annoy her. He often pointed out that she was repeating the same mistakes that had been done in the last two trips. It irked Kshama, partly because Abhay had not even been a part of those trips and partly because he was stating the truth.

But Kshama's ego refused to admit it. Abhay's opinions based on his extensive travel experience with many different agencies, made Kshama feel inadequate. Sometimes she raised her voice just to exert her authority but Abhay's calm demeanor only made her feel worse. On rare occasions, Abhay too shot back which made Kshama feel triumphant. Whether the goal was to exert dominance or simply break his calm, nonchalant attitude, she did not know. When their discussions repeatedly turned into heated arguments, Prajwal politely asked them to meet elsewhere.

After that, every alternate weekend, Kshama travelled from Ranachatti to Dehradun and met Abhay. Sometimes Abhay visited her and they discussed their plan in a small restaurant in Barkot. Public places made it hard for them to argue openly and the disagreements seemed to resolve faster.

During one of their conversation, Kshama learned that Abhay was two years her junior. After which, she found it even more infuriating when he disagreed with her. She knew it made no sense. She did not believe in ageism. She herself had challenged many of Prajwal's ways of dealing with customers. He was her senior not only in age but experience as well. But there was something about Abhay that got on her nerves.

Abhay had travelled more, was well-educated, and had lived in places like Mumbai, Bangalore, and even London. She also learned that his accent was not fake. It had blended into his speech after living in London on and off for the most part of his adult life.

"Why did you return back to India? That too Dehradun?" Kshama asked one day.

"Why do you say it like Dehradun is a bad place?"

"Well, it's certainly not what it used to be," Kshama replied. Abhay nodded in agreement.

"I guess, I wanted to come back and do something for my country. Contribute to its progress. You know like Mohan Bhargava in *Swades*[6]," Abhay feigned sincerity. Kshama rolled her eyes.

"Mohan Bhargava in Swades was a scientist."

"Do you mean only scientists and people from serious professions can be patriotic?" Abhay pretended to be hurt by Kshama's words. Then he broke into a grin.

"Okay, Okay. I came back for Ma. She is getting old and has been feeling lonely. I am the only remaining family she has. Ma expressed how tired she was of doing it all on her own and was thinking of handing over our business to someone else. When I completed my course in London and everyone was talking about entrepreneurship and being your own boss, I realized there was no point in handing over my family's business to someone else and starting anew." This time Abhay's smile was genuine. His words stuck a chord in Kshama as memories of her relationship with her own mother resurfaced.

"You know, I lost my father when I was twelve. After that, it has just been me and my mother. She is my best friend and my biggest inspiration. Had she not taken father's place and prevented the business from crumbling, I don't know where I would be now." Abhay's words made Kshama wonder if she had misunderstood Abhay's attitude towards her as signs of patriarchal behavior.

"What about your family? Are you close with your mother?"

Kshama looked at Abhay for a long moment. Over the last several meetings, intentionally or unintentionally, the two had learned many things about each other – likes, dislikes, opinions, values and experiences. Yet, Kshama had never revealed anything about her buried past. Other than Amruta, no one knew who Kshama had been before she moved to Ranachatti. It was best if Abhay too did not know of it.

---

[6] Bollywood film focusing on a NASA scientist's journey back to his roots in rural India.

"I'm an orphan," Kshama said without meeting his eyes.

"Oh, I'm sorry, Kshama," Abhay said softly placing his hand on hers. Kshama did not pull her hand back.

"So, Prajwal Uncle tells me you were only twenty-one when you decided to join him. He also told me you are the first woman travel organizer and guide in Dehradun. You know, I have always found it inspiring to see women make their own mark, especially in a country like ours where women have to work twice as hard to reach half as far." Kshama smiled as she listened to Abhay's honest words. There was no sign of flattery.

When they were done for the day, Abhay offered to drop Kshama to Prajwal's house where she would stay for the day. Kshama politely declined. Something in her told her it was best to maintain her distance from Abhay.

"C'mon, Kshama. I'm sure you can tolerate me for a few more minutes," Abhay insisted, lightly holding her elbow and guiding her towards his car. As Kshama sat in the car, she felt her senses tingle with Abhay's scent. What was wrong with her?

As they drove out of the crowded marketplace and passed by serene neighborhoods that were lined by tall trees, Abhay turned on the music. They drove in silence while Kshama tried to comprehend why she was feeling the way she was. For the most part of the drive, she kept her gaze outside the window but she could feel his eyes on her. Whenever she adjusted herself to look ahead, she found Abhay shift his gaze and suppress a smile.

After what felt like hours, Abhay stopped the car in front of Prajwal's house. Kshama thanked him and got down.

"By the way, Ma insists that you come home on the last Saturday of the month. It is her birthday and we celebrate it with a small Pooja followed by dinner every year. I have already informed Prajwal. Please join us. She will love it," Abhay looking outside the window. Kshama frowned and began to protest but Abhay cut her off.

"Don't worry she won't try to fix us together or something."

Before Kshama could respond, Abhay grinned at her and drove away.

Kshama stood there a moment longer wondering. What the hell did he mean?

For as long as Kshama could remember, she had not tried to dress well for any occasion. She chose comfort over fashion and often found herself wearing loose trousers and sweaters. Even during the festivals, she let Amruta or Gitanjali decide for her and wore heavy, uncomfortable attire for their sake.

But now as she looked into the mirror, she could not help but see herself from Abhay's eyes. It was as if a part of her mind actually cared to look good for him. It scared her. These emotions stirring within her were akin to plunging back into the deep waters after surviving a near-drowning experience, a mixture of fear and exhilaration.

You're not a teenager, Kshama. Get a hold of yourself.

Kshama was dressed in a simple collared blue Salwar Kameez. Her curls loosely hung over her shoulders and a stone *Bindi*[7] sat on her temple. With a tissue in her hand, she contemplated removing her *Kohl*[8] and lipstick, not wanting to look like she had dressed up for Abhay. Over the last several meet-ups, not once had she applied makeup or dressed in anything other than her usual sweaters and trousers. If she made an effort to look nice today, Abhay would definitely notice. Did she want that? On the other hand, Kshama did not want to be underdressed for the party knowing the guests would all be high-profile people.

A soft whistle behind her made Kshama wince. She turned around and crossed her arms defensively as Amruta, standing at the door, grinned.

"You look nice, babe," she said plopping on the bed, "Let me guess. Date night with Abhay?" asked Amruta settling on Kshama's bed. Kshama reminded herself to change the spot in the garden where she kept her spare key.

---

[7] : Ornamental mark worn on the forehead

[8] : Traditional eye cosmetic

Every time after an exhausting day meeting Abhay and arguing over every aspect of the impending trip, Kshama vented her frustration to Amruta. Who after the first two times had declared that Abhay annoyed her because he was attracted to her. Kshama had dismissed the Kindergarten norm and stopped sharing details about her meetups with Abhay to Amruta.

"His mother's birthday lunch," Kshama replied, softly wiping the lipstick off her lips so that only a dull hint of the colour remained.

"Different names, same game," Amruta rolled her eyes, "He knew you would refuse to go on a date with him so he came up with the excuse of his mother's birthday."

"Why are you here?" Kshama asked annoyed.

"Ma asked me to help you get ready. She was worried you would attend the party in your usual clothes and miss the opportunity of making a good impression."

"Good impression- " Kshama's eyes widened, "What did you tell Gitanjali *Masi*[9]?"

"Well-"

"Amruta…"

"Okay. I'm sorry but she had not spoken to me properly ever since I told her about the divorce. I missed talking to her and sharing juicy gossip. So when she heard about your meetings with Abhay from Chachu and could not handle not knowing what was happening between the two of you, she reached out to me."

"And you decided to fan the spark…"

"I'm sorry," Amruta pursed her lips not really apologetic, "But is it really that bad? I can clearly see something is going on between the two of you. Agreed that I have met him only a couple of times but he seems like a good man. The twinkle in his eyes, when you are around, says a lot about how he feels about you."

---

[9] : Maternal aunt

Kshama took a deep breath and shook her head. She had no answer to Amruta's questions. "Kshama, it's been more than fifteen years. For how long are you planning to hold on to the past? You don't meet men like Abhay very often. Don't miss this opportunity to start something beautiful because some boy in the past did not see your worth. You need to stop punishing yourself and take a second chance."

Kshama did not respond for several minutes.

"How do you do this, Amruta? After all that you've been through, you still haven't lost faith in love," Kshama asked as she sat down next to Amruta.

Amruta had left behind everything for Rishi. At twenty two when she married Rishi against her parent's will and decided to leave Ranachatti, she had believed their love would be enough. The arguments and prolonged silences had begun only a year later. The second year, Amruta had come to live with Kshama for two weeks before Rishi came to take her back. This happened a couple of times in the following years and during one such stay, Amruta had managed to get Gitanjali's forgiveness for marrying against their will.

When Gitanjali learned about Amruta's strained marital situation, she suggested an age-old remedy: having a child that would foster a stronger bond between them and make it more difficult to separate. Although this advice seemed illogical to Kshama, Amruta, who was still deeply in love with Rishi, believed it was the right course of action. However, the mounting stress and recurring disappointment month after month ultimately shattered the remaining threads holding their dwindling relationship together.

"Kshama, today Rishi and I might have separated. But I will never regret falling in love with him. It's the best feeling – being loved and cared for."

"Why then…"

"Rishi is a good man. He always treated me right. But he is still tangled in his conservative roots. After the initial spark died, I realized his goodness of heart was not enough for me. I valued my freedom more than our relationship," Amruta replied. Kshama nodded in understanding.

"Kshama, you must promise me to let your heart decide for you. Give Abhay a chance if he takes the first step. Don't be afraid just because some moron took you for granted a million years ago."

On reaching Dehradun, Kshama stepped out of the jeep and thanked the driver, who had become a familiar face during her many trips between Dehradun and Ranachatti over the years. She hailed a rickshaw and made her way to Prajwal's house, spending the afternoon there. In the evening, Prajwal returned from the agency, and together they headed towards Abhay's house.

As Prajwal maneuvered his car out of the bustling market area, entering Rajpur Road and then into a tranquil neighborhood adorned with grand mansions and elegant villas, Kshama's nerves escalated. Suddenly, she found herself questioning whether her attire was suitable or if she would be the only one dressed modestly amidst a gathering of affluent and fashionable individuals from Dehradun's high society. She glanced at Prajwal, who appeared as composed as ever.

It was natural for Prajwal to feel at ease. He had spent his entire adult life among these people, boasting a thriving business and a diverse range of travel experiences that made him an intriguing personality. On the contrary, Kshama felt like a fraud who had nothing to offer. She pondered how she would introduce herself if prompted to do so. She certainly couldn't delve into her past or talk about her family. What would people's reactions be if they discovered she was an orphan, who had relied on the generosity of Amruta's family for many years until Prajwal decided to give her a chance?

Kshama couldn't fathom what led Amruta to believe Abhay would have any interest in her. Abhay held a Master's degree from a premier institute in London, while she didn't even have her twelfth-grade marks card. Abhay was not only handsome but also affluent, whereas Kshama saw herself as neither. Abhay lived in this mansion, surrounded by maids and servants. She lived by herself in a wooden cottage at the edge of a forest.

As Prajwal drove through the gates of Brij Vatika, revealing a beautiful white villa surrounded by a meticulously maintained garden, Kshama realized that coming here might have been a mistake. She feared becoming a subject of ridicule and suspected Abhay's intention behind inviting her to the party. It was to assert his social status, whether to impress or intimidate her—she couldn't be certain. Above all, Kshama feared getting her heart broken again.

As Kshama and Prajwal stepped into Abhay's house, Kshama was taken aback to find only a small gathering of people in the living room. Seated gracefully on an antique-looking armchair was a woman in her early sixties, radiating an air of wisdom. Flanking her on either side were two other women of similar age. Prajwal proceeded to introduce Kshama to the three women. The woman in the middle, as expected, was Sumitra – Abhay's mother and Prajwal's old friend. The other two women were her friends – Julia and Rama. All the three ladies were dressed in simple yet elegant silk sarees with intricate, expensive jewelry.

Kshama exchanged pleasantries with the women and sat down on the sofa opposite them while Prajwal proceeded to meet the two men who stood in the balcony, smoking. Kshama guessed them to be Rama and Julia's husbands.

A few minutes later Abhay descended from the stairs and extended a warm welcome to both of them. He was dressed in a suit, had a light stubble and his otherwise unruly hair was combed back. It made him look older – more mature and serious. He shook hands with Prajwal and pleasantly surprised Kshama by giving her a quick hug.

With the realization that no more guests were expected, Kshama felt a sense of ease settle within her. The lunch, crafted to Sumitra's preferences, took on an intimate atmosphere. Sumitra, with warmth in her eyes, expressed her delight at Kshama's presence. "I'm so glad you came, Kshama. I've heard so much about you." Kshama wondered if Sumitra had heard about her from Prajwal or from Abhay.

"I had wanted this to be a small get-together. To be honest, I didn't even want to celebrate this day at all. I sometimes feel I'm too old for such festivities. But Abhay wouldn't listen," Sumitra shared with a chuckle, "So, I eventually agreed, but on the condition that he could only invite few of his close friends. Otherwise, our house would be overflowing with guests by now." Sumitra laughed heartily at the thought.

In that moment, Kshama's heart leaped inside her chest. Abhay had invited her as one of his close friends. Tearing her eyes away from Sumitra, she locked gazes with Abhay, who was already looking at her. A subtle smile passed between them.

A few minutes later Abhay's other guest arrived and Kshama found her heart drop. A young woman, possibly in her mid-twenties, walked in and everyone in the room turned in her direction. She was slim, stylish, and walked with an air of supremacy. Kshama did not have to ponder much to guess her profession – she was either a model or a budding actress.

Abhay walked to greet her at the entrance and the two embraced each other for a long moment. The duo walked together closing the distance towards Sumitra. Kshama felt a pang of jealousy as she observed the effortless chemistry between the two. The young woman embraced Sumitra and they spoke for several minutes before moving around to greet the other guests. Everyone seemed mesmerized by the girl's presence.

Kshama placed her spoon in the bowl of half-eaten ice cream and tried to smile as Sumitra walked up to her and introduced her to the young woman – Prachi who as guessed was a model, soon to debut in a Bollywood movie. Kshama realized she was the only one there who did not recognize Prachi.

An hour later Prajwal suggested that it was time to leave. Kshama was more than ready. Sumitra called for Abhay who excused himself from the other guests and appeared before Kshama. He smiled at her but Kshama pretended to not notice which made him frown. He escorted them to their car and when Prajwal turned on the engine, Abhay peeped into the passenger seat window.

"I hope you had a good time," Abhay said. Kshama smiled in response and thanked him half-heartedly.

Kshama slept fitfully that night unable to comprehend her feelings. How had she fallen into this trap again? Had she not learned anything from her past?

As the first sunlight streamed into the room, Kshama made a decision. She would keep things professional with Abhay for the next two weeks, until the Second Innings trip ended. After that, she planned to talk to Prajwal and make sure Abhay wouldn't join her on future trips. Kshama hoped that with time, her feelings would fade, and everything would go back to normal.

During the next two weeks, Kshama and Abhay met only once, which, upon Kshama's insistence was scheduled at Prajwal's agency. If Abhay had sensed her hesitance in meeting him like before, he had not expressed it. It made Kshama wonder if everything she had felt between them was in fact just in her head.

On reaching Goa, the group of fifteen – six senior couples and three septuagenarian women who were childhood friends – were picked up from the airport in a Volvo bus and dropped off at the hotel where they were to rest for the day.

The tour began the next day when the group embarked on their journey to explore the temples in North Goa. Their first stop was the magnificent Mangeshi Temple, known for its stunning architecture and spiritual significance. Kshama, with her deep knowledge of the temple's history, tried to impress the customers by narrating captivating tales and anecdotes about the deities worshipped there but it was Abhay's charismatic presence and infectious sense of humor that the tourists seemed to be interested in.

Next, they visited the serene Shantadurga Temple, where the group marveled at the divine ambiance and sought blessings from the goddess. This was followed by a visit to Ramnathi Temple where the group had their lunch and then continued their visit to all the surrounding temples until sunset.

By the end of the day, Kshama felt sidelined. No one seemed to be interested in the information she had prepared about the history or cultural significance of these temples. Abhay on the other hand had become the heart of the group. His humorous remarks and playful interactions with the tourists brought smiles to their faces and fostered a sense of camaraderie within the group creating a lasting impression on the senior couples and the septuagenarian women, especially Rajashri, who found his stories and attentiveness endearing.

On day two, the group visited the Basilica of Bom Jesus followed by Archaeological Museum and Portrait Gallery and then Reis Magos Fort where the group almost left behind Kshama, lost in their childish games thanks to Abhay's silly yet amusing ideas of entertainment. Luckily, the bus driver reminded everyone of the missing guide and Abhay promptly located Kshama and brought her back.

For the rest of the day, this incident became a source of amusement. They playfully teased each other, reminding everyone to stay close and not wander off, especially when Abhay was about to share another intriguing tale. Although irked and disappointed, Kshama managed to feign humor and half-heartedly joined in the laughter.

In the noon when they stopped for lunch, Kshama heard the women talk in the washroom.

"Abhay is doing a great job. I can't remember the last time I had so much fun on a package tour."

"I agree," another woman added. "But I wonder what the girl's role in all of this is. I mean, he can clearly manage the entire trip on his own."

"Maybe he is training her," the first one replied, "Apna Travels is doing well now, so they might be hiring new guides."

"Hmmm… maybe," the second one said, "But I don't see how she is going to become anything like Abhay. Some qualities are ingrained. You can't teach people to be jovial and fun."

The day ended with a stroll through Fontainhas - Latin Quarter in Panaji, known for its well-preserved Portuguese-style houses, narrow streets, and vibrant colors. Kshama was grateful to return to her room after that.

The next morning.

"What do you mean we have to cancel Tambdi Surla?" Kshama asked.

"We have already seen so much of heritage sites and temples. I think we need to give the group some time to relax on the beach and enjoy a free day," Abhay replied sitting on Kshama's bed. It was the morning of day three and Abhay had arrived in her room unannounced asking for a quick chat.

"Are you saying, the trip has been hectic?" Kshama tried to keep the irritation out of her voice. It was clear that the group would agree to whatever Abhay suggested. In the last two days, Abhay had certainly become a favorite. One of them had said Abhay reminded her of her son while Rajashri– had said Abhay reminded her of her high school sweetheart.

"Well… yes," Abhay replied, "It would have been perfect for youngsters but these are senior citizens. One of them is close to eighty. I just feel we are focusing on covering too many places in less time and not giving enough time for them to make good memories."

"Abhay, this is my third trip with a senior group. I had planned the first one keeping their age in mind. The feedback I received was that there was enough time to cover several more places instead we chose to spend more time in one place in order to save money."

"I understand. But that is where customization comes into the picture. I'm sure not all seniors think the same way." Abhay's tone struck Kshama's already irritated mind as undeniably condescending.

"Fine! If you think you can do this better. Let's do it your way," Kshama said more harshly than she intended to. Abhay was taken aback momentarily.

"Why do you have to be like that? It's a team work. If I had to do it my way, I would not have come here to consult you," Abhay replied. Kshama narrowed her eyes, not falling for his charming words.

"Consult? Team work? Do you take me for a fool? Do you think I'm blind not to see how you are taking over everything? They seem to hardy notice I'm here."

"Is that what this is about? You being visible?"

"No…" Kshama turned away from Abhay and busied herself leafing through the hotel menu. Abhay stood up and gently turned Kshama towards him. Taking the menu from her hand, he placed it on the table and sighed deeply before speaking.

"Then what is it, Kshama? Why are you trying to pick fights with me at every chance you get? I understand this was how we started but I thought we had become friends," Abhay smiled, hoping for Kshama to soften, "These last two days I have seen nothing but coldness and indifference from you."

"Did I do something to upset you? Please tell me, Kshama," Abhay asked when Kshama refused to reply. A moment later, Kshama lifted her eyes and locked gaze with him.

"You don't understand, Abhay. You have everything – Family, money, education and travel experience. This job is all I have. I know I'm not yet as good as you're at winning over customers. But I'm trying. And your presence here worries me. I'm worried that I will lose the only good thing I have in my life."

The tenderness Kshama saw in Abhay's eyes made her regret her harshness. Kshama tore her eyes from Abhay and sat down on the bed looking outside the window. Kshama had never felt so vulnerable before. She had just shared her biggest fear with a man she had only met a few weeks ago. Abhay did not say anything for several minutes. They just sat next to each other trying to wrap their mind around what the other was feeling. After what felt like hours, Abhay stood up.

"I'm sorry, Kshama. I didn't realize how my sudden interference in your job might affect you. But I promise you've nothing to worry about. This is your trip and these are your customers. My intention was never to replace you," Abhay said softly, "When I first met Prajwal, the plan was to only be a part of this one trip. Just to get an idea of how things are done at Apna Travels. But when I met you and our spirited conversations began, I realized we make a good team and together we could expand this business. But now I feel I have overstepped."

"Trust me, you have nothing to worry about," Abhay repeated, "From now on this is going to be yours alone. I will not join you on any trips unless you want me to."

Abhay's words should have relieved Kshama of her worry. It is what she had wanted all this while. To be able to do things her way without any interference. Instead the thought of Abhay not being around in the future brought a sense of loss.

"Okay, if you're really that upset, I can leave now." Kshama realized Abhay was getting impatient. "You can finish the trip by yourself. But please don't be like this. Say something," Abhay added.

"Thank you," Kshama said after a long moment and hesitantly added, "But you don't have to leave."

"Are you sure?"

"Yes, I worry the women in the group might drop out if you leave," Kshama smiled but her smile did not reach her eyes instead tears that she had been blinking back throughout the conversation escaped, leaving a trail on her cheeks.

"Kshama…" Abhay held her hand. Kshama tried hard to break their gaze but failed to do so.

Suddenly the image of a seventeen-year-old girl experiencing love for the first time came to Kshama's mind. The feeling enveloped her like a delicate, fluttering butterfly taking flight within her chest. It was a sensation of pure innocence, untainted by the complexities of the world. But then an ominous silence settled around her and mistakes of the past came rushing towards her like a warning sign.

But before Kshama could pull back, she found Abhay's lips on hers. Her mind shut down and her body seemed to make decisions on its own. Her eyes closed and after a moment of hesitation, her lips moved in sync with Abhay's. Her hands found their way around his neck, while his strong arms held her against his body as though in fear of losing her. They stayed that way for what seemed like hours when the sound of a metal glass drop startled them out of their world.

At the door was Rajashri, eyes wide like buttons and an expression of disbelief on her face which slowly transformed into a mischievous grin. The metal glass continued to rotate on the floor, coming to a slow stop after a few seconds.

"You have broken my tender heart. I thought you were mine and only mine," The old woman sang and walked away in mock- anger. Kshama tried to hide her embarrassment but failed.

"I better go console her," Abhay said without meeting her eyes and rushed out of the room, a hint of a blush playing on his cheeks.

After breakfast, Kshama gathered the group together and conducted a vote. They decided to skip Tambdi Surla based on the majority. Surprisingly, she did not feel disappointed or hurt at the group's decision to skip the Mahadev temple, which was her suggestion, and choose Abhay's option of a jeep safari to Dudhsagar Falls. Somehow, Abhay's sensitive response to her concerns and the kiss, of course, had changed Kshama's perception towards him. Abhay, too, ensured that he did not sideline Kshama at any point.

On reaching Mollem village area, Kshama once again asked the group if any of them had any concerning medical issues that prevented them from taking the bumpy jeep ride. The three septuagenarian women – Rajashri and her friends decided to stay back at the hotel and visit the nearby beach. The rest of the group assured Kshama and Abhay that they were in good health and eagerly looking forward to the jeep safari to Dudhsagar Falls. With enthusiasm palpable, the group boarded the jeeps, ready for the exhilarating journey ahead.

As the jeeps navigated through the rugged terrain, a sense of adventure filled the air. The bumpy ride added an extra layer of excitement, and the travellers held on tightly, their anticipation growing with each passing minute. The journey took them through dense forests, offering glimpses of wildlife and the serene beauty of nature. The group marveled at the lush greenery, the sound of chirping birds, and the occasional glimpses of monkeys swinging from tree to tree.

As they approached Dudhsagar Falls, the distant sound of cascading water grew louder, heightening their excitement. The jeeps were parked at a designated area, and the group embarked on a short hike to reach the mesmerizing waterfall.

And there it was, Dudhsagar Falls, a sight to behold. The majestic waterfall, with its white milky (Hence the name) cascades plunging from a great height, left everyone in awe. The sheer power and beauty of the falls were truly breathtaking. The group found a spot to sit and immerse themselves in the mesmerizing views, feeling the refreshing mist on their faces.

"We need to talk about what happened," Kshama said taking a seat beside Abhay on a rock facing the mighty falls.

"What do you mean?" Abhay asked a smile playing on his lips. But Kshama's face was serious.

"Did it happen in the heat of the moment or…"

"Of course not. Kshama, I like you, and although I was not planning on it to happen so fast, I wanted us to become more than just friends eventually," Abhay replied, holding Kshama's hand in his but Kshama seemed unconvinced.

"Are you saying you never felt anything between us these last few weeks?"

"I don't know what I felt, Abhay. I'm very confused."

"Why?"

"Because of all the mixed signals?"

"Mixed signals?"

"Assuming we go ahead with this. What about Prachi?" Kshama asked unable to comprehend the overwhelming feelings. She knew she had to get everything straight before making any decisions. She could not afford to repeat the mistake the seventeen-year-old her had made.

"What about her?" Abhay looked confused and then his expression changed to shock, "Oh my God! Is that why you have been so distant from me ever since the party?" Abhay slapped his temple "Shit…"

Kshama turned towards the waterfall and waved at the seniors who were seated on different rocks and were posing for a photograph. One of them signaled for them to join, and Kshama gestured to wait a minute.

"Prachi is my childhood friend who visits us once a year on my mother's birthday," Abhay paused waiting for the 'once a year' bit to sync in. "She is special to my family because we grew up together and our fathers strived hard together against poverty during their initial years. Yes, it is true that Ma wanted us to get married but neither of us want that. She has a long way to go in her career."

"And you?" Kshama asked still not convinced.

"And me what?" Abhay's smile had disappeared and his words were laced with a hint of irritation.

"Why don't you want to get married to her?" Kshama asked brazenly, "I mean she is perfect in every way. I don't see why anyone, especially someone good looking and wealthy like you would choose me over her." Kshama knew she was pushing too hard, jeopardizing everything that could be hers. But she had to be certain about what was on Abhay's mind. She knew what her teenage-self did not. Love, though often portrayed as a selfless union, thrives on the intertwining desires and needs of two imperfect individuals. But what happens once the desires and needs are fulfilled?

"Because she is not you, dammit! Because I don't love her. I love you!" As Abhay's words reverberated merging with the symphony of the waterfall, Kshama's heart skipped a beat. Abhay himself stood stunned for a moment at his own revelation.

After what felt like an eternity had passed, Abhay shifted his gaze at Kshama, his eyes seeking a response. But the weight of his words hung heavy in the silence between them. When Kshama did not respond, Abhay walked away from the water into the mud road where the jeeps were parked.

Snaping out of the initial shock, Kshama followed him after quickly making sure the seniors were all seated and in no danger of slipping into the water and breaking a bone.

Kshama found Abhay inside one of the jeeps they had come in. She got in and sat beside him unsure of what to say. The word love should have made butterflies flutter in her stomach and her heart drum against her chest. Instead it made her anxious.

"I was attracted to you the moment I saw you in the agency. But I was sure it would pass within a few days. When I first heard about you from Prajwal, I saw inspiration in you and eventually a good friend. But it's these last few days, when you turned cold and distant from me, that I realized this was something more than friendship," Abhay turned towards Kshama not minding the tourists who gave them weird looks and held her hand, "Yes, Prachi is perfect," he said, "But she is not you."

The butterflies fluttered. Kshama stared at the man in front of her whom she had despised from the moment he had entered Prajwal's office. She had loathed his accent, his confidence and the effortless charm that seemed to draw everyone towards him. She hated it that he was secure in his personality while she struggled with hers. She hated it that he had no burden of the past to carry nor the necessity to prove himself.

But then she had found in him someone who challenged her not to impart dominance but because he considered her an equal, someone capable of holding her ground and standing up to what she believed was right. Kshama knew she would never fall in love with someone like she did all those years ago. She would never jeopardize her happiness or future for a man. But Abhay did not ask for any of that and she knew if she let him go, she would regret it.

So just as Abhay broke their eye contact and tried to leave the jeep, Kshama held his face and placed her lips on his. She placed her hand on his chest and felt his heart, like hers, drumming in excitement. A moment later, Kshama sensed his smile against her lips.

That night, sleep eluded Kshama as she found herself tangled in a web of emotions. Once more, after what seemed like an eternity, an inexplicable warmth enveloped her mind. Her past, shrouded in fog, appeared to fade away, making room for Abhay and the promise of a shared future. Excitement and anticipation danced in her thoughts, yet they were accompanied by a subtle undercurrent of fear. The fear of losing Abhay, of relinquishing a carefully guarded independence in the pursuit of happiness.

For almost seventeen years, Kshama had shielded herself from these kinds of emotions, building a protective barrier around her heart. Yet, Abhay had skillfully broken through, stirring up feelings she thought were long gone. Now, she was caught between the excitement of a fresh start and the worry of potential heartache.

As she tossed and turned in her bed, she wondered if Abhay was also feeling the same. There was only a thin wall separating the two. If she pressed her ear to the wall, she could hear him move around. She got up from her bed and poured a glass of water. She shrugged and walked to the wall and pressed her ear against it. Silence. He must have fallen asleep, she thought.

When sleep evaded her for another hour, Kshama decided to go out for a walk and calm her mind in the cool December air. Outside, the crickets chirped, piercing the silence of the night. The guards at the entrance were asleep. A stray dog stirred from her sleep and looked up at Kshama but did not move, mindful not to disturb her sleeping puppies. Kshama smiled at her and walked into the little ornamental garden in front of the building.

After strolling in the garden for a while, Kshama felt better and decided to return to her room. As she walked up the two flight of stairs and reached her door, she heard Abhay's door open.

"Kshama…"

"Abhay, why are you up?"

"I couldn't sleep," he grinned and ran a hand through his hair. Kshama felt a blush creep up her face and realized a little part of the delusional teenage girl was still alive somewhere within her.

"Me neither," Kshama replied.

The two stood in the silence of the hallway, eyes locked, wondering what to speak. For the last several months, whether developing a plan or getting into a heated argument, they had never run out of words.

"Do you want to watch a movie together?" Abhay finally broke the silence. Kshama frowned. Abhay was not a fan of movies. He found it hard to sit glued in front of the TV for hours at a stretch. Kshama wondered if it was hint to spend the night together. The thought made her nervous.

Say No. the seventeen-year-old girl in her mind whispered. *What will the others think when they find out?*

But Kshama knew she no longer had to worry about what others thought of her or her actions. She was a thirty-four-year-old, independent woman. She could do whatever she wished without concerning herself with the world's opinion. She had learned this the hard way. Kshama looked at Abhay's soft eyes and the hint of the grin that was playing on his lips.

"Okay," Kshama replied and followed him into the room, her heart hammering in her chest like a caged bird.

Once inside, Abhay asked her to make herself comfortable on the couch and pick a movie from the five CDs on the table while he got the popcorn.

"Where did you get these?"

"I rented them from the CD place opposite to the hotel. I wasn't sure which one you would like," he smiled.

Kshama found herself smiling when she realized Abhay simply wanted to just watch a movie with her.

"So you knew I wouldn't be able to sleep," Kshama teased him.

"I was hoping so."

On closer inspection, Kshama realized that Abhay had chosen all of her favorite movies. During their meetups before the trip, Kshama had shared her favorite movies with Abhay, all of which were related to travel. She had been surprised that despite being a traveller himself, Abhay hadn't seen any of them. The conversation had then moved to books. But Abhay had made a mental note of her favourite movies and had taken the trouble to rent it out for her tonight. It was a sweet gesture that once again awoke the butterflies.

A little after an hour later, they were almost at the end of 'The Bucket List', when Kshama realized Abhay was fighting back his tears. It made her smile. She grabbed a tissue from the table and offered it to him. He smiled embarrassed but took it anyway. As the rolling titles appeared, a yawn escaped her.

"I think I should go now," Kshama said, standing up. Abhay nodded and rose, accompanying her to the door. As she reached the doorway, Kshama remembered leaving her purse on the couch, turned around and nearly collided with Abhay. With their faces just inches apart, Kshama found it easier to drown out the warning voice in her head. Before Abhay could move away, she placed her lip on his. He smiled and kissed her back, first gently and then passionately. When things got heated up, Abhay pulled back.

"Are you sure?" he asked holding her hands in his and locking eyes with her. Seeing the genuine concern in his eyes, Kshama knew she could not be more sure. She nodded as a blush creeped up her cheeks.

"You can tell me to stop anytime you want," Abhay said before placing his lips on her once again.

As the first rays of sunlight streamed through the window, Kshama woke up in Abhay's arms. Their bodies tangled between the sheets and for the first time in years, she smiled, feeling not just at peace but genuinely happy.

Kshama and Abhay spent the next two years either travelling or planning their next trips – partly to escape the watchful eyes of Abhay's mother, Sumitra and Amruta's mother, Gitanjali who would force them to get married the moment they learnt of the budding romance. Prajwal on the other hand vowed to keep their relationship a secret as long as they desired. In return, he only asked the love birds to keep it decent when they travelled with his customers especially senior groups.

Together they organized trips all over India and across Asia. In India, they traversed the breathtaking landscapes, from the snow-capped peaks of the Himalayas to the golden sands of the Thar Desert. They guided their clients through the bustling streets of Delhi, the majestic forts of Rajasthan, the serene backwaters of Kerala and the cascading waterfalls of Meghalaya. Each trip was meticulously crafted, offering a harmonious blend of historical wonders, vibrant traditions, and authentic culinary experiences.

Across Asia, Kshama and Abhay curated journeys that immersed travellers in the exotic tapestry of cultures and landscapes. They led groups through the ancient temples of Cambodia, the floating markets of Vietnam, and the serene tea plantations of Sri Lanka. Their attention to detail and genuine love for the destinations they explored allowed their customers to experience the true essence of each place, leaving them with cherished memories and a desire to return. Naturally, Apna Travels flourished with four more branches in India's major cities.

While Kshama and Abhay reveled in their shared passion for travel, the secrecy surrounding their relationship added an extra layer of excitement and urgency. With each stolen moment, their love grew stronger, their connection deepened. They cherished these clandestine encounters, treasuring the stolen glances, the secret touches, and the moments of vulnerability they shared.

Presently, Kshama was back in Ranachatti for a week to meet Gitanjali and Amruta on the occasion of Gitanjali's birthday which she refused to celebrate. So, Kshama and Amruta decided to make the day special by giving Gitanjali the day off and cooking an elaborate meal for lunch, followed by a cheesy Bollywood movie that the family watched together on their newly installed LCD TV.

In the evening as the three women sat in the verandah sipping sweet tea and savouring the winter sun, Kshama knew what was coming.

"You have travelled around the world and yet found no suitable man in all these years," Gitanjali clucked her tongue in disappointment.

"How is it that you spend so much time with Abhay and don't find him attractive? It takes at least a week for the girls, women and even grannies here to stop talking about him after his visit," Gitanjali added. Between Gitanjali's suggestive words and Amruta's teasing glances, Kshama tried hard to hide her blush.

"I'll try to find a good man in the next trip," Kshama replied not very convincingly but it seemed to pacify Gitanjali.

Later, as Amruta and Kshama retired to Amruta's room, where they had planned a sleepover, Amruta grinned ear to ear making Kshama suspicious.

"Okay, I'm sorry but I can't hold it in anymore," Amruta confessed, her eyes gleaming with excitement.

"What is it, Amruta?" Kshama inquired.

"I was in Dehradun last evening to get Ma's chain fixed in the jewelry shop, and guess who I bumped into?" Amruta teased, her smile widening.

"Who?"

"Abhay!" Amruta exclaimed, unable to contain the surprise in her voice. Kshama frowned "And?"

"Guess what he was buying…" Amruta's voice lowered and Kshama realized why Amruta was so excited.

"A ring, babe! A ring. I think he is going to pro—"

"No," Kshama interrupted, her voice tinged with a mix of fear and uncertainty. Amruta frowned and then as she looked at the colour drained from Kshama's face, she realized how hard this might be for Kshama.

"Kshama, I know how you feel about marriage," Amruta began, her voice now laced with empathy. "But you are so in love with him. Marriage is just a formality. You two are already bound to each other. Honestly, I'm yet to see two people who are so deeply in love even after two years."

"I know," Kshama sighed, "But I'm scared. Scared that marriage will change everything we have. Why can't things just remain as they are? Why is this formality needed?"

"Because marriage is a beautiful union," Amruta smiled, "It's a celebration of love, a commitment to build a future together. You and Abhay share something extraordinary. Don't let fear hold you back from embracing that."

Kshama sighed, her mind clouded with memories of the past. An inexplicable fear bubbled within her whenever Abhay casually spoke about their future, about weddings and children. It resurfaced the bitter memories of the past, leaving her questioning if she would ever be ready to fully commit herself to someone in that manner.

"Okay, I might have mistaken," Amruta smiled, attempting to uplift Kshama's spirits, "Also, the ring didn't seem like an engagement ring. I mean, who buys an Amethyst ring? Especially not Abhay. He can probably buy the biggest diamond in the store..."

Amruta's voice buzzed in the background as yet another whirlwind of emotions swept through Kshama's mind. *Amethyst.* The word echoed in her thoughts, triggering a vivid memory of a drunken night during one of their trips.

Kshama and Abhay had indulged in a little too much wine, and they found themselves sitting on the balcony of their hotel room, gazing at the starry night sky. In their intoxicated state, the topic of weddings and marriage had emerged, and Kshama, in a playful manner, had joked about diamond rings being overrated. She had confessed her affinity for amethyst, finding it more unique and enchanting. They had shared a hearty laugh, and Kshama had assumed that it was a forgotten moment, lost in the haze of that tipsy night. But now, when Amruta mentioned an amethyst ring, doubt crept into her heart. Had Abhay remembered that conversation?

Kshama smiled at Amruta, and the duo moved on to less serious topics talking their hearts out with endless cups of hot tea before falling asleep in the early hours of the morning.

In the coming days, whenever Abhay and Kshama spoke over the phone or exchanged countless messages on the popular messaging app, WhatsApp, which had become a sensation among teenagers in recent years, Kshama found herself growing increasingly anxious. Thoughts swirled in her mind, pondering what she would do if Abhay were to propose. The idea of rejecting him seemed unimaginable, as it would mean losing everything she held dear. There was truly no valid reason for her to say no, except for the lingering shadow of the past that occasionally engulfed her present, suffocating her with doubt.

As the days turned into a week and Abhay remained silent on the matter, Kshama began to believe it was all a misunderstanding. Perhaps the ring he had bought was intended for a friend, and maybe it wasn't even an amethyst ring after all. Amruta, bless her heart, had never been one to pay close attention to details. Consequently, when Abhay called her two weeks later, proposing an impromptu trip to their favorite hideaway, Jibhi—a secluded hill station in Himachal Pradesh where they often sought refuge in a friend's cozy wooden café —Kshama hastily packed her bag and made her way to Dehradun, leaving all her anxious thoughts behind.

Jibhi.

As Kshama broke the kiss and nestled closer to Abhay, all her fears had vanished. She knew this was where she belonged. In Abhay's arms, away from the world and its stereotypical norms. Honestly, at the moment, whether from the post- sex oxytocin or from the proximity to Abhay, the man she truly loved, Kshama felt her reservations about marriage fade away. She surprised herself as she daydreamed of the proposal and the prospect of a union with Abhay for a lifetime.

"What are you thinking?" Abhay's voice slowly brought her back to the present, and she realized he had been watching her all along.

"Nothing," Kshama replied quickly, "What do you want to do today?"

"Well…"

"Not that.." Kshama swatted his arm playfully, "I mean, not just that," she added with a blush.

"I was thinking of a short hike to the Jalori Pass. We haven't been there in a while," Abhay suggested.

After a refreshing hike, Kshama and Abhay found themselves sitting in a serene spot, facing the majestic snow-capped mountains that stood tall in all their glory. The air was crisp, carrying a hint of adventure and tranquility. Kshama took a moment to soak in the breathtaking view, the mountains seemingly whispering tales of timeless beauty.

As Kshama raised her water bottle and took a sip, her eyes caught a glimmer of movement. She turned her gaze towards Abhay, and her heart skipped a beat as she noticed him pulling out a small box from his pocket. The unmistakable shape of a ring box sent a surge of emotions coursing through her veins.

In that pivotal moment, Abhay's eyes met Kshama's with tenderness and warmth. Sensing her surprise, he gently held her hand, his smile offering reassurance. "Please don't panic. I know how you feel about this, and that's precisely why I wanted to keep it simple."

Kshama's mind raced, a whirlwind of thoughts and emotions converging within her. "But, Kshama, I want you to know that I'm ready, and I am willing to wait for as long as you need. I love you, and I cannot imagine spending the rest of my life without you."

Abhay's simple yet heartfelt confession touched Kshama's heart, soothing her fears and doubts. She found it hard to respond. She broke her gaze from Abhay and looked at the small box in his hands.

"To avoid bruising my tender heart any further, I'm going to pull out the ring only after you say yes," Abhay added, a playful sparkle in his eyes. Kshama laughed softly at his words, any lingering uncertainty slowly melting away.

"I think you should take it out," Kshama smiled and held her left hand out "I've always wanted an Amethyst ring."

Abhay placed the ring on her finger and then kissed her deeply. There was no need for any words. They sat there, holding hands watching the serene view when suddenly Abhay turned towards Kshama.

"Wait... how did you know it was an Amethyst?"

"I have my ways," Kshama shrugged.

"Ah…" A moment later, realization hit Abhay. "I knew Amruta had spotted me much before I saw her at the shop. Keeping a secret is not that girl's strongest suit."

CHAPTER 3

Present Day, Ranachatti.

Kshama wiped her tears as she got down from the taxi and walked into Prajwal's house, where Amruta was already waiting for her with worried eyes. Upon seeing Kshama's wet eyelashes and long face, Amruta pulled her into a warm hug. Amruta did not ask her anything, and for that, Kshama was grateful. The next morning, the two bid goodbye to Prajwal, promising to contact him soon with a good plan for the very first Dinnala Bugiyal Trek. By evening, they were back in the serene lap of Ranachatti.

After warming up in front of the crackling fire on the verandah and savoring hot tea, Kshama and Amruta made their way into the kitchen, where Gitanjali was busy preparing dinner. They knew they had to overcome the first and most significant hurdle, and win the favor of the most important player in their new venture.

"Total strangers staying here?" Gitanjali exclaimed. "And in your house where you live alone? Are you out of your mind?" she asked Kshama, who pursed her lips. Gitanjali, Kshama, and Amruta were seated on the wooden-carpeted floor in Gitanjali's little, ill-ventilated kitchen. It was past sunset, and the temperature had fallen to single digits. Gitanjali was making *rotis*[10] and *daal*[11] over the *chullah*[12] while Amruta adjusted the firewood below to keep the

---

[10] : Traditional Indian flatbread

[11] : Nutritious and flavorful lentil dish

[12] : Traditional Indian stove

52

fire going. The gas stove – a recent addition to the kitchen – was reserved for making morning tea only.

"I cannot agree to this. You girls might have grown up in age, but your mind still works as irresponsibly as teenagers," Gitanjali clucked her tongue in disapproval. Kshama and Amruta exchanged worried looks.

Gitanjali, Amruta's mother, was one of the strongest and kindest women Kshama had ever met. When Kshama had first come to Ranachatti, she had wondered how Amruta's parents would react to her intrusion. But Gitanjali had nothing but love and warmth to offer. It was much later that Kshama learned about Gitanjali's second daughter, who had passed away in infancy. Gitanjali saw her little daughter in Kshama.

While Gitanjali was soft-natured and timid, she was also fiercely physically strong. At only five feet, with a lean body, Gitanjali managed to carry hay loads that weighed as much as her from the mountaintops every day in the pre-winter months to feed the mules during the harsh winter. During summer, Gitanjali and the other women in the neighbourhood worked in the fields to grow cabbages, cauliflowers, and potatoes that would sustain them for a few months. When the finances became extremely strained, Gitanjali climbed to the forests above to collect lichens known locally as Jhula Ghas, which she sold to licensed buyers who used it in traditional medicines and dyes. It was a strenuous job, identifying the mossy herb and scraping it carefully off dry barks. It left her exhausted by the end of the day. Yet, not once had anyone in the family gone to sleep on an empty stomach.

"But Ma, listen to our plan. Kshama has a lot of experience in this—" Amruta began to explain.

"I still don't understand why you insist on living up there alone when we have so many rooms vacant here. Is this old house not good enough for you now? Haan… Miss International?" Gitanjali half-teased, half-scolded Kshama.

"You know this will always be my home, Masi. My true home is where you are," Kshama replied honestly. Gitanjali suppressed a smile. Amruta gave Kshama a thumbs up.

For the first three years since starting a new life in Ranachatti, Kshama had lived a hermit life with no purpose, no ambitions, and no direction. Then one day Amruta introduced her to Prajwal's Apna Travels and Kshama once again dared to dream.

Apna Travels had given her that purpose and with the purpose came dreams and materialistic goals. At the top of this list sat the desire to own a house that was just hers. It was not that Kshama did not think of Amruta's house as her own. Amruta's home had welcomed her with open arms when she had had nowhere else to go. It would always remain her beloved home.

But at twenty-five, having travelled a fair deal and saved enough, Kshama had inadvertently begun to dream of building and decorating her own home. Saanidhya – her little blue cottage at the very top of Ranachatti—was the outcome of that dream. Gitanjali who secretly admired Kshama for achieving her dream, did not approve of a young woman living alone in a house at the edge of the forest. She had somewhat relaxed after Harper was adopted.

"Okay assuming I agree to this, are you going to let strange boys and men live with you in your house?"

"There will be girls and women in the group too, Masi," Kshama replied.

"And you will be in charge of allocating the rooms, Ma. You can let the girls stay with Kshama and we can have the boys here," Amruta suggested. "And of course, Gattu will stay here for protection," she quickly added before Gitanjali's wide eyes could pop out.

"I'm not sure if this is a good idea. There are so many things that could go wrong."

"Masi, let's go through your concerns one by one. We can decide at the end if we should take it forward."

"What if one of them falls sick in the cold? We don't even have a hospital close by."

"We will talk to Bhuvan Kaka and ask him to keep one of his jeeps here. He can take the patient to Barkot. Next." Amruta replied rather haughtily. Kshama glared at her.

"And what if they get drunk and create a nuisance? How will the neighbors react?"

"We will make sure they do not get access to *Raksi*[13] or any kind of alcohol. I will make sure Gattu or Rakesh *Masa*[14] don't indulge in it during the trek." Kshama replied.

Gitanjali smirked at Kshama's assurance. There was no way the men, especially her husband, could stay away from Raksi for even a day during the winter months. Rakesh Rana, Gitanjali's husband, who had once taken pride in being one among the few teetotaler men in the village, now indulged in the intoxicating brew like a captivated connoisseur. It was one of the reasons he refused to work during the off-season. Gitanjali blamed Raksi and the Nepali brewer who lived in the forest for Rakesh's change in habits.

"And the food? Do I have to cook for all of them three times a day?"

Kshama knew Gitanjali was simply using cooking as an excuse. She loved cooking and would do so every day even for the sake of complete strangers. She believed in feeding the hungry to be the greatest of all karmas.

"Think of all the extra income, Ma. You know we need it," Amruta pulled out her trump card when she sensed they were losing the argument. After some more coaxing by Amruta and a lot of assurance from Kshama, Gitanjali reluctantly agreed to host one trekking group at her home after the first snowfall on the condition that only girls would sleep in Kshama's house while she boarded the boys. Kshama and Amruta hugged Gitanjali gratefully and then walked back to the verandah discussing the next steps.

Kshama and Amruta had two months to make all preparations – identifying the most scenic trail, safe pit stops, building make-shift restrooms at the base and the peak, and arrangements to carry tents, sleeping bags, and food. All of this had to be done before the first snowfall. They had to learn what other trekking clubs were offering and had to do better within the same budget. Above all, Kshama had to brace herself, mentally and physically, for

---

[13] : Strong liquor made from fermented grains

[14] : Maternal uncle

a snow trek, an adventure she had last undertaken over seven years ago.

Someone yelled *Gattimela*[15]. Someone else thrust the garland into her hand. All around her, people spoke in excited tones. A moment of silence and then the wedding song boomed. In the commotion, Kshama looked up from her feet and met the groom's twinkling eyes. A face she had known for as long as she could remember, yet had truly known only when things began to fall apart.

Kshama's heart was beating fast and her feet ran cold. The realization hit hard, she was a seventeen-year-old bride. She had sacrificed her dreams, her education, and her freedom – all for a boy she wasn't even sure she loved. Kshama's eyes darted towards the garland in the groom's hand, only there was no garland. Instead, there was a thick iron shackle.

Kshama stepped back. This was a trap. What had she done? She tried to turn around and escape but the ladies with caked faces and kohled eyes held her in position. The groom's father gestured for the groom to put the shackles around her neck. Kshama opened her mouth to scream but no voice came. She looked around to call her family for help. A moment later, her blood froze. She had no family. All of them had died.

The groom took a step forward and placed the icy cold shackle around her neck. Everyone clapped and hooted. He held one end of the chain and dragged Kshama behind him. His family followed. No one heard her silent plea. No one shed a tear for her broken dream.

Kshama woke up with a start and sat up in her bed. She touched her neck and breathed a sigh of relief when she found no shackles. She looked at the clock. It was 4: 00 AM. A nightmare that she had not had for many years now.

Kshama did not go back to sleep. Instead she sat at her desk and went through the pending tasks that needed to be worked on before the group

---

[15] : Wedding in Kannada

arrived. She had to make it a success. She owed it to Prajwal, who had placed his faith in her. She owed it to Gitanjali, who was striving hard for her family's well-being. She owed it to the people of this little mountain village who had welcomed her with open arms and made her one among them. Above all, she owed it to the seventeen-year-old girl who had believed in herself enough to leave behind everything she had ever known and make a life for herself.

Two days later.

Kshama winced as she placed her foot on a loose stone and stumbled. But she did not stop to check on her leg. Instead, she continued to cross the stream that was overflowing with icy water from the mountain tops. She had to reach the base and return before sunset.

After a day's break, she would repeat the trek and strive to cover it in a shorter duration. Building her stamina was crucial. Seven years ago, she had been a pro, but now the gap years had reset her to the starting point in terms of endurance, strength, and the lung capacity required for high-altitude treks. Kshama shook her head to dispel the memories. It was not the time to reminisce about the dreadful day when, for the second time in her life, she had lost everything. Stamina was the least of her losses.

If Kshama were to lead the first-ever trek across Dinnala Bugiyal to Jindi Peak and back, she must be mentally and physically prepared. Her energy and speed would serve as a guiding light for the trekkers, inspiring them to surpass their limits. If she were to slow down or stop for her own sake, it would dampen the collective energy. This would not only be a setback for Prajwal's agency but also for the few women trekking guides in the region.

While Kshama and Amruta spent three or four days a week preparing themselves physically, they spent the rest setting up the rooms that would house the trekkers, arranging for tents, firewood, and groceries all of which had to be either brought from the Barkot market or collected from the forests above. They also had to make sure the only doctor in Ranachatti—Dr. Bhuvan would be available during the trekking season and that he would have all the necessary medicines needed should anyone fall sick or get hurt.

In the last week of September, Ranachatti bid farewell to the Yamuna yatra, and the pilgrimage season came to a close. The once bustling village now saw the departure of all tourists and pilgrims, leaving behind a sense of emptiness and quietness. While the pilgrims returned to their homes with memories and blessings, the villagers, especially the men, wore somber expressions. The closure of the yatra marked the end of their main source of income for the year. With the pilgrimage season over, most villagers, who relied on the influx of travellers to sustain their livelihoods, now faced uncertainty. Finding odd jobs during these months was challenging, and the savings were often not enough to sustain their families through the lean period.

As November rolled in, there was a subtle shift in the weather. The temperature dropped, and the chilling wind blew through the streets of Ranachatti. The days still presented clear skies, but the absence of visitors made the village seem quieter than ever before. With the onset of winter, the village's landscape slowly transformed; trees shed their leaves, and the surrounding mountains stood tall, their peaks awaiting the first snowfall.

By mid-November, Kshama had the itinerary ready. The trek would be three days long – two to ascend and one to descend –each following a different route so that both sides of the scenic mountains and rivers could be covered. Gattu and Rakesh would carry the groceries and utensils to cook meals for the group. After the trek, the group would spend a day in Ranachatti recovering and then visit the famous Yamuna temple at Janaki Chatti, where the trip would conclude. The team would be picked up in a Bolero by their local driver from the Apna Travels office in Dehradun and dropped back after the trek.

Amruta and Kshama had decided to set the price of the trek just enough to cover the expenses made plus a decent amount to pay Gitanjali, Rakesh, and Gattu for their efforts. Apna Travels would not make any profit from this first trip, which allowed them to set a competitive price.

On the first try, it took Kshama more than seven hours to reach the base, which was how long it had taken her to climb it the very first time more than a decade ago. From what she could recall, nothing significant had changed on the trail. The tall pine and walnut trees still lined the less-travelled path. The forest floors were still covered with crunchy brown and gray leaves. Icy water from the Yamuna still flowed in delicate streams, and little wildflowers peeked from nooks as she passed by. Ranachatti was truly timeless. As she passed by these familiar spots, savoring their serenity, once again Kshama's thoughts of apprehension returned. Was she knowingly becoming a catalyst in the degradation of this place in the name of development?

On reaching the base, Kshama sat down. It was growing dark, and the forests would not be safe after sunset if she were alone. She would have to start her return journey soon, but her legs seemed to have turned into jelly and refused to stand up. There was a drumroll in her chest, and her lungs burned from taking in deep breaths of crisp mountain air. The sweat had drenched her thermals and was now causing her back to feel numb. Taking her phone out, Kshama looked at herself. Her face had turned pink, and she was gasping for breath. Definitely, not something people would want to witness in someone leading the trek through the jungles and unknown mountains.

Each of the seven trekkers who had enrolled had asked Kshama or Prajwal who would be leading the trek. They had all sounded a little disappointed when they realized it would be a woman. They had managed to convince the trekkers by saying two other men from the mountains would accompany them. Kshama wondered what the trekkers would say if they realized their guide was not only a woman but also someone who had not trekked in seven years and could barely make it to the base without taking a dozen breaks.

As Kshama pushed against the ground, carrying the hay-filled gear on her back, she wondered if she had made a mistake by agreeing to Prajwal. If the trekkers returned unsatisfied with the experience, Apna Travels' business would take a hit.

It was too late to have second thoughts, Kshama told herself. The group had already enrolled, Prajwal had made his investments and the weather predictions had been made. The first snowfall was expected during the second week of December. Kshama had four weeks to prepare herself.

CHAPTER 4

Bengaluru, 2022.

❝Vidvath, I'm afraid I can't let you take any more leaves this year," Vidvath's boss, Zoya, said in a tone of finality. They were seated opposite each other in her cabin. Behind her, Vidvath watched the patches of the evening sky – barely visible in between tall buildings of concrete and glass – transform from orange to gray as though being consumed by the dominant color in the scene. It was well past six in the evening and Vidvath with most of his team would be working for a couple of hours more to make a high-priority fix in their software. The software they delivered last week had been rejected by the customer on account of incomplete and buggy implementation.

It was only Monday and Vidvath was already fatigued. Of course, he could not blame it completely on work. He had spent the weekend trekking the Kodachadri hills – a 22km moderately difficult trek in the western ghats, 400kms from the city - and had travelled last night, reaching Bengaluru only in the early hours. After a fitful sleep of barely three hours, his manager, Zoya woke him up to inform him about the rejection of their software. There was a mixture of irritation and disappointment in her voice and Vidvath felt guilty. He knew deep down that he was not taking his job seriously – not out of disregard but out of lack of passion.

"I know I have exhausted all my privilege leaves. But can I not apply for a few days of LOP next month? I have already booked the flight tickets and paid for the trek. You know I have been planning this for several years now,"

Vidvath replied, unable to meet Zoya's eyes. Zoya who had not long ago been in the same cadre as Vidvath, had climbed the corporate ladder faster through sheer dedication and skill. Despite having to report to a toxic boss for some part of her career, she had never treated her subordinates the way she had been. Vidvath had on many occasions, taken advantage of Zoya's kindness.

"Vidvath, you're a Team Lead now. The team looks up to you. If you keep going away every now and then, it affects their productivity. I also see a change of attitude in some of them. They are taking deadlines lightly and are not punctual in their signing in as well."

Vidvath knew it was true. He barely knew the names of his team members and had not even met the interns yet.

"I could not let you take the leaves in December, even if I wished to. The customer is really disappointed and is expecting meticulous work from us in the next software that has to be delivered before they go on their Christmas vacation. They also want you to be available during the last week of the year because they don't believe the software is going to be as expected in the first go," Zoya said, leaning back in her chair and rubbing her temples.

"I can't stay here during the last week. That's when the trek commences."

"I could have let you take leaves if you had a genuine reason – medical, family or so. But your reasons are not considered valid by the higher management."

"How is taking care of your mental health not valid?"

"Are you seeing a psychiatrist? Did they recommend you to go on these treks every month?" the vein popping on Zoya's forehead warned Vidvath against further argument.

Zoya sighed, "Vidvath, I understand that you feel the need to escape from here every now and then. Honestly, I sometimes envy you for being able to do that. But this year I feel you're jeopardizing your career. You have not met many of your goals for the year yet, and those completed have been done so in haste. I simply cannot let you do this. As your friend and your boss."

Vidvath stood up and walked towards the door, wondering what he would do now.

"I also suggest you seek help. I don't think running away to the mountains is a solution to what you're feeling," Zoya said turning back to her laptop screen.

That night lying on his bed in the two-bedroom flat that he had once shared with two others, Vidvath found himself unable to sleep despite his exhaustion. He got up, poured himself a drink and stood by the window. From his vantage point, he could see the entrance of the Tech Park where his office was located. Beyond it, a backdrop of high-rise buildings from other tech parks, apartment complexes, a small lake at a distance, and a few patches of green formed the city scape.

In front of the tech park, bright streetlights illuminated the multi-lane road, accentuating the mad rush of honking, racing vehicles entering and exiting various office buildings. The scene vividly represented the bustling part of the city that never slept.

Vidvath sighed and went back to bed. As he lay down watching the rusted blades of the ceiling fan, gleaming in the ambient lights of passing vehicles, he wondered why he was still there. Why had he stayed in this city where he had no one to call his own – no friends, no family. Was it his job? While Vidvath was thankful for the job and the handsome salary he earned, he felt no real passion for his work. Was it because he was too scared to return to his village or to start life elsewhere?

Picking his phone from the nightstand, Vidvath opened the trek poster and smiled. In the background were the snow-capped mountains shining brightly in the early morning light that rendered them golden. The trail was covered with knee-deep snow and trekkers bundled in layers of clothes, carrying huge gears on their backs were making their way up the mountain like ants on a mission. The sight filled Vidvath with a sudden surge of adrenaline as he pictured himself in their shoes, conquering the challenging terrain and experiencing the thrill of adventure. He knew this trek would be a test of his endurance as well as a journey of self-discovery and personal growth.

Going on a snow trek had been Vidvath's dream since the first time he had heard about it over five years ago. Saurav, his colleague and an experienced trekker from Nepal had introduced it to him. In the last few years, snow treks had become a trend and Vidvath longed to be part of one.

At first, he had been skeptical of his ability to survive in near-zero and sometimes sub-zero temperatures. On Saurav's suggestion, Vidvath had started running every morning and even joined the gym to build his stamina. Every month, he went on a trek around Bengaluru with local trek groups. He took care of his diet and sleep cycles. By the end of the year, Vidvath had gained both stamina and confidence to enroll for a winter trek. But that year, he had to let go of the opportunity as his elder sister, Yashodha, decided to get married around the same time. Being her only true family, Vidvath had to spend the month preparing for the wedding. His ailing father, who strongly condemned remarriage, had refused to be a part of it.

The following year, Vidvath trained harder and read everything there was to read about winter treks in the Himalayas. He chose Uttarakhand and spoke to many agencies and clubs that offered a snow-trek package. However, that year, his father passed away after falling prey to COVID-19 - the devastating second wave of the pandemic that left the country shaken.

A few weeks ago, Saurav, who now lived in Nepal with his wife Leena, shared the poster with him. He had explained to Vidvath how this Trek – Dinnala Bugiyal Jindi – would be perfect for him. An unexplored part of Garhwal Himalayas, considered a hidden treasure of the Himalayan trail. Saurav, who had been on many such lesser-known and unknown snow treks, had recommended this one because he believed that most well-known treks like Kedarkantha, Kush Kalyan, Gulabi kantha were now crowded, commercialized, and failed to deliver the raw trekking experience.

"It's unexplored and only the people of Ranachatti and neighboring villages know about it. It's a moderate trek with breathtaking views. Plus you'll be staying with the nice mountain people and experiencing their simple yet rich life firsthand," he had explained. "Prajwal, a friend of my father is starting a trekking club under the banner of his thirty-year-old travel agency, Apna

Travels. His team, formed by the local mountain people of Ranachatti, will take good care of you." Saurav had assured. "Who knows, you might find a nice Pahari girl there and finally decide to leave Bengaluru for good."

Recalling Saurav's light-hearted comment, Vidvath's mind influenced by the drink he had just had, wandered to a part of his past that he had managed to suppress for many years now.

Jogibettu, 2005.

Nine months had passed since the fateful day when Vidvath's world had fallen apart. Radhika – his love turned fiancé – had died. Her entire family had been killed. Her body had not been found and the authorities had all but stopped looking. Suman, Radhika's older cousin, and a member of the District's Nari Shakti Women's Welfare Association had left no stones unturned to locate Radhika but in vain.

For the people of Jogibettu, life returned to normal after a few days. The only thing in the village that reminded people of the family was the house. Recently, Radhika's distant uncle had announced that he was selling it. To everyone's surprise, Suman – the closest living relative – had not protested. What would she do with an empty house where she had never been welcome? The keys to the house were temporarily handed to Vidvath's father, the Sarpanch. A new postmaster had been appointed in place of Radhika's father, and life continued to go on in the little village, presently abuzz in preparation for the annual Cart festival.

But for Vidvath, life had come to a complete stop. It had all happened so fast. It seemed as though one day their families were celebrating their engagement and making plans for the future, and the next day, Radhika and her family had vanished. Vidvath had been in the spotlight for many days after that. Everyone pitied him and some, not so subtly, blamed his father's ill-doings for Vidvath's ugly turn of fate. Some who knew his family closely pondered aloud if death was a better fate for the poor girl than joining his family.

With each passing day, regret gnawed deeper at Vidvath. He knew he had failed Radhika on more than one occasion. He had been a coward, and Radhika had paid heavily for his cowardice. But what pained him the most was that fate had not even given him a chance to atone.

"Vidvath, my son, you can't continue to live like this. You need to move on." Vidvath's mother, Vinaya's voice brought him back from his train of thought. How long had she been here? Vidvath wondered. They were in Vidvath's room, where he now spent most of his days. Every day, his mother came to his room to check on her grieving son. Vidvath had transformed from a carefree lad to a conscious, self-introspecting man in less than a year.

"I'm worried for you, Vidvath. How many more months are you going to grieve her death?" Vidvath once again noticed how his mother still could not utter Radhika's name. It brought along too much pain.

"*Amma*[16], you won't understand…"

"Yes. Maybe I don't. I have never known love. All I have known is a sense of dutifulness. It is for this reason that I was happy for you even when I felt you two were too young to get married. It made me happy that you would be spending your life with someone you loved." Vidvath watched the tears pool in his mother's eyes. He wondered how ill fated they both were. One had lost their love, the other had never found theirs.

"Anyways, I'm here to tell you something important. Vidvath, your father has been patient all this while. In fact, this is the most patient I have ever seen him. But now I sense he is not going to be quiet."

"What do you mean, Amma?"

"Have you decided what you want to do in life?"

Vidvath did not reply. Instead, he looked outside his window at the changing sky. He wished to go to the pond in the forest and watch the evening sky transform into night. The pond with its clear water, little guppies, and picturesque view had been *their* spot. It was where Vidvath had confessed his

---

[16] : Mother

feelings for Radhika. It was where the incident that shook their world had taken place. Vidvath had not visited the place since Radhika's death.

"Remember this, Vidvath. When you don't make your own decisions, others will make them for you," Vinaya said when Vidvath did not answer. "Your friend Ranjan is moving to Bengaluru for his higher studies. They have found a good college where he plans to study computers."

Vidvath looked at his mother with surprise. Ranjan had been Vidvath's classmate throughout school. Academically, they had been together in the lower rungs and had really not put much effort into climbing higher. Like Vidvath, Ranjan too was expected to follow in his father's footsteps.

"Your father and I think you too should move to the city and restart your studies. You have been home for three years now. Your educational qualification as a twelfth pass does not amount to much in today's world. Everyone is talking about graduation and post-graduation," Vinaya said, "Also, I think it will be good for you, away from all this."

"No, Amma. I don't want to go. I can't. After all this, I can't continue my life like nothing ever happened. It's been only a few months. Radhika does not deserve to be forgotten so easily."

"Don't be stupid, Vidvath. You're only twenty-one. You have a long life ahead, and you cannot spend it thinking about her," Vinaya said rather sternly and sighed when she saw Vidvath's sad eyes, "I understand what you're feeling, Vidvath. Trust me. I too have lost a loved one. Padmini's death still feels like a nightmare that I will wake up from any minute. But there is nothing we can do to bring them back. We can only pray that they have peacefully moved on and that we will meet again in another life," Vinaya added as she remembered her childhood friend and Radhika's mother, Padmini.

"I want you to think about it. Make a decision on what you want to do in life. Do you want to stay back here and follow in the footsteps of your father? Do you want to be a man of power who is feared by the entire village and respected by barely a few?" Vinaya's voice dropped to a whisper when she said this, and her eyes glanced at the door. Vidvath managed to smile, witnessing for the first time, his mother's brave side.

"Or do you want to go away when you still have a chance and start life afresh? Study what you wish to and make a living of your choice. Live life without any restrictions where you get to make all your decisions on your own." Vinaya's words rang true to Vidvath. If he lived here longer, his father would rope him into his tangled web of politics, from which he would never be able to escape. And before he knew it, he would become like his father whose reality Vidvath had begun to understand in the last few months.

Two days later, Vidvath's father – Raghupathi Rao, called for his son. When Vidvath entered the living room, his father had a proud smile on his face.

"Son, I have managed to get you a seat in one of the good colleges in Bengaluru. It cost me a fortune, but I would like to think of it as an investment in the future leader of this village. Once you return from Bengaluru as a graduate, the villagers will respect our family even more."

Vidvath's father had not asked him if he wished to go. He had not asked him what he wanted to study or which college he had in mind. He had simply gone and bought a seat. This did not dishearten Vidvath; instead, he felt more confident of his decision. His mother was right, he had to leave before it was too late.

A week later.

Summer in Jogibettu, like many other coastal villages, was sweltering with the temperatures well above 35 degrees during its peak. When the heat became unbearable, the rain gods showed mercy and it poured heavily. On those rainy days, the weather was pleasant, only for the scorching heat to return the following day. While the rain and sun gods played hide and seek, children in the village made the best of both days. When the skies were clear, they visited the beach and on rainy days they gathered in the verandah of one of their houses and played *Chowkabara*[17], *Ali Guli Mane*[18], and other board games.

---

[17] : Traditional board game played in India

[18] : Another traditional board game

During the monsoon, as the rains lingered, the children indulged in cheap thrills from stories about haunted houses and ghostly tales. The sleepless nights followed narrow escapes, as whispers of forbidden places grew, in the passing from one child to another. Adults added their two cents to keep the excitement alive. In the end, it all became woven into the fabric of their cherished childhood memories.

Vidvath's early years were no exception. Today, however, as an adult, Vidvath for the first time understood what walking into a haunted house felt like. Standing at the threshold, he wondered how many times as a child he had barged into the house, sometimes straight to the kitchen, demanding to be fed. As a teenager, the innumerable times he and Avinash had tip-toed out of the back door to fiddle with a stolen *beedi*[19]. As a young adult, the hours he had spent across the street waiting to catch a glimpse of Radhika. The bittersweet memories came flooding into his mind.

Vidvath held the wall beside him for support. He had half a mind to turn around and leave. But he couldn't. This was his last chance to witness it all and get some closure before attempting to start afresh. He had already spent several months trying to find the slightest ray of hope, but in vain. She was gone and there was nothing he could do to bring her back.

With a deep breath, Vidvath took a step inside the house. The living room, once filled with laughter and festive sounds during his last visit, was now engulfed in an ominous silence. The auspicious day the elders had chosen to formalize their relationship felt like a distant memory. Subconsciously, Vidvath touched the ring on his finger – the one Radhika had placed there.

Some of the decorations from their engagement day still adorned the walls. Lifeless flowers hung from dust-covered threads above the Pooja room. The *Naandi Kalasha*[20] placed in the Pooja room for the wedding ceremony to happen without any hurdles was still there. The mango leaves and flowers had withered. Vidvath swallowed the lump in his throat and crossed

---

[19] : Hand-rolled Indian cigarette wrapped in tendu leaf

[20] : Traditional ceremonial pot used in Hindu rituals for auspicious occasions

the living room towards the kitchen.

Walking into the kitchen, the aroma of freshly brewed coffee welcomed him momentarily only to transform into an odor of rotting fruits and vegetables that were meant to be left alone for only for a week. The little kitchen table was a graveyard of upturned cups and glasses that had been left to dry weeks ago. He picked up the fist-sized black crushing stone from the counter and carried it with him. An heirloom that Radhika's mother had inherited from her grandmother, Vidvath recalled from one of the many childhood stories she had narrated. It surprised him how much he knew about the family yet so little of Radhika.

After a final glance at the kitchen, Vidvath walked out towards Radhika's room. In a parallel world, where the great tragedy had not taken place, this moment would have been exciting. Vidvath's first entry into Radhika's room in all these years. But now their worlds had turned upside down. Radhika's room was just yet another reminder of their relationship that fate had crushed even before it had begun.

On reaching the door, he took a deep breath and pushed it open. A gush of wind welcomed him from the little window on the opposite wall. With it came the sweet fragrance of Radhika's perfume – sandalwood. The expensive one that she only used on special occasions. Like the day of their engagement, two weeks ago. Vidvath fought back the welling tears, his movements around the room slow and deliberate, as if desperately searching for a connection with Radhika beyond the tangible. With a heavy heart, he gathered an armful of books from the shelf—novels, short stories, poetry collections, fragments of her world. Tenderly, he arranged them on Radhika's bed, each volume a silent witness to her presence. A sharp pang of emotion pierced him when he uncovered a copy of Rumi—his gift to Radhika that she had kept. Inside, his fingers traced a poem he had highlighted, not fully comprehending its depth at the time, but now acutely feeling its resonance in the void left by her absence.

He looked around the little room. It was surreal that he had never been here before. It was only something he had sneaked a peek at whenever he came to visit Avinash. Avinash, the responsible elder brother that he was always made sure Vidvath and the other boys only sat in the living room.

For Avinash, Vidvath cried at the loss of a brother whom he had known all his life, with whom he had shared all his good and bad moments. But with Radhika, he cried for the memories he never got to make, for the girl he believed was the love of his life yet knew hardly anything about. The pain was real but was it selfless? As selfless as true love is supposed to be? Was he crying for the young girl full of dreams who died tragically having not lived her life at all? Or was he crying for himself, mourning the lost opportunity to repent for his actions?

Walking to Radhika's study desk, Vidvath picked up the photo frame that held her family photo. There was a scrapbook that had messages and signatures of her friends from school and a stash of letters from someone named Binya. Vidvath collected as many of Radhika's things as he could—her stamp collection, her stationery box, her collection of earring and bangles and the brown stuffed bear that he had won for her at the village fair. He placed them all on the bed and carefully packed them into the cardboard box he had brought along. Vidvath wished he could pack everything in the house and carry it with him to a safe place where the memories would live forever.

Just before leaving the room, his eyes caught a decorated shoe box under Radhika's bed. Placing the cardboard box on the floor, he picked up the shoe box jeweled with little stars and golden strips of paper. Fresh tears pooled in his eyes as he leafed through dozens of maps and travel articles cut out from magazines and newspapers within the box. There were names and places he had never heard of. Sunsets, beaches, monuments, pyramids, deserts, snowy mountains—the little box contained the world. A world that Radhika yearned to explore. A dream she had often talked to him about and he had dismissed with a laugh.

"It is an impossible dream, Radhika. We cannot afford to travel to so many places in one lifetime. Isn't it enough that we live together here, being each other's world?" Radhika had always replied with an understanding smile. As he skimmed through its contents, Vidvath found a stash of unopened letters—his letters that he had sent through Tara, Radhika's best friend. Radhika had not opened any of them.

Vidvath carefully placed the shoebox into the larger cardboard box. He walked out of the house, securing the lock on the main door after one last glance at the place. A memory that he knew would haunt him for the rest of his life. Vidvath had no idea what he was going to do with the box or why he had collected all those things in the first place. Was it to save it from perishing? Or was it a hope that someday he would get a chance to return it to its rightful owner? A small voice in his mind refused to believe Radhika was gone forever.

Returning home, Vidvath walked straight to his room and opened the old trunk from under his bed. He carefully placed the cardboard box inside it. Longingly moving his fingers over the box one last time, he locked the trunk and pushed it back under the bed—to be safe and forgotten.

A year later.

For the young man who had lived all his life in a little coastal village, surrounded by lush greenery, clear skies, and the sound of the ocean, life in Bengaluru had not been easy to adapt to at first. Vidvath, Ranjan, and Saurav— a boy from Nepal whom they had befriended during orientation—had moved together into a PG (Paying Guest Service) run by a middle-aged spinster named Bhagyalakshmi, located in a building just outside the college.

After six months of living at Bhagayalakshmi's, Vidvath experienced frequent episodes of a stomach infection while Ranjan began feeling homesick. Finally, on Saurav's suggestion, the trio rented a flat close by that would be their home for the next three years. Saurav, who was two years their senior and had lived all his adult life by himself, taught them many important life skills. While Saurav cooked, Vidvath and Ranjan took turns chopping vegetables, cleaning and washing the dishes.

Saurav who had come from a culture where men enjoyed cooking and taking care of themselves and their families, openly criticized Vidvath and Ranjan when he learned about the rigid gender roles practiced in their families. While Ranjan did his share of chores grudgingly, Vidvath learned to embrace this new mindset. He learned some basic recipes from Saurav and discovered that he actually enjoyed cooking.

When Vidvath visited Jogibettu during the semester break, he was a transformed man. To his father's disappointment, he began spending more time in the kitchen, watching his mother cook and taking notes of the traditional recipes that he missed greatly in the city. Vinaya's heart swelled with pride when Vidvath prepared her delicious recipes that he had learned from Saurav. He no longer hesitated to talk to Yashodha, his ostracized elder sister. Vidvath spent hours talking to Yashodha, taking her to the city for movies and meals at fancy restaurants. He even convinced her to complete her education through a long-distance learning program and helped her enroll in it.

Back in Bengaluru, the trio explored the city outskirts during weekends and roamed around the city, trying street food, and watched movies after class. Occasionally they went to a dance club, but Vidvath did not enjoy the loud music and ambiance. Sometimes two girls who knew Saurav – Pooja and Leena – joined them. Before they knew the five of them had become a close-knit group. Vidvath soon learned that Leena and Saurav were in a relationship, and Ranjan was trying hard to impress Pooja. After that, Vidvath became a third wheel in the group. Vidvath began to feel lonely again. When Leena suggested introducing a friend of hers to Vidvath, Vidvath politely declined. It was then that Vidvath realized he was not yet ready to forget Radhika. Whether out of love or guilt, he did not know. He was however grateful to Ranjan for not revealing Vidvath's past to the group.

By the end of the second academic year, Vidvath had learned how to live with his pain whose edges time had blunted. The nightmares had reduced and Vidvath sometimes woke up from a dream where he was living a happy, content life. When Pooja broke up with Ranjan and Leena graduated from college and moved away, Vidvath could not help but feel a little relieved.

Three years passed by quickly and the trio despite a few setbacks, graduated with a Bachelor's degree in Computer Applications and a decent job in one of the many software companies that recruited freshers during on-campus placement drives. Holding the offer letter in hand, Vidvath knew he was never going back to Jogibettu and his father would never again be able to force him to do anything against his will.

A year had passed since Vidvath's graduation. Vidvath, Ranjan, and Saurav worked in the same company although in different departments. For them, life had not changed much. They often felt like they were still in college except now there were no exams and assignments. There was free food, longer weekends, and better pay. The only sad part was there were no semester breaks and more accountability.

While Saurav enjoyed his work and often spent his free time learning new coding techniques and tools, Ranjan found it hard to even finish the allotted work on time. He hated the job and his manager had begun to sense it. Vidvath managed to finish his work on time and became a valued asset to his team. But he refused to spend his weekends and free time on anything even remotely related to his work.

Through the company's Cultural and Sports Club, Vidvath was introduced to the world of treks and hikes. One weekend, the club organized an easy-to-moderate trek to Antargange in the Kolar district of Karnataka. Having never trekked before, Vidvath found the climb excruciating. His lungs burned from lack of oxygen, his feet ached and cramped. He was the slowest in the group. Yet, he knew he had found his escape. The physical pain soothed his mental chaos, kept him focused, and cleared his thoughts even if only for a few hours. Hiking through dense plantation, small caves and rocky boulders, Vidvath for the first time in many years felt alive. It was also the first time he had spent an entire day without thinking about the past even once.

Vidvath returned home that evening tanned and exhausted from the trek. But his heart was filled with satisfaction and exhilaration. His legs ached, and he had pulled a muscle in his back, but he had no regrets. He had fi-nally found an escape where his mind and body were engaged for hours at a stretch with no time or energy left to dwell on the past. He knew this was what he wanted to do— trek, hike, and exhaust his body enough so his mind does not get a chance to wander.

When Vidvath pulled his phone out from his backpack, he was surprised to see five missed calls from his home. He called back, and his father received the call on the second ring.

"Vidvath, why aren't you here yet? We were expecting you. The election is only a month away," Vidvath's father's voice was stern and borderline threat-ening. It was the first time his father had called him in a year. It was always his mother who called to check on him.

"I'm not coming, Appa." A few years ago, a phone call from his angry father would leave Vidvath nervous and afraid. He would have immediately jumped to pacify his father with an apology and left for his village as instruct-ed. But not anymore. The time away in a big city like Bengaluru had shown Vidvath how small and powerless his father, or any other self-proclaimed powerful man in Jogibettu was in comparison. He had also learned that his financial independence had paved the way for all other forms of indepen-dence. Finally, he had realized why Radhika had fought so hard for her future.

"What do you mean? Is your boss not letting you take leaves? Then leave the job—,"

"No. It's not my boss. I don't want to come." Vidvath smiled. It felt good to stand up for himself.

"Vidvath!" His father's tone was now low and warning.

"Appa, I am not interested in parading around Jogibettu with your goons, holding banners and placards. I don't want to bribe the naïve people, give them false hopes, or threaten them. I refuse to be the cause of their helpless-ness or the fear in their eyes. What you're doing is wrong. I'm sorry, Appa, but I won't be a part of this."

The line went silent for a few seconds and Vidvath wondered if his father had disconnected the call. Then he heard a deep breath and he knew from experience that it was the silence before the storm.

"How dare you, Vidvath! You ungrateful son of—" Vidvath's father's voice was raised several notches.

"Enough Appa!" Vidvath roared. "I'm not scared of you anymore. If you really want an heir to your so-called legacy, I suggest you ask Yashodha *Akka*[21]. She is educated and has far more life experience. She understands society and its crooked ways better than you or I do. She will be a good leader. And maybe our family will finally earn some respect from the people."

Vidvath disconnected the call before his father could reply. He knew he had wounded his father's ego, but it was necessary. Without a male heir for support, his father would become vulnerable, and perhaps a better candidate would get the opportunity to do something for their beloved village.

The following week, Ranjan resigned and went back to Jogibettu. Apparently, his father, Taranath had decided to contest against Vidvath's father, Raghupathi Rao, in the upcoming elections. Ranjan wished to be there for his father. This further angered Raghupathi Rao, who declared he had no son.

A month later, Raghupathi Rao lost the Gram Panchayat election by a long shot, and to everyone's surprise, even though Taranath made it as one of the nine Panchayat members, he was not elected as the leader. For the first time in the history of Jogibettu, a woman had become the Sarpanch.

---

[21] : Elder sister

CHAPTER 5

Ranachatti, 2022.

In the last week of December, Ranachatti welcomed its first snowfall of the season. The tranquil landscape underwent a gradual transformation as delicate snowflakes danced in the air. Yet, the majority of the village was still covered in dry grass, bare trees, and rocky terrain. It would take a day or two for the snow to settle.

Kshama woke up to the view outside her window and smiled. The elements were with her. Prajwal had informed her the previous day that the group of seven trekkers had arrived and would leave for Ranachatti early the next morning. They would reach the village a little after sunset. Kshama smiled, hoping that by the time the group began their trek the next day, the forests above and the entire trail to Jindi would be covered in ankle-deep snow.

Kshama freshened up, dressed in layers, and put the leash on Harper, who, despite his tiredness, looked happy at the prospect of walking in the cold weather. Even with his thick fur, Kshama dressed him in an insulated coat and boots. After making sure he was comfortable, the two of them walked out of the house and started along the downward stone path connecting their house to that of Amruta's.

The air outside was filled with a crisp chill, and the village exuded a sense of quiet anticipation. Kshama pulled her woolen cap further over her ears and tucked her gloved hands into her pockets. Amruta waved at Kshama as she approached.

"It snowed!" Amruta exclaimed, hugging Kshama. According to the initial weather forecast, snow was expected during the second week of December as it happened every year. However, it had been delayed this year, and Prajwal had to inform the trekkers about the postponement. They were disappointed but agreed to reschedule.

Throughout the rest of the day, Kshama and Amruta meticulously reviewed their plan, double-checking on Gattu's preparations and reminding both him and Rakesh once more not to carry any Raksi or Sher Beedis with them. Kshama knew from experience, that once night descended in the forest, the biting cold could be intolerable for city dwellers. Their resolve might weaken, leading them to resort to desperate measures to ward off the chill. There had been cases in the past where trekkers on nearby trails had become unruly after a few gulps of local alcohol.

The girls travelled to Barkot market and arranged for one more tent and a sleeping bag, realizing that the eighth trekker who had contacted Prajwal at the last moment would not be comfortable sharing the tent with the others. They also purchased some gloves and warmers, just in case.

Kshama and Amruta were disappointed when the little snow that had accumulated began to melt, and there was no sign of any snowfall for the day.

"Are you sure some of them are not beginners?" Kshama asked as they climbed the upward trail from the road towards Amruta's house. They slipped a few times, stepping on thin ice that had formed overnight on the rocks. While Kshama had taken up the responsibility of setting the budget, deciding the meal plans, and marketing, Amruta, who enjoyed building acquaintances with new people, took up the task of getting to know the trekkers—making note of their special requests and medical concerns.

"Well, three of them—two girls and the boy who is travelling separately from Bengaluru—have never been on a snow trek, but they have trekked longer, more strenuous ones in the Western Ghats," Amruta replied from memory. Kshama nodded.

"So what are their names and where are they from?" Kshama asked, suddenly curious. Until now, she had considered the group as one unit, rather than eight individuals from different parts of the country with diverse travel and trek experiences. This perception had made planning and visualization easier, but now it made her nervous as she realized she had not dealt with strangers in a long time.

"Well, they are all in their twenties except for the recent addition. The girls are cousins from Kerala—Reetha, Trisha and Nitya. Arjun is Trisha's elder brother who is bringing along his friend Piyush from Andhra Pradesh. That's five of them. Sushant and Seema are a couple from Mumbai. Sushant is mute but can hear and is the most experienced trekker of them all. The last one is the older man from Bengaluru, he is thirty-six and I have spoken to him only once so far. His name is Vi—"

"Thank God! You girls have returned!" Gitanjali's voice echoed from a few steps above as the duo approached Amruta's house. "Harper isn't eating anything. He just moans and turns his face away when I try to feed him. He thinks you abandoned him." Gitanjali was upset and jittery, as she always was when it came to someone in the house not eating well.

"Masi, he has been doing that a lot lately. He is old and— " Kshama tried to console Gitanjali as she made her way towards Harper, who was sound asleep near the fire.

"He is only fourteen," Gitanjali said.

"That's seventy-two in human years," Amruta replied, earning a glare from Gitanjali.

"We are the mountain people. Seventy-two is middle age for us!" Gitanjali replied, "I'm going to go boil some eggs for him. You girls make sure he eats it before he goes to sleep again," she added walking into the kitchen.

"She didn't even ask if we had eaten anything," Amruta grumbled.

An hour later, Amruta received a call from one of the girls, Reetha, that they had arrived.

"Welcome to Ranachatti," greeted Amruta as the group got down from the jeep. The crisp air hit them as they stepped onto the snowy ground, and their breaths formed puffs of mist in the chilly atmosphere. Standing beside them, Kshama tried to see Ranachatti and its surroundings from their eyes.

The village was now covered in a thin blanket of snow, and the landscape looked like a winter wonderland, with rooftops and trees adorned in patches of glistening white. The surrounding mountains stood tall and majestic, their peaks teasingly frosted with snow. Despite the cold, there was an air of excitement among the trekkers as they took in the enchanting sight before them.

"Thank you," smiled Piyush, extending his hand to shake Amruta's. The others followed suit, their faces reflecting wonder and amazement at the picturesque scene.

"This place is so beautiful!" exclaimed Reetha as she looked around. "Makes the long journey totally worth it." Nithya nodded in agreement, her eyes reflecting the snow-capped mountains and the dim light that painted the landscape with a soft glow.

"I cannot wait to see what lies above in the mountains," added Trisha, handing over her gear to Arjun, her elder brother, who narrowed his eyes at her but took it anyway. Trisha rubbed her hands together and tucked them into her jacket's pockets. All of them were dressed in several layers of warm clothes and waterproof jackets as advised.

"This madam here gets cold easily," teased Piyush, and then continued to ask Amruta a series of questions about the mountains, the yatra season, the Yamuna and everything in between.

"Don't worry. You will feel warmer as you start climbing. Once we reach home, you can warm up by the fireside and have hot tea," said Amruta, leading them towards her home.

"You must be Seema and Sushant," said Kshama as she approached the couple walking quietly at the back of the chatty group. Seema smiled in response and shook Kshama's hand. Sushant gestured at something in sign language and Seema translated it: "He says your village is lovely."

As the group approached Amruta's house, they were met with a warm and welcoming sight. The verandah was adorned with twinkling fairy lights, casting a cozy glow over the surroundings. Gitanjali came out to greet them first, her cheeks rosy from the cold. She smiled at the sight of the trekkers and welcomed them.

The group dropped their gear in the verandah and settled down in front of the fire, which crackled and emitted comforting warmth. Gitanjali served them steaming cups of tea and biscuits, and the aroma filled the air with a delightful fragrance. The group introduced themselves to Gitanjali, who was relieved to know that all of them understood Hindi, with some, like Seema and Piyush, speaking the language fluently. The conversation flowed easily, and the trekkers felt a sense of camaraderie settling in.

The group befriended Harper, who appeared livelier on seeing many new faces. He, too, settled by the fireside with the group, where Rakesh told them interesting stories about the village festivals and the treks he had been on. He showed them photographs on his phone and was satisfied by the groups awestruck response. Soon Gattu, Rakesh's trusted help, joined them.

When the night grew cold, Gitanjali invited the group into the kitchen where she was preparing rotis and rajma curry on the firewood stove. The girls huddled together by the fireside and moaned from the momentary relief from the biting cold. Reluctantly, they washed their hands in lukewarm water outside and returned to the kitchen for dinner. The boys continued to sit in the verandah, where Piyush, Gattu and Rakesh secretly shared a beedi while Arjun tried to communicate with Sushant and learn the sign language he found intriguing. The men were served dinner, which they chose to have outside in the verandah.

As Kshama moved between the kitchen and the verandah informing the group about the next day's plan, she found herself relaxing at how well the group was adjusting. It reminded her of her initial days in the strange, secluded village and how she had struggled to accept it. But she knew it was different for them. They were here for a few days, mentally prepared to adjust to anything new or strange, knowing that their families were waiting back home with whom they would share the memories of this adventure. To her it had been a new beginning from which there was no turning back.

Exhausted from the long journey and the bone-chilling cold, the group retired for the night early. They convinced Kshama that they would all adjust to staying in two rooms as none of them were ready to climb up till the top to sleep in Kshama's home. Gitanjali convinced Kshama to sleep here as well. Kshama noticed how gleeful Gitanjali had turned to see the full house.

Santosh and Gattu slept in the spare room after relishing their last bottle of Raksi which as promised, they wouldn't touch until the group left the village. Gitanjali, Kshama and Amruta sat in the kitchen taking advantage of the heat from the last bits of lit firewood.

"The group adjusted well, I must say. They are not fussy and seem comfortable," Kshama said.

"Some of them are rather too comfortable I would say," added Amruta.

"Yes, that lanky boy… Piyush is it? He seemed very interested in impressing you," said Gitanjali.

"I don't think he is particularly interested in anyone. He was flirting with all the girls. Even with you," Amruta replied with a grin.

"Amruta!" Gitanjali mock scolded as she tried hard to not blush. She walked out of the kitchen to make sure the lights in the verandah were turned off.

"So when are we expecting the other guy?" Kshama asked.

"I called Chachu sometime back. He said the man missed his flight and had to take the next one which led to a delay in the entire plan. He is in Dehradun now at Chachu's house. He will only be reaching here tomorrow evening."

"Okay. But we cannot start the trek a day late because of him."

"I know. That's why I have a plan. You, Gattu and Papa take the group tomorrow and I will meet you at the base the following day. We will start early, take the shortcut and catch up with you guys so that we can all climb to the summit together. The bugger better be a fast walker."

"The short cut? Won't that be wrong. He will miss out on many beautiful views."

"I will convince him. If he is fast, we can take the scenic route and still reach the base by noon. If he wants to go slow then we have no option but to take the short cut."

"I guess that makes sense."

"Girls, it's late. You have to start early so get some sleep," said Gitanjali as the last of the firewood hissed and turned cold.

On the day of the trek, Kshama woke up to the sound of Gitanjali heating water in the kitchen. Kshama and Amruta had stayed up late into the night revisiting the change in plans now that they could not start the trek together with the entire team. Kshama was nervous, knowing Amruta would not be around on the first day.

Getting out of bed, Kshama put on her coat, neck warmer and gloves. When her feet touched the stone floor outside, a chill ran up her spine. She warmed her feet near the fire that Rakesh had lit in the verandah. Overnight, there had been some snowfall that had dropped a thin veil on Ranachatti. Kshama hoped there would be more snow as they climbed. She squinted her eyes at the snowcapped mountains and realized it had already begun to snow heavily at the top. By early next week, Ranachatti would be covered in ankle-deep snow.

Kshama had lived in Ranachatti for seventeen years. Yet every winter somehow felt new, romantic at first and then ruthless. Putting on her socks, she walked around knocking at the doors to wake up the trekkers. She knew it would take them more than an hour to freshen up and get ready.

Thirty minutes later, when none of the group members came out, Amruta banged on their doors and warned the trekkers about having to take the less scenic shortcut in case they started late. One by one, the men came out of their rooms, groaning, rubbing their hands, cursing the chilly air, and jumping when the lukewarm water turned ice cold on contact with their skin. They freshened up in haste and refused to take a bath. The girls, however, managed to take a quick shower and were ready to leave on time.

Kshama, Amruta, and Gitanjali packed groceries for the day. Gattu, to everyone's utter disbelief, carried three tents and the grocery bag on his back and walked with ease. Rakesh arranged for walking sticks from the dried trees nearby and handed them to everyone. Everyone carried their own backpack with their sleeping bag, water bottles, and snacks. They bid Gitanjali and Amruta goodbye, and followed Gattu to the top of Ranachatti, where the trek would begin.

Fifteen minutes later, the group was outside the last house of the village, having passed the curious eyes of its people, shaggy dogs, and bored Khacchars or mules. As they huffed and wheezed along the way, the trekkers witnessed women half their size walk down the mountains with hay loads on their back, smiling and talking to each other with ease. They stopped to exchange greeting with Rakesh and Kshama.

"What do they eat? How are they doing it so easily?" asked Trisha, sitting down on a flat stone by the side of the road, catching her breath.

"Practice," Kshama replied, " And survival. If they don't wake up early and get the hay before the snow accumulates, their mules will have nothing to eat during the winter months. If the mules fall ill or die, the villagers will lose their main source of income during the Yamunotri pilgrimage months. These mules need to be strong and sturdy to carry the tourists to the mountain top and back every day during the yatra," Kshama explained.

"Why don't the men do it? I'm sure it would easier for them to carry the loads. I don't see a single man here," asked Nithya, looking at Gattu's speedily retreating figure as she helped Trisha back on her feet.

"Same reason why so many men all over the country refuse to work," Piyush replied nonchalantly. Kshama nodded in agreement.

"Don't the women rebel?" asked Reetha.

"A few do. Thanks to social media and high-speed internet these days that shows them how women in the towns and cities live their lives. But their rebellion does not have an effect here. The men don't care, and the only ones to suffer from their rebellion are the mules due to starvation and the children from poverty," Kshama replied. "If they don't make enough money during the pilgrimage season, they won't be able to sustain for the rest of the year. There are not many odd jobs to generate enough income here during the off-season."

"Then how did you manage to get Rakesh and Gattu to work for you?" asked Trisha, falling in step with the rest of them.

"I pay them well. They think of this as a man's job to climb these mountains and exhibit their strength. It gives them a chance to impress the city people like you with their familiarity and knowledge of the mountains," Kshama replied. "Ask Rakesh Masa how Ranachatti got its name."

"Sir," Reetha called out, rather sweetly. Rakesh halted in his step and turned around with a smile. Kshama wondered if anyone had ever called him Sir before.

"Can you tell us how Ranachatti got its name?"

Rakesh pretended to think for a moment. "It was our family. The original dwellers who built this village on this mountain. We are the Rana family. My ancestors were the first people to have settled here. The temple below where you people got down yesterday is also said to belong to our family," Rakesh said with great pride. Kshama suppressed a chuckle, recalling how she too had believed in awe when she first heard this from Rakesh many years ago. It was Amruta who later told her there was no documentation to prove the claim. It could be true, but mostly it was just a coincidence. The chances of naming an entire village based on one family were slim. Either way, the story added a nice touch to the trekking experience.

An hour later, Kshama announced a break, and everyone settled down at a scenic spot facing a stream and icy mountain tops in the far distance. Rakesh and Gattu collected dried branches and twigs to make a fire. The group huddled close to the fire. Gattu collected water from the stream and handed Kshama a packet of instant noodles. For the next fifteen minutes, everyone devoured the spicy noodles and sipped on icy water from the stream. It was 10:30 AM, and the sun was fully out, yet it did very little to drive away the cold.

"Our next stop will be in two hours at a small hut, three kilometers from here. We will rest there for an hour, have lunch, and then trek to the base, where we will camp for the night," Kshama announced as she stood up and urged everyone to clear the litter and pack their belongings. Just then, a group of men on their horses waved and hooted at the group as they passed by.

"The whole place has turned white at the top! It must have snowed heavily last night," a man on horseback hollered as he passed by the group. The group hooted in response.

For the next two hours, the trekkers marveled at literally everything—frozen water streams, wild Buran flowers, little waterfalls, wild birds, and little animals that scurried around as the trekkers walked through the imaginary trail behind Rakesh.

"I'm surprised the path is so clean. I haven't seen a single plastic wrapper or bottle along the way," Arjun exclaimed as he clicked pictures of the most unusual of things – insects, a dried leaf, a crack in the ice. Piyush played melodious songs on his portable speaker that soothed the exhausted group. Trisha, Seema, and Reetha were a few meters behind, bonding over the exhaustion they felt. Piyush and Sushant walked with Rakesh, trying to match his pace and hoping to learn more about mountain life. Arjun and Nitya walked with Kshama.

"I'm glad you brought up the point. Our intention behind not conducting this trek before was the same. You must have seen how the main road below Ranachatti is littered by tourists. It has been months since they left at the end of the pilgrimage season, but the litter is still clogging our drains and water bodies. If we are finding it hard to keep the village clean, imagine how much worse it would be if tourists littered the forests and water bodies in the mountains," Kshama explained. She had observed the group from the beginning of the trek. They were responsible trekkers. They had two waste bags tied to their backpacks in which they collected wrappers, covers, and tissues. Each of them had carried a metal water bottle and cutlery.

A little after 1 PM, Kshama announced lunch break, and the group dropped to the ground outside a stone hut surrounded by wild flowering plants. The house, albeit dark and spooky inside, had a rustic appeal. A short, stout man welcomed them and offered them piping hot cups of watery tea. Even as the sun sat above their heads, the temperature did not seem to soar.

"His name is Girvesh. He moved here from Nepal twenty years ago and has been living in this house ever since. He specializes in making Raksi and Sher beedi from forest herbs, millets, and jaggery," Rakesh narrated Girvesh's story while the group helped themselves to some instant noodles, this time with a few pieces of onion and tomatoes.

"I haven't had noodles for breakfast and lunch since my hostel days," Sushant signed, and Seema translated.

"Don't worry, Sushant. The mountain water, fresh air, and the climb will compensate for any unhealthy food you eat," Kshama assured.

An hour later, the group thanked Girvesh and continued trekking up the mountain.

"We need to fasten our pace. The sun sets by 4:30 PM these days, and climbing in the dark is risky. Heavy snowfall is expected tonight. So hurry up," Kshama announced as she moved to the head of the group beside Rakesh.

After walking for another two hours, the group reached the base just in time for the sky to turn dark. The campsite was covered in dried grass and patches of snow. Gattu and the boys began setting up tents while Rakesh created a makeshift toilet at the far end of the field. Kshama started a fire at the designated spot and arranged the groceries. Soon, Gattu and Rakesh would start cooking dinner.

A few minutes later, Kshama heard a scream. The group rushed to the spot behind tall trees on the west side to find a shivering Trisha. In front of her was scattered pieces of animal skeleton. Upon closer inspection, Piyush declared it was a cow or a buffalo. Kshama moved the group back to the campfire.

"Don't worry. It must be a bears work," Rakesh said nonchalantly.

"Gee, thanks. I'm not so worried anymore," Trisha replied, and Rakesh grinned.

"Will the bear attack us?" asked Seema. Sushant nodded no, pointing to the fire.

"He is right. Animals do not come anywhere near the fire," Kshama assured the group.

"And what happens in the night when the fire goes off?" asked Arjun.

"Well, don't come out of the tent at night if you hear anything. Finish all your business before nightfall," Rakesh replied, pointing towards the make-shift toilet.

"Masa, enough," Kshama said, glaring at Rakesh. "You guys have nothing to worry about. I promise. We have come here over a dozen times these last few months and have never spotted a bear or any other wild animal. Also, bears hibernate during winters. The skeleton is very old. It must have been kill—died during the monsoon."

"Have you come face to face with a bear at any time, Sir?" Reetha asked Rakesh.

"No," Rakesh replied, stealing a glance at Kshama who was explaining something to Trisha.

"But a few years ago, a snow leopard walked past me when I came to collect firewood," added Gattu as he approached the group dragging a large tree trunk for firewood behind him. Kshama narrowed her eyes at him. She missed Amruta.

"It was on another mountain on the other side," Rakesh quickly added and walked away.

After warming up in front of the fire, the group slowly came to life. It was then that they realized they had lost their cellphone networks. Piyush, who had come prepared, had an offline playlist on his phone, which he played on the speaker. One by one, they began singing and dancing. Bears and snow leopards forgotten. Every half an hour or so, Rakesh walked to the forest behind the campsite and brought fresh firewood to keep the campfire alive. Sushant, who was a freelance blogger, had many questions for Kshama which he signed and Seema translated. Kshama was happy to answer them all in detail. Later, Kshama and Rakesh served them dinner which the group devoured.

"I can't believe you managed to cook rice, dal, roti, and *sabji*[22] here in the woods," Arjun exclaimed as he took pictures of their makeshift chulha on which sat a burnt pressure cooker.

After dinner, everyone sat around the fire, hoping to warm up enough before retreating to their tents. Crickets creaked on the treetops and wind whooshed every now and then. Above them, the sky had turned into a carpet of little diamonds.

"If you sit still and observe, you can differentiate the satellites from the stars. Satellites move faster and are slightly brighter," Kshama said, pointing out some constellations she had learned to identify. The group lied down on foam mats spread across the ground and watched the sky in silence. If Kshama saw Nithya's hand slip into Arjun's as they lay side by side, she pretended not to notice. She, however, could not help the emotions that stirred in her chest. It reminded her of the time she and Abhay had come here the first time.

At little past ten, they called it a night and retired to their respective tents. The girls shared one, the boys another, and Kshama had her own tent which she was supposed to share with Amruta, and a small one in which Rakesh and Gattu slept. Kshama, however, tossed and turned for several hours. It had been years since she had last slept in a tent. The last time she had slept in the campsite, she had fallen asleep tucked in Abhay's arms without a care in the world.

---

[22] : Indian vegetable dish cooked with spices

The next morning, Kshama woke up to the commotion outside her tent. It was still dark, with the first rays of sunlight slowly piercing through the clouds. As she unzipped her tent and stepped outside, she was awestruck by the view. In front of her, for as far as the eyes could see, the ground was covered in thick layers of snow with the last of the snowflakes dancing in the air. Streams of water from the mountain tops were frozen.

Gattu and Rakesh were making a fire, while the group played around in the snow. At the far end, the mountains of Swarga Rohini, Bandarpunch and Bali Pass glistened under the morning light.

Vidvath woke up to the sound of his alarm and shivered as he got out of the thick blankets. It was 6:00 AM. Outside, it was as dark as midnight with not even a hint of sunrise. Vidvath had never experienced such cold in his life and it felt surreal. Last night, he had carried a cup of piping hot water to his room from the kitchen. It had turned lukewarm in less than a minute. His toes, despite two layers of protection, felt numb; his nose and eyes were watery, and no amount of moisturizer seemed to help the cracked skin on his face.

Walking out of the room, he was greeted by Gitanjali who was heating a bucket of water using a homemade electric coil. It was a simple device—two insulated wires connected to the ends of a copper wire gummed to a wooden board. The wires did not have a plug; instead she directly inserted them into the socket holes. There were two more placed outside the kitchen.

"Are you sure you want to start this early? It's going to be very cold up there until sunrise," asked Amruta as she entered the verandah, pulling her coat tightly around her body. She was dressed and ready to go.

"Yes, I don't want to keep the group waiting. I'll fresh up quickly and then we can start. I'll try my best to climb as fast as I can," Vidvath replied, rushing past her towards the bucket of hot water.

Thirty minutes later, they were out of the house, picking up their respective gear and beginning their climb. Although at first Vidvath's feet ached at every step, he soon felt warmth seep into his shoes as he continued to climb. By the time they reached the top of the village, Vidvath no longer felt cold. He was sweating through the four layers of clothes and felt the adrenaline rush through his body.

"If you keep up this speed, I think we can take the regular route and still reach on time. The others will be at the base until noon. I have informed them to wait, " Amruta said encouragingly. Vidvath noticed that she was not out of breath like him.

Two hours later, after a quick break for breakfast, they continued their climb. By mid-morning, Vidvath sensed his energy dropping. The cold air made it hard to breathe, and the cramp in his left leg did not seem to loosen.

"So, where are you from? Have you always lived in Bengaluru?" Vidvath smiled, realizing Amruta was trying to distract him from the pain.

"No, I moved to Bengaluru for college and then settled there after I was offered a job. I'm from a small village in South of Karnataka called Jogibettu," Vidvath replied. For a brief moment, he saw a flash of surprise on Amruta's face. Before he could inquire further, she had composed herself.

"Is Jogibettu a common name there? Like how we have Chatti here. You know Ranachatti, Janaki Chatti, Hanumanchatti…" Amruta asked.

"Hmmm," Vidvath wondered. "Yes, we have a couple of villages in the district ending with bettu. But I have not come across any other village named Jogibettu." Amruta nodded.

"Why do you ask?"

"Oh, nothing. I have never been to the south of the country so I try to understand about the places there through the tourists who come here," Amruta quickly replied, and then continued, "So, you're more of a beach person then."

"I think I'm an anything-close-to-nature person. A decade in an IT job can do that to anyone," Vidvath chuckled. They had now reached the part of the trail that was submerged in silence. The floor was covered with a thin layer of snow above a bed of dry leaves that crunched with each footstep. The wind had died down, and soft rays of sunlight seeped through the canopy of trees.

"I think it must have snowed heavily at the campsite last night," Amruta said as she saw chunks of snow accumulated on the forest floor. Vidvath, having never witnessed snowfall before, smiled giddily.

"What about you? Have you lived here all your life?"

"I lived in Delhi for a few years and then moved back here. I do freelance work now," Amruta replied.

"You're living the dream of an entire generation. Living amidst nature, adventure treks and freelance work. No boss, no leave applications, no EMIs. Sometimes I wish I had the courage to quit and move back to Jogibettu. Start something of my own."

At Dinnala Base.

"I think I found a spot. I see a single bar," said Nithya, standing on the other side of the frozen stream. Her phone pointed at an unusual angle towards the sky. Kshama was beside her, refreshing her chat. Amruta had messaged her early this morning, informing her that they had started and would reach the base by noon. Another message received two hours later said they might reach earlier than expected. The man was fast.

Just as Kshama was about to put her phone back in her jacket pocket, another message chimed.

You guys go ahead. We will be late. Will see you at the top. Kshama frowned. She quickly replied back.

Is anyone hurt? Should I send Gattu?

No. We are okay. Just tired and took few breaks.

Something about Amruta's message did not feel right. It was as if she did not want to join the group. Had she developed a crush on this last trekker?

Was she hoping to spend some alone time with him? Kshama smiled at the thought.

"Guys, time to start packing. Let's fold the tents and sleeping bags. We will start in exactly an hour. Amruta and the other trekker will join us at the top. They are running late," Kshama announced, just realizing she still did not know the name of the last trekker.

An hour later, the group began its trek across the snow-laden path, following Rakesh who seemed to continue at the same pace as the day before despite the thick snow. Gattu was a tiny silhouette several meters away, once again carrying most of the load.

"That there are the peaks of Bandarpunch mountain. The highest one is called the main peak, to the left is the white peak and to the right is the black peak. Does anyone know what Bandarpunch stands for?" asked Rakesh.

"Monkey's tale," Arjun replied. "I'm guessing there is a story related to Lord Hanuman here. Did any part of the Ramayana take place here, Sir?"

"Not Ramayan, but Mahabharat. Somewhere in these mountain ranges, Bheem is believed to have met his older half-brother, Lord Hanuman."

"Wow!" Trisha exclaimed.

"But Ramayana was several hundred years before Mahabharata. How can Lord Hanuman be present in both?" asked Rakesh.

"There is no information of Hanuman ji's demise anywhere in the scriptures. He is an immortal. Even today, we do not speak of him in past tense."

"So, what is the story of their meeting?" asked Reetha.

"It was during the Vanavas period of the Pandavas. One day, Draupadi wished for the Saugandhika flower, known for its enchanting fragrance and beauty. Bheem left in search of the flower and came across a path blocked by a long tail. Coming closer, he saw an old monkey resting on the side with its tail across the path. He requested the monkey to move its tail aside so that he could pass. The monkey denied and asked Bheem to move it by himself. Having never experienced defeat when it came to matters of strength, Bheem tried to lift the monkey's tail with all his might but failed. When he accepted his defeat and asked the monkey who he really was, the monkey transformed into lord Hanuman and introduced himself as Bheem's older half-brother. It is said that Lord Hanuman wanted to teach his younger brother the importance of staying humble. Later, Lord Hanuman protected Arjun's chariot by residing in the chariot's flag during the war of Kurukshetra." The group listened in awe as Rakesh narrated the story with great pride.

"Have you been there, Kshama?" asked Nithya falling into step beside Kshama.

"Once, many years ago. It is the toughest trek I have ever attempted, and by God's grace, completed. It takes seven to eight days to reach the summit. The route is heavily crevasse-infested, and the weather conditions can get unpredictable." Kshama replied as the memories came flooding to her mind. Although it was her idea to trek to Bandarpunch, it was Abhay who had been her rock during those moments of self-doubt and panic. He had constantly reassured her, reminding her of her resilience and strength. Then he held her close when she had burst into tears of happiness on reaching the top.

"It is very inspiring you know, seeing you organize and guide these difficult treks. I know it sounds misogynistic, but I'm sure doing something like this must be more difficult being a woman."

"It is actually true. Not many women take up this profession. Mainly because most trekkers are skeptical when they hear a woman would be leading it. But if you think of it, the mountains do not differentiate. If nature was were to take its course, even the strongest, fittest of men will not stand a chance."

"Oh no!" Trisha exclaimed, looking back at Kshama and Nithya.

"What happened?" asked Kshama.

"I think I left my phone at the campsite."

"I'll go back and check. You guys continue. I'll catch up with you. Don't wander away. Stay with Rakesh Masa," Kshama instructed as she turned around. It would take her half an hour to go back. Hopefully, Amruta and the last trekker would reach the base by then.

"I'm sorry, Kshama," she heard Trisha behind her.

"It's okay. Don't worry about it."

Despite the biting cold and exhaustion, Vidvath felt alive. His dream of several years had finally come true. He had trekked for close to six hours, something he could not have imagined three years ago when he first decided to go for a winter trek.

As he reached the base, with Amruta a few steps ahead, he felt exhilarated. As though destined, fresh snowflakes began to descend. It was the first time Vidvath was experiencing a snowfall, and it made him feel enchanted. He stretched out a gloved hand, and a snowflake landed on his palm, exhibiting its crystalline beauty. For that moment, his legs did not ache, his hands and feet did not feel numb, and his lungs did not burn. His mind was busy taking in the serenity and vastness of his surroundings. Amruta explained to him the different mountain peaks that were visible and their stories. She showed him around the place, telling him what the group did last night when they camped here.

"I wish we had reached a little earlier. We could have caught up with the group," Vidvath said as he sat down on the ground and watched the mountains. Amruta did not respond and looked away. During the last two hours or so, Vidvath sensed that Amruta was in no rush to reach the base on time. More than once, she had asked for a break and had assured him it was okay if they did not join the others. It felt strange, but Vidvath let it pass. Maybe she wasn't feeling her best.

"Thanks for staying back for my sake. I was really worried I had missed the entire trek," Vidvath said.

"Don't worry about it, we are glad you could make it," Amruta replied. "We will meet the others tonight at the summit. The view from there is amazing."

"Who is leading the rest of the group?"

"My friend, who is also a guide at Apna Travels, joined by my father and his friend, all of whom know the mountains well."

"Oh yes, I think the manager at Apna Travels had told me her name, – Kshama right?" Vidvath recalled. Amruta nodded.

"You guys are an inspiration. Back where I come from, women are still struggling to find acceptance in male-dominated professions. Here, you are climbing mountains and guiding trekkers from all over the country."

Vidvath sat down at a spot from where several peaks of snow-capped mountains were clearly visible. Amruta pointed out each one of them and explained the story behind their names. Vidvath listened to her intently, trying to make a mental note of them all. He pulled out his camera from his bag, and started clicking pictures. Amruta excused herself and walked to the frozen stream on the other side of the campsite.

Vidvath noticed the remnants of burnt firewood at two distinct spots and smiled, as he imagined the warmth and camaraderie shared around a bonfire the previous night. He hoped the one tonight at Jindi summit would be even more spectacular—flames dancing in harmony under the expansive, star-studded canvas above.

Vidvath knew they would have to start walking soon if they planned to reach the summit before nightfall. When he turned towards Amruta to inform her that he was ready to start again, he found her squinting at the forest. A silhouette appeared from behind the trees and waved at them.

Kshama smiled and waved as she approached Amruta and the last trekker from the group. But her smile quickly waned as her eyes shifted from Amruta to the man standing behind her. Her heart skipped a beat as a wave of dread washed over her. It was impossible to deny who he was, even before his face fully came into view. Kshama's world seemed to freeze, caught in an agonizing moment. Her worst fear, buried deep in her heart, had not only surfaced but was now moving steadily closer to her. The air around her grew heavier with anticipation, as Kshama realized that her carefully guarded secret was on the precipice of exposure.

PART 2

CHAPTER 1

Jogibettu, 2002.

Deva Deva, you're drinking coffee again? Have you no shame disobeying me after all that I have done for you?" said Suman through gritted teeth, imitating, Radhika's mother, Padmini.

"Coffee will not make me any darker than I already am, Amma. Dark skin is beautiful. There is nothing to be ashamed of," replied Radhika in a calm, practiced tone as she tried hard to suppress her laughter.

"And who is filling this rubbish in your head? Suman? That witch is spoiling our girls, I tell you," spat Suman, scrunching her face in disgust, mimicking their grandmother Jayalakshmi. At Suman's uncanny imitation of her grandmother, Radhika lost her composure and burst out laughing.

Every Thursday, when Radhika's school bell rang an hour early, she rushed to her cousin Suman's house, where she felt most at home. The duo often reenacted everyday conversations at Radhika's house, like the one today, and had a great laugh.

Suman was Radhika's first cousin, and her parents had moved to Mangaluru city when she was still a young girl. She completed her education there and became a teacher. After a short-lived marriage and her parents' untimely death a few years later, Suman decided to move back to Jogibettu and contribute to the education of young minds there.

While the rest of the village saw the thirty-four-year-old divorcee - the first of her kind in the village - Suman as an outcast, Radhika and a few other students in her class admired their English teacher. Whether the respect was due to the strong and independent woman Suman was, or because of the language she taught, at school was unclear. There were not many fluent speakers of the English language in their little coastal village of Jogibettu. In addition to this, Suman contributed to the local newspaper and was an important member of Nari Shakti, the district's Women Welfare Association, making the villagers fear her as much as they disliked her.

Despite Radhika's mother Padmini's innumerable attempts to keep her daughter away from Suman, the two developed a deep bond built on their shared love for literature and disdain for misogyny.

"Suman Akka, I finally received my first letter yesterday!" While at Suman's place, Radhika spoke to her in English. It had started as a way to help Radhika get better acquainted with the language when she was younger. Now, she spoke it with as much confidence and fluency as she did her mother tongue, Kannada. But the two had grown comfortable talking in English. It especially helped when Radhika wished to share something with Suman at a family gathering. Radhika loved watching her mother grit her teeth in anger and confusion, unable to comprehend their conversation.

"That's nice. Who is it from?" It was Suman who had introduced Radhika to novels. She often let her borrow them from her home library. Radhika's thirst for reading had outgrown the school library many years ago. In one of the books she had recently read, Radhika had come across the term 'pen friends'. After learning from Suman about what it was and how it worked, Radhika wanted nothing more than to have a pen friend. Suman had reluctantly agreed, knowing Radhika's parents would not be happy to know that their teenage daughter was writing to a stranger far away.

"She calls herself Binya, as in Binya from Ruskin Bond's The Blue Umbrella. She does not want to disclose her real name yet. But I promise, she is a girl," Radhika spoke hurriedly, hoping to convince Suman that she was safe.

"Tell me more," Suman smiled.

"She is my age and lives with her family in a small village called Ranachatti in Uttarakhand," replied Radhika. "Her village is situated along the path to Yamunotri. It takes around six hours from Dehradun. She says she loves reading and dreams of seeing the world someday. But she hasn't been anywhere beyond Dehradun. She hasn't heard of Mangaluru or even Karnataka. She said she was excited that she now had a 'Madrasi' friend." Radhika rolled her eyes at the last bit.

"Although it's been just one letter, Suman Akka, I already feel like she is my kindred spirit," Radhika's wide smile reached her eyes. She carefully folded the letter and placed it between the pages of her notebook. Suman knew what it was to be a teenager exposed to new experiences: the thrill, the carefreeness, and the newfound desire to explore. But it was important to caution Radhika about the other side of the equation.

"Radhika, it is nice that you now have a friend outside this little village. But you are smart enough to know that the world out there could be dangerous. You need to be careful about what you share in your letters."

"I understand, Akka. I will be careful, promise," Radhika nodded.

"Speaking of dreams, have you made up your mind about what stream you're going to choose after graduation?" asked Suman. Radhika was a student in the tenth grade and would be done with her boards in a few months. Being a bright student, not just academically but also in logical reasoning and communication, Suman was sure Radhika could become anything she set her mind to. Very early in her childhood, Suman had realized Jogibettu would not be enough for Radhika.

"At this point, Suman Akka, I think I will choose the stream that takes the longest time to graduate," Radhika chuckled but was not able to hide the sadness behind the thought. Suman frowned.

"I overheard Amma and *Ajji*[23] talking about marriage proposals for me after my degree." Radhika pursed her lips. "Ajji said if the proposal is good, they could have the engagement before the final year as well." She shook her head. "Suman Akka, it's like waking up one day and realizing I have only four years, five at best, to live before my life is handed over to a stranger and his

---

[23] : Grandmother

family."

Suman thought for a long moment and then smiled. "Don't worry about that now. When the time comes, we will make sure your education and career are not compromised. For now, focus on what you want to do."

"I like Arts, but considering our financial situation, I feel taking up Science and then pursuing Engineering or Medicine will be a better choice," Radhika replied. Suman smiled.

"Why are you smiling?"

"Generally, I advise students to choose what they really want to study rather than what can potentially make more money. But this thought is overshadowed by your intention of wanting to help your family's financial situation," Suman replied. Most girls in Jogibettu chose relatively easier streams just for the sake of possessing a Bachelor's degree, which would help them in the marriage negotiations that followed soon after their graduation. "It also helps that an Engineering degree is a year longer than a BA. And I have heard of some ridiculous things, like the dowry demanded is significantly less for a girl with a science degree."

"Why is that?"

"Families now want to look modern in society, so they are marrying their sons to girls whom they plan to 'allow' to work after marriage. Now, a degree in science usually gets higher pay, which means a lifelong income for the family rather than a lump sum amount at the beginning." Suman shrugged. When Radhika first began to grasp misogyny, Suman's casually unagitated responses to her questions had irked her. But now, Radhika understood it was mere exhaustion from having witnessed so many avatars—small and big—of this patriarchal society.

"Radhika, if you had all the freedom in the world – financial and otherwise—what would you really want to study?"

"Honestly, I don't know," Radhika replied, fidgeting with her fingers. How was she supposed to decide what she wanted to do for the rest of her life or what was best when her knowledge of careers was confined within Jogibettu's limited number of educated individuals? In Jogibettu, most students stopped studying after twelfth grade and assisted their fathers in the family business or stores. Some, mostly boys, moved to the cities to apply for government jobs or join engineering colleges. But the number of girls who did this was still small.

"Hmmm..." Suman smiled. "Radhika, you're not the only one who is going through this. Everyone standing at the threshold between school and college is in the same dilemma." She assured Radhika. "Think of what your interests are. What is it that you like doing enough that the thought of doing it for the rest of your life does not scare you?"

Radhika thought for a long moment. "I could read books for a living or maybe travel to a new place every month and learn about their cultures," Radhika replied honestly. "I know these are unrealistic..."

"Not really. There are many professions that pay you for travelling and reading. Journalism for example. But of course it is not as fun as it sounds. It is hard work and there are risks involved."

"What other travel-related professions are out there, Suman Akka?"

"Let's see," Suman replied. "In tourism there are jobs as tour guides. Wild life and nature Photography, I heard, is also a serious profession now. Travel writing – this is where your love for writing and travelling comes together. Here you get paid to travel to a particular place and write articles about your experiences there," Suman added. "From what I know, most of the time these are not stable jobs. You get paid based on the size of your assignment and your readership. There might be times when you don't have enough work."

"All of these sound like a dream, Suman Akka. But I know they are not for me. I need to choose something stable so that I can help Appa and Amma with the finances. Despite our modest condition, they have managed to provide a good life for me and Anna. I don't want them to strain under the weight of my marriage expenses and dowry," Radhika replied. Suman nodded understandingly.

There was a skip in Radhika's steps as she walked home from Suman's place. After promising Suman that she would be careful about what she shared with her pen friend, Radhika had coaxed Suman into sharing her experiences with writing to strangers when she was younger. Suman had reluctantly agreed and shared many interesting bits from the letters she had received.

Suman's letters were from places Radhika had never heard of—Hanoi, Frankfurt, Osaka. There was one particular pen-friend that Radhika wanted to know more about. A French baker, Lyam, referred to Suman as Mademoiselle in his letters. Radhika had found it all very romantic—a foreigner, a baker, the French terms he used – until she realized Lyam was seventy-five and a father of three daughters whom he also addressed as Mademoiselle.

As she walked along the potholed roads bordered by tall trees on one side and a garbage-strewn gutter on the other, Radhika wondered if she too would someday find someone special through these letters. A relationship built on love for the written word. It would make a great love story.

Radhika knew she could only dream of something like that happening in her life. She would be lucky if she wasn't betrothed to a stranger before she even graduated. While her parents valued her education, it would not surprise her if they yielded under society's pressure. But her teenage mind was hopeful. Fueled with love stories from novels she devoured regularly, the possibility of a beautiful love story seemed more real.

As though pulling her back to reality, a shooting pain punched through Radhika's stomach. She clutched her stomach and took a deep breath, waiting for the pain to subside. She began walking again. A few steps later, the pain returned. Radhika knew what was happening, yet she felt panic rise in the pit of her stomach. Oh no, not now. Not here.

Consciously, she loosened the buckles of her backpack and lowered it to cover her skirt. She walked home in hurried steps between the shots of pain. On reaching home, she stood at the threshold of the main door and watched her mother serve Avinash his evening snacks. With one look at Radhika's pale face and lowered bag, Padmini knew what had happened.

"Here she comes. Done with the gossip session with your dear Suman Akka?" Avinash teased as always. He frowned when Radhika did not retort.

"Are you okay?" Padmini whispered as she approached Radhika.

Radhika did not reply. All she wanted to do was run to her room and lie on her bed with a hot water bag and wait for the excruciating pain to stop. But she knew there were rules to be followed. Rules she did not agree with but would not be given a choice. So she stood at the threshold, clutching her stomach, waiting for her mother's instructions.

"What's wrong with her?" Avinash asked as he watched his sister's pale face.

"Why are you wearing your bag so low?" he asked, walking towards Radhika.

"That's enough, Avinash. Finish eating and leave," Padmini replied sternly, and gestured for Radhika to follow her into the spare room outside the house next to the verandah.

Five days later.

"I know this is not something you would have chosen. But it is an old tradition in the village, and we must respect that," Suman said to Radhika, who frowned as Suman helped dry her hair.

"Of all the people here, I can't believe I'm hearing this from you, Suman Akka. I thought at least you would oppose this," Radhika huffed.

"I understand this is embarrassing for you now, Radhika. But *Ritushuddi*[24] is a progressive idea if you think about it," Suman replied. Radhika scrunched her eyebrows in confusion. Earlier, a few women close to the family, had come together and bathed her in turmeric water. They had bombarded her and her mother with do's and don'ts based on their experiences. Renuka, her

---

[24] Traditional ritual marking the onset of menstruation for young girls

mother's friend, warned her not to touch any plants during her 'sick' days, as they would wither and die. A few others agreed. Someone asked her not to eat pickles or tamarind, and someone else warned her not to even touch pickles as they would turn bad. After a while, Radhika stopped listening.

Namitha, Radhika's maternal aunt had gifted her a gorgeous silk saree as was the tradition. Radhika was to wear this saree for the rest of the ceremony.

"Through this ceremony, we are normalizing the idea of menstruation. Instead of hiding it, we are celebrating womanhood. The tradition is centuries old, originating in the times when girls lacked the knowledge about puberty that we have now. Women came together to impart knowledge based on their experience to the young girls and bless them," Suman explained, though she knew what was coming next.

"If it is a celebration, then why am I treated like an outcast in my own house? Why am I made to sleep on a mat on the floor in a separate room and eat from a different set of utensils? Don't these menstruation experts know that it is not a contagious disease?"

"That is something I'm not happy about either," Suman replied with a smile. "Like all traditions, people have forgotten to adapt and change with changing times." Radhika blinked back tears of anger and frustration.

"Just bear it for this time. From next month, you can come stay with me," Suman said. Radhika's face lit up at the words. "It's okay if you don't want to. You are a woman now and may not want to get into bad influence," Suman teased. Radhika rolled her eyes and managed to smile.

"You think Amma will agree? Five full days with you every month?" Radhika asked, rubbing her eyes.

"We will think of something."

Radhika smiled at the thought. She loved Suman Akka more than anyone else in the family. Spending five days with her instead of just one hour every week seemed like a good deal in exchange for the discomfort and pain she would have to endure during that time. Radhika began to make a mental list of all the things she would do while at Suman's place.

Draped in the silk saree and adorned with her mother's gold jewelry, Radhika was led out into the frontyard where a makeshift stage was set up. She was asked to sit on a low wooden stool beside one of dolls she played with as a child. This Radhika learned symbolized the end of her childhood and the onset of puberty.

Women from the neighboring houses and a few older men had been invited, along with many of Radhika's friends. Everyone arrived bearing gifts and enjoyed a scrumptious meal. Just as Radhika was beginning to feel better about the whole business, she spotted Vidvath in the last row with Avinash beside him. What was he doing here? Were boys even allowed? Did they know about menstruation and this ceremony? A hundred questions spiraled through her mind, while embarrassment began to bubble in the pit of her stomach.

Vidvath, who was Radhika's senior by two years was also Avinash's best friend. This in addition to the fact that Radhika's mother Padmini and Vidvath's mother Vinaya had been friends since their school days, had somewhat bridged the gap in the financial status between the two families. Needless to say, like most men in Jogibettu, the fathers did not mingle in the same social circle.

Radhika harbored a childhood dislike for Vidvath, rooted in their history of teasing and provoking each other. In their younger years, Vidvath and Avinash often engaged in mischievous antics that left Radhika fuming. As they grew up, Radhika began to realize how different Vidvath's life as the sole heir to his booming family business was compared to her modest upbringing.

Vidvath, the sole heir to a thriving family business, seemed to navigate life with apparent ease that came with affluence. He often got away with mischief in school and outside, and was even promoted to higher classes despite failing many subjects. Rumors had it that the school benefited from donations periodically made by his father.

Yet, as the years passed, Radhika observed a more complex facet of Vidvath. Beyond the wealth and privilege, she witnessed a young man who cherished his friendship with Avinash and held a genuine respect for her parents.

The teasing and provocation ceased over time, replaced by a more amiable demeanor that, to Radhika's surprise, no longer irked her as it once had.

"Are you okay?" it was Radhika's best friend Tara's voice that shook her out of her train of thoughts. Radhika quickly tore her eyes off Vidvath and cleared her throat. " Yes… why?"

"Nothing. Just that you have been staring at Vidvath for over five minutes now," Tara grinned, wriggling her eyebrows.

"They say it is common to feel this way… now that…" Tara continued.

"Oh… shut up."

September 2002

Twilight spread its golden glow over Jogibettu that evening. The sky painted a palette of gold and blue as day transformed into night.

Seventeen-year-old Vidvath passed by his best friend's house on his brand-new motorcycle for the seventh time that evening. Each time he circled, he slowed down in front of the tiled-roof house, stealing glances towards Radhika's room, which faced the road. His heart drummed in his chest like a caged bird trying to escape. He knew this was wrong. Stalking a girl and loitering outside her house after sundown were behaviors frowned upon by people from families like his. But he couldn't help himself. He had to see her.

It had been three days since Vidvath had last seen Radhika. It was on the last day of school before Dasara vacations. She had smiled back at him in the hallway, causing his heart to flutter. The feeling had left him restless. It wasn't as if he was seeing Radhika for the first time. They had practically spent their entire childhood together. When they were very young, Radhika had made them fake tea and snacks with her play kitchen set. Vidvath and Avinash had played pranks on her—hiding her toys and scaring her with ghost tales. Vidvath had wiped away her tears and made her laugh. Then in middle school, they had fought several times, both physically and verbally, only to turn around and tattle on each other to the elders.

So now, this unusual feeling made no sense to him. Everything the movies claimed was happening to him. Suddenly, the romantic scenes that he cringed at as a child, made him blush.

It had all started on the day he had been forced by his mother to attend Radhika's Ritushuddi ceremony. He knew it was a ceremony held when a girl became a woman. They had held one for his sister many years ago, but he did not know what 'becoming a woman' exactly meant. He was too embarrassed to ask anyone about this in his family. But Radhika had appeared different that day.

Vidvath had learned from Avinash that the family was leaving to visit their maternal grandmother in Mangaluru the next day and would only return a week later. Vidvath knew he had to see Radhika before she left, or else he would have to spend the week sleepless like he did the last three days.

As he slowed down in front of the house for the eighth time, he saw Radhika walk out with a lamp in her hand. She looked serene in its soft glow, and Vidvath could not help but watch her, mesmerized. Her freshly washed hair was wound loosely in a towel. A few loose strands carelessly hung over her plump cheeks. Her button nose, adorned with a small pin, glowed softly in the lamp's light. The soft sound of her anklets chimed through the front-yard. She placed the lamp in front of the holy *Tulsi Brindavan*[25] and chanted a short prayer before turning around and walking into the house.

Vidvath stood there for a moment longer before starting his bike and heading home, a smile plastered to his face.

---

[25] : A sacred place or structure dedicated to the holy basil plant

Dear Radhika,

I apologize for not replying to your letter sooner. My days and nights seem to have merged into one. Our quiet Ranchatti has been buzzing with people from all over the country and some from outside these last several weeks. The road below our house that leads to Janaki Chatti —where the yatra to Yamunotri begins —is crowded all the time. Every day, thousands of people on foot, in Palkis, and on Khacchars (mules – I learnt this from my English teacher) travel to Yamunotri, the source of the river Yamuna and the seat of Goddess Yamuna. I wish you were here to witness her splendor.

There are guests at my house too. My little room is now occupied by eight of my cousins. All the men are busy taking Yatris[26] to the peak and back. This is the only time in the year when we locals can make some money and sustain ourselves for the rest of the year when there is no source of income.

One of my cousins, Rani, is extremely nosy and prying. Doing anything without her on my tail is impossible. This is one of the reasons for my delayed response to your letter. I'm writing this to you at 4 in the morning just so that I can have a little peace and privacy.

I am sitting on the topmost platform of our village. It is where our primary school is. There is a little terrace garden here which is in full bloom with a variety of wildflowers. Next to me are our mules, Raja and Rani. I named them. No points for guessing why I chose the second one.

In front of me, a mountain stands tall and mighty. After the yatra ends, the women in my village will start walking up the mountains in the early hours and return with stacks of hay by noon. This is for the mules who cannot go up the mountains to graze in the winter. Mother wants me to join her this year. If she found out that I have woken up this early, she might ask me to start today.

The weather has been pleasant these last few months but soon the merciless winter will

---

[26] : Pilgrims

be upon us. So for the next couple of weeks, everyone will make trips up the mountain to Dinnala and collect firewood that will keep us warm in the cold months.

In your last letter, you mentioned about Summer Holidays. It is the first time, I hear about it. Here we have holidays during peak winter months when the temperature falls below zero. Sometimes when we wake up in the morning, our front yard is covered with knee-deep snow. It is my most favorite time of the year. After all the crowd has moved away and the yatra is closed for the year, Ranachatti returns to its quiet and serene self. I spend these months, wrapped in layers of blankets, sipping hot tea and reading my novels. My Chacha (My father's older brother)- who lives in Dehradun gifted me a set of Ruskin Bond books during his last visit. I hope it lasts the entire winter season. I have run out of books to read.

There is so much I want to tell you and so much more I want to know about your village where the sun shines throughout the year. I wish I had a camera with me so I could add photos to these letters and share a glimpse of my world with you and maybe you could do the same?

Cannot wait to hear from you soon. My mother still does not know about you. I drop the letters in the post box below when I go to the temple or grocery store. Does your family know about me? If yes, convey my regards to them.

Love,

Binya.

CHAPTER 2

A week later.

With each passing minute, Vidvath's newfound attraction towards Radhika was increasing. The more he thought about her, the more he found himself restless to meet her, talk to her, and eventually confess his feelings for her. The thought made his heart skip a beat both in excitement and fear. If his father caught wind of what he was thinking he would be flayed with the black leather belt that he had witnessed his father use several times on his mother. But there were ways to get around quietly until he was older and strong enough to withstand his father. Only a few more years, he thought.

For now, he eagerly waited for the holidays to end and school to begin when he would see Radhika again. Vidvath tossed in his bed, squinting at the sunlight that poured through the window. He looked at the clock beside him. It was almost 9 AM. He wondered why his mother had not woken him up. He decided to use this opportunity to daydream as he had done these last few days.

Last evening, the village boys had invited him for a not-so-friendly match of cricket with the boys of Perdur, a neighboring village. A battle in disguise of a match, between two rival groups that passed down from generation to generation. Normally, Vidvath eagerly waited for an event like this, where he would get a chance to show his machismo. This time, however, Vidvath had excused himself on account of a bad stomach. Instead, he had spent the evening skimming through old photo albums, reminiscing about his childhood days with Avinash and Radhika. He chuckled, recalling how even as a little girl Radhika used big, fancy words confidently despite the temporary lisp. He made a mental note to use these memories as icebreakers when he had the chance to speak to her in private.

As he continued to dream, Vidvath heard a commotion in the living room. Upon careful listening, he realized it was his father yelling at someone. He got up and sprinted towards the door when he heard a heartbreaking wail. Even before opening the door, he knew it was his older sister Yashodha. And even before his grandmother showered unspeakable words on her, Vidvath knew his sister had come home forever.

Vidvath did not leave the room until he heard his father's jeep drive away. He could not help but feel like a coward for doing so, which made him wonder if he would ever develop the courage to go against his father and his cruel ways.

Raghupathi Rao, Vidvath's father, was someone who was feared by not just the people of Jogibettu but all the neighboring villages. The family-owned Mahalakshmi Chemicals and Fertilizers had acquired a monopoly in the entire Taluk. Raghupathi Rao had made sure no other competitor set foot in his territory, and in his time alone he had quadrupled the business, earning both name and wealth along the way.

When Vidvath stepped into the huge courtyard, the air was stiff with tension. His grandmother, Anasuya, had calmed down and was now mumbling incoherently as she sat on the antique carved wooden swing and continued to weave a jasmine garland for the evening pooja to Goddess Sharadha on account of the last day of Dasara. Vinaya, Vidvath's mother, was in the kitchen, sniffing silently. Vidvath was sure she too had fallen prey to his father's wrath. After all, only a mother is accountable for her daughter's barrenness, isn't she?

Vidvath walked to the spare room where he knew Yashodha would be staying. Her room on the first floor had been turned into a guest room, many years ago. Inside the dimly lit room, Vidvath spotted Yashodha unpacking her bag, setting her meager belongings inside the old, worn-out cupboard that had once belonged to him. An old mattress was rolled up against the wall, and a single plastic chair sat in the corner of the room. This is where Yashodha would be spending most of her life from now on. The thought made Vidvath shudder.

"Akka," Vidvath managed to whisper, swallowing the lump in his throat. Yashodha turned around and walked towards him. After a moment of hesitation, she held him in an embrace, and cried her heart out. Vidvath held her, something he had not done for many years, and blinked back the tears. He realized how his once bubbly and full-of-life sister, only ten years his senior, had aged so quickly. She had lost weight and had bags under her eyes. She hardly spoke, and when she did it was only a notch higher than a whisper. There were scars on her forehead and arms that she no longer tried to hide with makeup.

In the last ten years, Yashodha had visited only thrice. The first time, she had been treated like a queen. For the six months she had stayed, Vidvath had envied the treatment she had received. It had all ended when she gave birth to a stillborn baby girl. The second time, she had miscarried, and the third time she had been dropped off by her husband, Purushottam, who needed time and space for his second wedding. After accepting a second dowry from Yashodha's father, Purushottam had agreed to take her back if only to help his second, much younger wife with the household chores.

"He kicked me out, Vidhu. Just like that. Ten years of our relationship meant nothing to him," Yashodha sobbed on his shoulder. Vidvath stood there, tears pooling in his eyes, anger bubbling in his heart as words failed him. But his silence did not bother Yashodha. She knew she was now a burden not only to her father but her brother as well.

"Why?" Vidvath managed to ask. Before Yashodha could reply, Anasuya walked into the room.

"Vidhu, go back to your room. There is no need for you to meddle in her sob story. She is here because of her own ill-doing," Vidvath knew if he did not obey, his grandmother would create a scene—the second one that day—and his mother and sister would fall prey to it. So, with an apologetic glance at his sister, he walked out of the room.

It was later, when Anasuya had retired to her room, that Vidvath learned the truth from his mother. Purushottam had lost all his wealth to gambling, and for the last few months, Yashodha had become an extra mouth to feed. He and his second wife had been plotting to get rid of her. So, one day, when his second wife complained of a missing piece of jewelry from her safe, Purushottam searched Yashodha's room. As expected, the ring was found in one of Yashodha's drawers where they had planted it earlier when Yashodha was busy tending to their infant son. Now labeled a thief in addition to barren and cursed, Yashodha had been stripped of the last shred of dignity and returned to her home.

It was the first time, Vidvath found himself reflecting on how society treated a woman—how his own father treated his mother and sister. As a child, before learning the difference between a man's and a woman's role in society, Vidvath had looked up to his multi-talented sister for everything. In school, she had always managed to top the class. She had won competitions in art and music as well. It was Yashodha who had introduced chess and sudoku to Vidvath when he was eight. Naturally, everyone in her class and her juniors respected her. Vidvath had been proud of being her little brother.

Today, she was nothing but a failure in society. A burden to her parents and her husband. All because she could not produce an heir. Would a man in her place be treated the same way? Vidvath wondered. His mind wandered to another woman, who had been in a similar situation yet with a very different attitude: his English teacher, Miss Suman.

On many occasions, Vidvath had heard his father and grandmother talk about Miss Suman with disdain. But he had also seen his mother and sister secretly admire the bold woman whom everyone in the village feared and respected. Vidvath wondered if someday Yashodha, too, would find it in herself to become like Suman. Vidvath promised himself that he would do everything in his power to stand with Yashodha when that day came.

Radhika's grandmother, Jayalakshmi, came limping into the living room after her short evening walk and sat on the worn-out charpoy. She pouted her lips and spat into the brass spitting bowl that sat on a stool next to her. She then opened her silver circular box, thoughtfully pulled out a *paan*[27], and placed it between her red lips.

"Radhika!" she called for her granddaughter.

Radhika walked into the living room, trying hard not to groan. She knew why her grandmother was calling her. Avinash, who was sitting on the sofa watching India's cricket ODI against England, chuckled. Radhika walked over to her grandmother, sat at her feet, and began kneading her grandmother's knotted, plump legs. Jayalakshmi moaned and chewed at her paan alternately. Radhika chose to remain silent for fear of being sprayed red from above.

Fifteen minutes later, Radhika heard her grandmother snore. Avinash was immersed in the match that seemed to be getting interesting by the minute, and Radhika's mother, Padmini, had still not returned from the temple. Her father, Srinivas Prasad, who worked as the village's postmaster, would not return till sunset. Radhika realized it was the right opportunity to visit Suman and gather some important information that she had been dying to know all week.

"It was amazing, Suman Akka! The procession, the costumes, the band, and the tiger dancers," exclaimed Radhika as she explained how she had celebrated Dasara at her maternal grandmother's house in Mangaluru.

"I know. I remember waiting for the procession to pass by our home

---

[27] : Betel leaf wrapped with areca nut and spices

when we lived there. Good old days," Suman replied, setting the table with tea and biscuits.

"Why don't you go now, Suman Akka?"

"It's too painful, Radhika. All my memories in the city are tied to my parents. They were all I had. Seeing the procession now, without them by my side, feels incomplete."

Radhika pursed her lips and scolded herself for being insensitive. She knew Suman had lost her parents when she was only twenty-one. Despite being alone, she had taken the bold step of walking out of an abusive marriage. She had then left her comfortable, well-paying job to return to Jogibettu with the intention of helping the women and children here. As a member of the Women's Welfare Association, she helped improve the quality of life of many women.

"I'm sorry, Akka."

"It's fine. It was a long time ago. The pain will always be there, but it gets better with time," Suman replied.

"Akka, did you hear about Yashodha Akka's return?" Radhika asked as she sipped her tea.

"Yes, I did," Suman replied curtly.

"Do you know what happened?" Radhika pressed.

"Yes," Suman picked up the newspaper, adjusted her spectacles and began to glance through it.

"Then tell me."

"No," Suman replied nonchalantly. Radhika lost her patience and pulled the newspaper down, making eye contact with Suman. "C'mon. I want to know. Everyone in school is talking about it but no one knows what exactly happened. Vidvath too isn't telling anyone anything."

"Good. Then the topic will die down in a few days," Suman pulled out a pen and began to work on the day's crossword.

"I want to know, Akka. Nothing interesting happens in this town. At least this…" Radhika tugged at Suman's hand impatiently. Suman squeezed her eyes shut.

"I said, no Radhika! Please drop it," Suman said sternly holding on to the last strands of self-control.

"C'mon. I'm sure sooner or later it will come out. Why not…"

"Shut up, Radhika!"

Radhika's eyes widened at Suman's harsh tone. "Akka… I…" It was the first time Radhika had witnessed Suman's anger. Even in school, when the children created a racket, she managed to quiet them down with a stern look. Sometimes just her presence was enough for the chaos to die down.

"Do you even realize what you are doing here, Radhika?" Suman asked, calming herself. Radhika decided it was best to keep quiet.

"You want me to share with you someone else's personal life, someone who is going through a lot of pain right now, just so you can become the center of attention tomorrow in your class? Is that what you've learned from me all these years?" Radhika lowered her eyes as realization struck hard.

"From the first time you came here, have I ever entertained you with any gossip?"

"But you sometimes ask me what people are saying about you behind your back…" Radhika mumbled, unable to hold her tongue.

"Yes, because of two things. One, it is about me. I'm the victim. Have I ever asked you how your grandmother or father is treating your mother? Or who in the village eloped with whom?" Suman knew this would strike a chord. This was not the first time Radhika had indulged in gossip. Suman knew it was the right time to make the teenager realize how gossip could cause irreparable damage to a person.

"Secondly, no matter what people are talking about me, I am strong enough to handle it. I cannot say the same about Yashodha. Her pain is fresh and she might be vulnerable. Even if that is not the case, we have no right to discuss her personal life in her absence and without her consent," Suman explained. Radhika felt her face heat up in embarrassment.

"How would you feel if I go behind your back and tell all your teachers that your grandmother abuses your mother and that your father chooses to give a deaf ear to it? Or tell your classmates that your school fee is being paid by a welfare scheme meant for children from families that cannot afford the tuition fee?" Suman knew her words were harsh, but it was the only way Radhika would remember the lesson for long. Her heart broke as she watched tears stream down Radhika's face. Suman stood up and walked to the sink with the tea cups.

"I'm sorry, Akka. I did not think it through. But, my intention was never to cause any pain to Yashodha Akka, I promise," Radhika said softly after a few minutes of introspection. Suman nodded in acknowledgment.

"There is no such thing as harmless gossip, Radhika. You never know how your one casual comment can destroy a person," Suman's voice was now soft, "A few years ago, I volunteered with an organization to help young girls who had been rape victims. One of them was extremely smart and had recovered enough to start showing great progress in school despite being the youngest in her class. Naturally, her classmates who came from better homes began to envy her. Somehow, one of her classmates found out about her past. Someone labeled her a prostitute. Someone else drew sketches of her and passed them around. The gossip spread like wildfire in the school and outside." Suman took a sip of water and cleared her throat. "A week before her 12th board exam, she was found hanging in her room. She had dreamed of becoming a doctor."

Never had Radhika felt so low about herself before this. The thought that her curiosity could cost someone their life made her feel sick. She knew she had to be very careful of what she said regarding other people.

"Radhika, I understand that gossip can sometimes serve as a burst of guilty pleasure. It can be addictive and compulsive. But we, as educated and compassionate people, should know where to draw the line. The Bible calls it a sin, and rightfully so. Is your momentary pleasure worth risking someone's life?" Radhika shook her head, trying to absorb it all.

"Here, I want you to read this. It is a brilliant book with a few lines on how gossip is the foundation of our species. Read it and reflect on how much we have evolved and how far we are yet to go," said Suman, placing a battered copy of Sapiens in front of Radhika. Radhika smiled thankfully. It was meetings like these with Suman that made her feel like she was learning and growing to become a better person.

Dear Radhika,

How have you been? The Dasara festival in your city sounds amazing. I wish I could be there. I was in Dehradun last week at my uncle's house. My grandmother had a stroke and needs help while she recovers so my mother and I went there to stay with her. She is recovering well and should be able to walk in a few months after her physiotherapy sessions. While I was there, I asked my uncle about the tiger dancers that I found intriguing in your letter. He showed me the pictures from one of his travel magazines. The costume, the colours, the energy everything looks so mesmerizing. Thank you for sharing this unique tradition with me.

Everything in Ranachatti is the same and will likely remain same till the next yatra season. Except for the temperature that seems to drop every day. The winter this year is expected to be early. In other news, a white man from American or Europe.. I'm not sure… is believed to have settled for a few months in our neighboring village. He is living with a local family. I wonder if he is a trekker waiting for the snowfall. They have this craze for trekking in the snow, I hear. The girls here are going crazy with this info. One of the girls in my class claim to have seen him and says he is the most handsome man she has ever seen.

In my wildest dreams, I am married to a Gora (White man) from a country far away where I live in a city bustling with life. Where parks and restaurants are open 24 hours and one can go shopping without having to plan it a week in advance and check for the availability of a jeep or bus. I wonder how much fun it would be to just get up, get dressed and go into the Bazaar without any escort. Is that how life is at Jogibettu?

This reminds me. Yesterday, my friend Seema got an earful from Jyothsna miss when she heard her playfully curse me that I would not get a Gora, instead I would be married to a Kallu (A Black man). We learned about racism and how its cruelty has destroyed so many lives. I think it was an important lesson to learn. Here, in our village when a child is born, the first thing people talk about is the gender and the second is the skin colour.

Radhika and Tara walked into their classroom talking, excitedly about everything under the sun. They were still coming to terms about how much life had changed after school. Three months had passed since they had joined the Pre University College, which was a stone's throw from their school. They were no longer school-going children who wore uniforms, braided their hair into two plaits, and polished their shoes every day.

In a span of months, everyone they knew had grown up. The boys, especially, were now a foot taller than they were only a couple of months ago. They flaunted longer hair, and many of them had managed to grow a slight beard. This naturally changed their overall demeanor. The girls wore makeup, had long colored nails, and wore heels.

Presently, Radhika spoke about the new book Suman had given her while Tara pretended to listen. Radhika and Tara were as different from each other as two people could be. Tara loved talking about clothes, jewelry, gossip, and food. Radhika, on the other hand, spoke passionately about art, literature, and travel. Radhika enjoyed the company of few, while Tara had an innate charisma that drew people towards her. She was tall and attractive, while Radhika was plain, average-looking. Yet, their unusual friendship, which had started in middle school when they were teamed together for a mutually hated sport, had blossomed over the years.

Radhika was busy looking for her 'class leader' badge in her bag when she heard her best friend's loud whistle. Radhika looked up, confused, and then traced Tara's line of sight. On the first desk, where Radhika and Tara always sat, was a bouquet of red roses and a small card. Before Radhika could think any further, Tara raced to the desk and read the card aloud.

"To Radhika. With Love," Tara sighed dramatically, placing a hand on her heart. Between the two, Tara had always been the openly romantic one. The only books she ever read for entertainment were romance novels. She dreamed of a man akin to the handsome, charming, flawless ones written by female authors. Unfortunately, Tara had not found a man even remotely close to these heroes in real life. She blamed the size of Jogibettu for this.

"Third one this week and fifth overall. I'm starting to feel a little jealous. Are you still clueless about who this Romeo is?"

When the first gift, a box of chocolates had been handed to her by a little girl from first grade with a similar card, Radhika had assumed it was one of her classmates playing a prank. Then the gifts kept coming – a bracelet, a heart-shaped love card, a bottle of pink nail paint that she despised - and Radhika began to worry.

Not many years ago, a boy from a neighboring village had begun to pursue a girl in Jogibettu's Government Degree College. Even after multiple rejections from her, the man refused to give up. He and his friends began bad mouthing the girl so that no one would marry her and eventually she would have to accept him. When the girl's parents caught word of this, they blamed the girl, stopped her education and got her married to someone in a faraway city. Radhika shuddered at the thought. There was no doubt, her parents would do the same if they found Radhika in similar situation. In Jogibettu, a girl's reputation outpaced her education by several miles.

When she heard the bell ring indicating the start of the first period, Radhika and Tara sat down at their desk and shoved the bouquet into Radhika's bag. By the time the last class of the day was done, Radhika was visibly stressed with all the overthinking she had done. When Radhika shared her fear with Tara at the end of the day, Tara promised to find out who this secret admirer was.

A week passed by. Three more gifts reached Radhika, each more intimate than the previous one. The last one was a fresh copy of Rumi's love poems translated in English. Radhika had seen one of these in Suman's restricted part of home library. It was a very old, battered copy that meant a great deal to Suman. Radhika now wondered if it had been gifted to Suman by someone special.

Taking the book from Radhika's hand, Tara swooned when she read one of the few highlighted poems.

I wait

with silent passion

for one gesture

one glance

from you

It was Rumi's poem. It should have made Radhika blush and feel butterflies flutter in her stomach. Instead, it made her worry more. Coming from a teenage boy conditioned by a patriarchal society like Jogibettu, the poem sounded like a threat. Several days had passed since the last gift, and Tara, through her vast network of school and college goers, had found a trail.

"Found your admirer," Tara said, fanning herself while Radhika stood in front of her, visibly nervous and impatient.

"Who is it?" asked Radhika, pulling Tara to a corner in the school corridor. She smiled at the girls passing by, trying hard to hide the worry etched on her face.

"Try guessing. You have three chances." It was moments like this that made Radhika wonder how the two had become best friends. If their roles were reversed and Tara had been the one being stalked, Radhika would still be the nervous wreck she was now, worrying about her friend's future, and Tara would remain cool as a cucumber.

"I'm in no mood for games, Tara! I haven't slept properly in days."

"C'mon, Just take a wild guess."

"Okay fine. Is it Amit?" Radhika replied with the first name that came to her mind. Of all the boys she knew, Amit was a safe bet. He was a decent, studious boy who came from a family like hers – respected and powerless. Also, Amit would never retaliate if she rejected him. Except maybe he would stop lending her notes when she missed classes.

"Oh God!"

"Oh God, what?"

"Logically, the first name you think of is the person you wish was your admirer."

"Stop calling him my admirer. He is a shameless stalker and your logic is rubbish."

"Seriously, Amit? That lanky nerdo?"

"He happens to be a good guy with an IQ greater than all other boys in the class put together"

"Agreed," Tara smiled enjoying Radhika being tortured. "But still, Amit?"

"Now tell me who it is before I suffer a panic attack."

"Stop being so dramatic. Here." Tara handed her the card from the bouquet and a photocopy of someone's scribbled class notes. The handwriting matched. On the top right corner of the notes was her stalker's name.

Radhika had assumed her first reaction to finding out who her stalker was would be anger. In a small village like Jogibettu, where words travelled faster than wildfire, stalking a girl and leaving anonymous gifts was an indecent thing to do. Even if someone had genuine feelings for a girl, the appropriate way was to wait for the right time, let the elders speak, and fix an alliance. This was the extent a love marriage was allowed to go in their society.

Yet, Radhika surprised herself by smiling. There was a skip in her heartbeat and a trace of relief when she realized it was her annoying brother's super annoying best friend – Vidvath.

Tara let out another loud whistle.

On Thursday, Radhika spent her weekly meetup hour with Suman, trying hard to act normal. Ever since she found out who her stalker was, Radhika felt self-conscious as she walked into class or along the corridor. It felt like everyone was pointing at her and whispering Vidvath's name. When she asked Tara about it, she dismissed the thought, saying Vidvath had not told anyone.

"Vidvath's best friend is your elder brother, do you really think Avinash would spare Vidvath if he knew?" Tara's words, although true, had been anything but comforting.

For the first time ever, Radhika waited for the clock to tick six so that she could leave Suman's house. Radhika's mind was too clouded with anxiety and worry to concentrate on what Suman was saying. It was something about a literature and art festival in Bengaluru that she was planning on attending. Finally, at six, when Radhika bid goodbye to Suman and rushed home, she felt the blood drain from her face.

In her living room, sitting opposite to her mother and Avinash, was Vidvath. It was at this moment that the gravity of the situation sunk in Radhika's mind. This was nothing like the love stories in her novels. There was no way Vidvath's family would accept her, the daughter of a Postmaster. Even now, as she watched Vidvath, dressed in casual yet expensive clothes, flaunting a thick gold chain and an expensive watch in her old, modest house, the stark difference between their worlds hit home.

At the very moment, Vidvath turned towards the door and locked eyes with her. He smiled softly. Something told Radhika that he knew she had found who her stalker was. Radhika did not smile back, nor did she look away, albeit he might mistake it for shyness.

"What are you doing standing there? Go freshen up. I have made hot *goli bajjis*[28]," Radhika's mother said, causing Vidvath and Radhika to tear away their gaze.

Radhika sat in her room, listening to the conversation outside. A few minutes later, Radhika heard her mother send Avinash to get milk from the shop. A moment later, Radhika's mother walked out of the backdoor to greet her neighbour, who had just returned from a long vacation. Radhika knew this was the right time to confront Vidvath. Picking up the plastic bag that she had loaded with all of Vidvath's gifts, she entered the living room. She looked around nervously, making sure no one was approaching them. Vidvath's face lit up seeing her. She walked towards him and then stopped a few feet away.

"What the hell is the matter with you?" Radhika said through gritted teeth as she pushed the plastic bag towards Vidvath. Radhika watched Vidvath's nervous smile fade.

"Radhi—"

"Vidvath, why are you doing this? You know what will happen to me and my family if word gets out. You are a man, the son of a powerful, wealthy person. No fingers will be pointed at you. But it's not the same for me."

"I don't know if this is a bet you have with your friends or if you are doing it just for the thrill of the chase, but I request you to please stop all this and let me be. The last thing I want is for my parents to stop my education and get me married to some stranger." Radhika quickly blinked back her tears and walked away as Avinash entered the living room.

Two months passed as Radhika acclimated to college life. There was a lot to learn, and unlike school, the teachers were less concerned about individ-

---

[28]: A popular South Indian deep-fried snack

ual student performances. Naturally, there was a lot of self-study to do, and Radhika found her schedule packed on most days.

Vidvath had not bothered her since the encounter at Radhika's home. He rarely visited their home, and when he did on Avinash's insistence, he made a conscious effort to keep his distance from Radhika. While this made Radhika less nervous around him, there was also a slight sense of loss. Vidvath's lack of persistence in this matter had developed a soft corner for him in Radhika's mind.

Presently, as Radhika and Tara walked past Vidvath's house on their way to school, they sensed something amiss. A crowd had gathered outside the house, and Vidvath's father's voice reverberated angrily as he spoke of how his reputation was going to the dogs. A few curious neighbors peeked through the front door and windows, anticipating some drama. Tara joined the on-lookers first, followed by Radhika, their curiosity getting the better of them.

Inside, the atmosphere in the Rao household was tense. Yashodha sat on a step leading to the courtyard, her pallor suggesting the life had drained from her. Wrapped in a wet blanket, she wept inconsolably. Vidvath stood solemn-ly by a wooden pillar, eyes fixed on the floor.

"How is it that you were unsuccessful even in killing yourself?" Anasuya - Vidvath's grandmother's words cut through the momentary silence in the courtyard like a knife.

"I have become a laughingstock in the eyes of the villagers. First, my mar-ried daughter is thrown out of her house for theft. Then she is seen flirting with a married man in the market. And now she tries to kill herself in broad daylight. What did you think was going to happen? Do you think the Wom-en's Welfare Association would let me stand in the elections if you had died?" Radhika had never seen Vidvath's father so angry.

"I wasn't flirting!" Yashodha's voice was loud but not confrontational. It was not to exert dominance but a plea to be heard. "Manoj was my classmate in school. I met him in the market and spoke a few words. What wrong have I done?"

"Shut up! You ungrateful bitch," Raghupathi Rao slapped his daughter across the face. There was no way he would tolerate someone, especially a woman, raising her voice in front of him. Everyone winced, but there was no sign of shock on Yashodha's face. Radhika realized it was not the first time this had happened.

"You should be happy you still have a roof over your head and food on your plate. What is the need for you to get out of the house and show your face in public? If you stay in the house, people will forget you exist, and we can all continue to live our lives peacefully."

As the tumultuous scene unfolded in the courtyard with shouting and pleading, Radhika found her thoughts inevitably drawn to Vidvath. Part of her fervently wished that he would summon the courage to stand by his sister, to confront the storm of accusations and injustice raining down upon Yashodha. However, a conflicting set of thoughts raced through Radhika's mind. Was Vidvath's seeming passivity a sign of cowardice, or was he trapped in a situation where any action could lead to dire consequences for both him and Yashodha?

A few moments later, Radhika was jolted from her thoughts when she realized Yashodha was being dragged by her father outside the house. Vidvath hadn't budged an inch, and his mother, defying all sense of embarrassment, pleaded with her husband to let her daughter go. Outside, Yashodha was thrown to the ground. Radhika stared in disbelief. When she turned to look at Vidvath, their eyes met. His held sadness but little else, as if the abuse was happening to a stranger, not his own sister. Radhika shook her head in disappointment, maintaining eye contact with him. Then she made up her mind to stand by Yashodha; No woman should have to face this alone.

A moment later, Vidvath emerged from the front door. As he approached, he discreetly signaled to Radhika, silently urging her not to get involved. Radhika nodded in agreement.

What unfolded next became Vidvath's worst nightmare.

Armed with a strange sense of determination, Vidvath walked to Yashodha and helped her off the ground. Ignoring his father's angry glares, he held her hand and began walking towards the house. Behind him, Raghupathi's angry tirade was a buzz. Everyone looked at Vidvath shocked. It was as if he had suddenly become visible, had stepped into the light out of his father's shadow. For that brief moment, Vidvath felt like the most powerful man in the village.

"Don't you dare step into my house with that disgrace of a girl," Raghupathi's words made Vidvath stop in his tracks. Did he have it in him to defy his father's ultimatum? If he backed down now, it would be a far greater humiliation than not doing anything at first. What would Radhika think of him? Taking a deep breath, Vidvath took a step forward.

"Vidvath, I'm warning you!" Vidvath's father spoke through gritted teeth. The number of people gathered to witness the scene were increasing by the minute. It was as if the entire village was at their door step. If Vidvath yielded now, he would forever be labelled as the coward he was. On the other hand, if he resisted his father, there was no telling what his father would do in fury.

Vidvath stopped and looked to his side, hoping to find some strength in Radhika. But she was nowhere to be seen. It is then he noticed her and Tara being escorted in the direction of the school by one of the teachers. Suddenly, Vidvath felt his energy drain, the courage leave his body, and fear grip him from within. His hand, that had only moments ago grasped Yashodha's firmly, now unraveled like grains of sand slipping through the crevices of a clenched fist. Yashodha looked at him, bewildered. Before Vidvath could decide his next step, he felt the searing pain of a leather belt lashing across his back. The sharp sting cut through him, leaving a burning sensation that radiated through his entire body.

"Who do you think you are?" Raghupathi's face was now same colour as Vidvath's angry bruises. "Your only identity is that you're my son and nothing more."

"Appa…" Yashodha pleaded at her father's feet, trying to halt the unrestrained lashes raining down on Vidvath. Vidvath, in an effort to shield her, gently pushed her away. Sensing an opportunity, Vidvath's mother seized Yashodha and pulled her away from the distressing scene.

"Do you truly believe you can defy me? You couldn't even pass your school exams on your own. Do you comprehend how many palms I had to grease to ensure you even reached twelfth class? And now, you attempt to challenge me! I've sired nothing but useless, ungrateful beings."

As the words left his father's lips, Vidvath felt them stab him all over his body. Suddenly, the lashes felt less painful. Vidvath squeezed his eyes shut, attempting to suppress the tears, acutely aware that many of his classmates and their parents were among the onlookers.

CHAPTER 3

A month later.

"Thank you for agreeing to meet me, Radhika," said Vidvath. Radhika nodded in response and quickly scanned the road behind them for the third time in the last five minutes. While she was excited to be on this 'date'—according to Tara— there was no telling what would happen if someone from the village saw them together, alone, here in this wilderness.

"Don't worry, Tara and Ram are standing guard there," Vidvath pointed in the direction of a tree. "They will give us a signal if they see someone coming our way." Radhika nodded. Ram was Tara's younger cousin from the city who had agreed to be a part of this because he was bored of having nothing to do in the village.

"I wanted to apologize to you, Radhika," Vidvath's voice had a seriousness to it, something Radhika had never heard before. His eyes traced the path of the birds far away in the sky, returning to their nest. "After what happened that day to Yashodha Akka for talking to her ex-classmate, I realized what a grave mistake I had committed by pursuing you."

"It would kill me if someone pointed fingers at your character because of my stupid mistake. I'm sorry, Radhika. I was naïve and blinded by this…" Vidvath was at a loss of words. "I don't have a word for what I feel for you."

A smile escaped Radhika's lips in response. She knew how hard it was for Vidvath, or any other man, to admit their mistake and apologize. Somehow, apologizing came easily to women.

"I forgive you, Vidvath," Radhika replied. Vidvath did not speak after that, and neither did Radhika. It was when Vidvath turned his face to look at the pond that Radhika noticed the scars on his arms and the base of his neck, where it escaped into his shirt. It made her wince as the memory of that horrific incident flashed before her eyes. For once, she was happy that she had been dragged away from the scene by her teacher and she had not witnessed Vidvath's pain and humiliation.

"I'm sorry too, Vidvath," Radhika said. Vidvath turned towards her and frowned.

"Had I not asked you to interfere that day at your home, this would not have happened," her eyes landed on his scars.

"It does not hurt anymore. The scars will go away in a few months," Vidvath said with a smile.

While Radhika's mind swirled with hundreds of thoughts mixed with the anxiety of being seen here with a boy, Vidvath could not help but sneak a glance at her every now and then from the corner of his eyes. He seemed more at peace. Why wouldn't he be? He was a boy, after all. If someone happened to see them together, it was she who would be questioned, blamed, and humiliated. She would be called a siren who lured this innocent young man out of his wealthy home. Despite knowing the consequences, Radhika felt safe with this boy, whom she had known all her life.

It was the end of the long, scorching summer and the beginning of the beloved monsoon. Ten kilometers from Jogibettu, surrounded by wilderness, the duo were seated on a lush green carpet of grass under the blue sky, spotted with white clouds. The breeze smelled sweet from the fragrance of the *champa*[29] flowers on a tree nearby. On three sides, they were surrounded by tall trees and overgrown bushes. A small pond sat to their right where little guppies and frogs swam. At a distance on the other side of the pond, was an old, dilapidated church that had stood witness to Jogibettu's affairs for over six decades. The white cross above it was an image that had been an integral part

---

[29]: A fragrant flowering plant

of everyone's life in the village. Behind them, facing the deserted road, was an old unused shed that was known as Ramanna's tea stall. A shop that had been there for close to thirty years, serving travellers a hot cup of tea or coffee, a beedi, and some snacks. After Ramanna's death, the tea stall had been abandoned. Now all that remained of it was the name and fleeting memories.

Vidvath's fake cough brought back Radhika from her train of thought. Of late, her mind had begun to wander at the smallest of chances.

"I have to leave in a few minutes," said Radhika. She had taken enough risk for one day.

"Stay for some more time, please" Vidvath replied with pleading eyes. Please. Another word men did not use very often. "What do you want to talk about?" asked Radhika.

"Nothing. I just want to spend time with you. To get to know you better and bring you here. This is my favorite place in Jogibettu. I come here when I am sad or angry or need some alone time," replied Vidvath, throwing little pebbles in the pond.

Radhika nodded. It was a beautiful place. She had never been here before. It was far from the core village and in the middle of nowhere. "But why?" Radhika could not resist the urge to tease him.

Vidvath did not answer. Instead, he stood up and walked towards the champa tree. He pulled out a single yellow flower and walked back to Radhika. With a soft smile and unmeeting eyes, he gave it to her. She accepted it with a smile and tucked it into her hair. A little green snake slid a few feet away from her, burying itself into the lush green grass. She watched it carefully, its camouflaged skin, the glistening eyes, and the gracious movement, its freedom.

Vidvath sat down beside her, now much closer. "There is a *jathre*[30] in Gundmi next weekend. Everyone from our class is going. Will you join us?" asked Vidvath.

---

[30] : A village fair

"I will have to ask Amma. Saturdays are usually reserved for helping her out with the house chores."

"Okay. The jathre starts only in the later afternoon. I think you can come with Avinash. He said he is coming."

"Of course, he is going." It's not like he has to spend his weekends helping at home or doing anything really useful, Radhika wanted to add.

Suddenly, plump raindrops splashed onto her forehead. When Radhika looked up, she saw the sky turning into a palette of white, grey, and purple. Trees around them swayed as the wind combed through them mercilessly. Somewhere, a thunder cracked. Within minutes, rain poured down. Vidvath got up first and extended his hand. When Radhika did not accept it, he took her hand in his and pulled her to her feet. Both of them rushed towards Ramanna's tea stall and stood under its creaking roof.

They sat down on the cracked bench and watched the rain and the transformation it brought along. Everything around them was ordinary yet beautiful. Rain in a place where the monsoons stayed for over 8 months a year could only seem extraordinary, and romantic to a teenager. Someone whose changing mind and body forced them to see the world around them differently, find beauty in the smallest of things, and find love in the simplest of words.

Radhika hopelessly wondered if someday the rain would change to snowfall, a childhood dream. No woman Radhika knew had ever stepped out beyond the district, except for that one girl, Gayathri who had married a man from Mumbai and settled there. Radhika wondered if she would be the first one from Jogibettu to see snow. Wouldn't that be wonderful?

"So you're coming," said Vidvath. Radhika looked at him confused momentarily, before realizing he was talking about the festival in Gundmi.

"I cannot promise, but I will try."

As the rain slowly reduced to a drizzle within minutes like it always did in the coastal region, Radhika waved goodbye to Vidvath. With Tara and Ram beside her, Radhika speed-walked home, putting one step as far away from the other, hoping to reach home before it turned dark. Her mind worked hard on making a believable excuse for returning home late; her heart, however, felt like a drumroll in her chest and not from her speed walk, but from the fluttering excitement of her new feelings.

Dear Radhika,

I'm so jealous! You have a secret admirer who is showering you with gifts! Why have you kept him a secret all this while? Reading about your first meeting with Vidvath makes me so happy for you. I hadn't thought of romance as a possibility in real life until now. In Ranchatti and all the surrounding villages, marriages have always been arranged, sometimes within families. There have been a few cases where young lovers have eloped and gotten married, but they do not come back to live here. I always pitied them assuming they must be leading a hard life away from friends and family. But now I wonder if their love for each other was enough, and they chose to start a new life somewhere far away from the judgmental society. Look what you have done, Radhika. You have made my movie dream realistic and tangible.

In other news, Ranchatti is covered in snow. There is white as far as the eyes can see. Again, it came as a surprise to me when you said you have never seen snow. So what does winter in Jogibettu look like? On second thoughts, maybe you never seeing snow is not as surprising considering I have never seen a beach or even a coconut tree!

Also, I apologize for addressing you as a Madrasi in my previous letter. It is what everyone here thinks of people from the South. I humored my mother by asking her what it meant. She said the whole of South India is called Madras and people there are called Madrasi. So this time when my Chacha, came to visit us, I asked him about South India. He has travelled all over India and is well-versed with many cultures and cuisines. He explained to me that like North India, South India too has many states. Mangaluru, the city you mentioned as nearest to Jogibettu, belongs to the state of Karnataka where Kannada is spoken by the majority. Madras (now Chennai), belongs to Tamil Nadu where people speak Tamil, arguably the oldest language in India. See, I did my homework!

Do keep me informed of how things progress between you and Vidvath. Also, thank Tara from my side for bringing you two together. Someday, I will definitely visit Jogibettu and meet you all in person. Till then you're my only window to this world of Jogibettu—so different from mine yet so alike.

Love,

Binya

On the day of the village fair, known as the jathre, Gundmi was adorned in vibrant colours. There was laughter and joy all around. The local school had declared a holiday and people from many nearby villages had come to join the celebration. The annual village fair commenced on the anniversary of the Shiva Temple opening. Small vendors selling sweets, ice creams, fritters, and fashion accessories had setup their stalls on the side of the roads. Teenage boys were hired to lure customers into these shops. The bangle and hair accessories stall was especially crowded, earning envious glares from all vendors. But they knew all of their goods would be sold out within the week. People were generous during such occasions.

"Who are you waiting for? Come, let's go to the soda shop," said one of the boys from Vidvath's group. They had all come together to Gundmi in the local bus.

"You go ahead, I'm waiting for Avinash," Vidvath replied, not moving his eyes from the entrance. He knew there was a very slim chance that Radhika would come. Their relationship had started on a wrong foot, and somewhere along the way, he had scared her. Although he had apologized to her and promised to be careful, he still sensed hesitation in Radhika when she was with him. Vidvath wanted to change that, ensure her that he was serious about her, that he would never do anything to jeopardize their relationship or her dignity. Yashodha's life had taught him what it meant for a woman to fall in the eyes of the society.

As minutes stretched into what felt like an interminable hour, Vidvath wrestled with the growing disappointment that he might not catch a glimpse of Radhika. Just as he was about to turn away, he saw a new group emerge through the gate. He smiled when he spotted Avinash. He waved at Avinash but his eyes continued to scan the crowd ignoring Avinash's confused frown. Vidvath's joy knew no bounds when he spotted Radhika at the entrance, a few steps behind her brother. Vidvath's heart skipped a beat.

Radhika, who usually dressed in a simple salwar suit with no makeup and minimal jewelry, had made efforts to look nice. She had applied kohl to her eyes that made them look bright and piercing. Vidvath tried hard not to look into her eyes. He was afraid he would not be able to pull away. As Avinash continued to chatter about a recent local cricket match, Vidvath continued to stare at Radhika while occasionally nodding in acknowledgment to whatever question Avinash was asking. Radhika had applied lip colour and a stone bindi. Her freshly washed hair was left open, something she rarely did. Had she really made an effort for his sake? Vidvath wondered.

"Let's go to the games stall," Avinash said as he dragged Vidvath with him. Radhika followed. It was at this moment that Vidvath realized if things did not go right, he would not only lose the person he believed was the love of his life but also his best friend.

"Amma asked me to let Radhika tag along. I know it's annoying, but I can't let her wander on her own here. I hope you don't mind"

"Of course," replied Vidvath looking behind and smiling at Radhika. Radhika smiled back after a quick glance at her brother.

Whenever Avinash was busy with a game or went away to buy something, Vidvath tried to speak to Radhika. Radhika pretended to not notice, but the blush that crept up her cheeks said a different story. With each passing minute, Vidvath was sure he was falling in love with her.

"Your turn," said Avinash, handing the fake gun to Vidvath. Vidvath accepted it and momentarily hesitated, wondering if Radhika would laugh at him if he missed the shot. After a couple of tries, Vidvath managed to hit the target and win a prize.

"Here, this one's for you, my love," Vidvath said, handing Avinash a brown stuffed bear that he had just won. Vidvath watched the color from Radhika's face drain momentarily on hearing the words.

"Don't you brag. Watch me now," replied Avinash, taking the bear from Vidvath and pushing it into Radhika's hand, before rushing to the game stall.

"Nicely done," Radhika managed to whisper to Vidvath. Vidvath grinned in response. Avinash played and lost three games before giving up, grunting that it was a stupid game anyway.

For the rest of the day, the trio moved around different stalls, ate snacks, played games, and stopped by to pray at the temple before calling it a day. At the crowded temple, Vidvath stalled, blocking Radhika's way and waiting for Avinash to be pushed further away by the crowd. When Avinash was far enough, Vidvath dared to hold Radhika's hand. He smiled when Radhika looked up at him. For a moment, Vidvath was speechless, and then someone yelled and pushed them further in the crowd. Radhika and Vidvath stood side by side and prayed to the Goddess in the sanctum sanctorum. Then they exited and took a detour, hoping to find some alone time before finding Avinash.

"You look beautiful," Vidvath whispered to Radhika as they approached a quieter spot. It was then that Vidvath caught a whiff of Radhika's sandalwood perfume, something he remembered she reserved for special occasions.

"Thank you," Radhika's voice was soft and her eyes were constantly scanning the place. Many families from Jogibettu were in Gundmi today. Vidvath knew her fear was justified but he could not stop himself from being near her. They sat under a tree away from the crowd, a respectful distance between them. Each more nervous than the other to talk. Vidvath had so much to say to Radhika but feared of saying something wrong. As if a single wrong word could shatter the fragile cocoon of anticipation that enveloped them.

"I want to buy you something. Come," he finally said. Radhika joined him at the bangle store where he let her choose. She chose a pair of simple earrings. She held one to her ear and looked in the mirror. Vidvath stood behind her and smiled at her reflection.

"There you are. What a crazy crowd. Didn't realize I had lost you guys until I reached the exit." Radhika and Vidvath jumped when they heard Avinash's voice behind them. Radhika quickly dropped the earrings and composed herself.

"Yes, we were looking for you actually," Vidvath replied.

"At the bangle store?" Avinash frowned.

"I wanted to check it out," said Radhika quickly. Avinash nodded.

"Vidvath, thanks for babysitting Radhika by the way," Avinash said as the trio started to exit the fair.

"Don't mention it," Vidvath replied grinning at Radhika.

"I don't need to be babysat."

"Tell that to Amma."

Ayear had passed since Radhika and Vidvath had first met at the pond outside Jogibettu. Like all teenage relationships, theirs had progressed rapidly. By the end of the first month, all of Vidvath's close friends knew about them. They feigned respect when they saw Radhika walking in the school hallway and teasingly addressed her as their 'Attige' or sister-in-law while talking among themselves. All of them were sworn to secrecy by Vidvath. Naturally, by the end of the third month, the entire school knew.

Radhika, however, had only openly confessed her feelings to Tara. The other girls learned about it from their brothers and friends in Vidvath's group. Every time Vidvath or one of his friends tried to talk to her or even smile at her outside school, Radhika's pulse quickened. Jogibettu was a small village where people loved to gossip, especially about love affairs involving children of wealthy families like Vidvath's. Radhika knew the risk associated with what she was doing but could not restrain her teen mind, which was like a rebellious flame, dancing in the face of caution, flickering with the audacity to challenge the cool winds of societal norms.

Radhika now visited Suman only on alternate Thursdays while she spent the others with Vidvath by the pond. It was the first time Radhika was doing something this rebellious. It was frightening and thrilling in equal measure. But she knew she had tested her luck enough. Her mother had showered her with questions the last time Radhika had come to meet Vidvath by lying to her mother that she was at Suman's place. Radhika's mother had seen Suman in the market around the same time and caught her lie. Fortunately, Radhika was able to convince her mother that the plan had changed at the last minute and that she had instead been to Tara's place.. Although her mother had dropped the topic there, it was evident from her face that she knew Radhika was lying. It was then that Radhika decided she had to stop these secret meetings with Vidvath and find a better, safer option.

"What is troubling you, Radhika?" inquired Vidvath as he tossed a pebble onto the placid surface of the pond, creating gentle ripples.

It made Radhika feel a little better that Vidvath was able to tell when she was upset even without her expressing it. It made it easier for her to say what she was going to say next.

"I think we should stop meeting like this, Vidvath." Vidvath's face changed from concern to worry. Radhika told Vidvath about what had happened with her mother after the last meeting.

"Are you breaking up with me?"

"Of course not," Radhika smiled reassuringly. "I just think we are risking too much. If anyone sees us here..."

"I think you're right. We need to find another place to meet."

"No, I don't think that's a permanent solution."

"What do you mean?"

"Vidvath, I'm seventeen and will be done with boards in a year. We could join the same college after that. In a few years, we both will be done with our graduation and get a job. We can then talk to our families about us, get married with their blessings, and start a new life"

"That has always been the plan, Radhika," replied Vidvath, placing his hand softly on hers. Radhika pulled away and scanned her surroundings. She had a bad feeling, as if someone was watching them, waiting for the right moment to catch them. Yet, despite this unsettling intuition, Radhika chose to put it aside, as she had done countless times before. This uneasy feeling had become a familiar companion, haunting their secret rendezvous like a silent specter that only she could sense.

"What if we get caught before that? What will we do then?" Radhika asked, a little irritated at Vidvath's calmness. It was evident that he was not as worried as she was. After all, he was a man, the son of a wealthy business-man. In society's eyes, she was the poor witch who had trapped the prince.

"So we don't see each other till then?" Vidvath asked, frowning.

"Not outside school. You can still see me when you come home to meet Avinash. We can see each other at village festivals and gatherings." Radhika had thought this through. Several times in the last few days.

"That won't be the same. You won't even talk to me when people are around."

"You must understand, Vidvath, the stakes are higher for me." Radhika sighed. "Also, we cannot let anything tarnish your father's reputation now." Vidvath's father, Raghupathi Rao, one of the wealthiest and most power-ful men in the village, had just submitted his nomination for the upcoming Panchayat elections. It was palpable that not only would he secure a victory, but he was also poised to be elected as the Sarpanch, a strategic move that aligned with his extensive political influence. But on the other side was an equally powerful man, Jagannath Sharma, known for this vast network in the political realm and his reputation for adeptly luring individuals into his fold and buying votes.

"Please, Vidvath. Try to see this from my place."

"Okay, if that is truly what you want," Vidvath finally conceded. "I don't know if I'll be able to stop myself from talking to you, but I'll try," he added softly, his hand extending towards Radhika's, seeking connection in the face of impending separation. Radhika did not pull away; instead, she looked into his eyes. They were soft, filled with longing and vulnerability. In that tender moment, she realized the gravity of their decision, understanding that this might well be the last time they would meet in private for quite a while.

Even as every sensible part of her mind urged her to pull away, Radhika found herself inexplicably drawn closer to him. The magnetic pull of their shared emotions overpowered rational thoughts. Before she could engage in further contemplation, Vidvath's lips tenderly met hers, creating a momentary haven that shielded them from the outside world.

Their kiss had the sweet awkwardness of most teenage first kisses. Yet, within that awkwardness, the emotions at play transformed the moment into something far more significant than its physical expression.

The spell was abruptly broken when they heard the rustling of bushes behind them. No one came to this secluded spot at this time of day, Vidvath had assured Radhika several times. Yet, Radhika knew the worst had happened even before it registered fully. Radhika's hands froze, and her eyes welled with tears of fright as they both turned to see the approaching men. It was Jagannath Sharma's men—Jogibettu's moral police. The malicious grin on Rampa's face, the leader of the group, told Radhika that her worst fear had come true.

If any other villager had caught Radhika and Vidvath by the pond, the news could have been contained between the two families and hushed up. However, Jagannath Sharma and his supporters had stumbled upon the spark with which they could potentially set ablaze Raghupathi Rao's reputation, consequently jeopardizing his chances of winning the election. In villages like Jogibettu, the moral conduct of the candidate's family often played a more significant role than the candidate's actual contributions to the village's welfare.

Radhika's relationship with her father mirrored the typical dynamic found in Jogibettu and neighboring villages. All communication between them was channeled through Radhika's mother, and her father only spoke directly to the children when absolutely necessary. Any words he did express directly were treated with the utmost gravity.

As Radhika witnessed her honest and hardworking father standing before Raghupathi Rao and his family, his eyes fixed on the ground, her heart ached. She felt the weight of responsibility for the situation; her impulsive actions had stained her family's reputation in the village. Tomorrow, as her father went from house to house delivering letters, she knew people would regard him with disrespect and pity.

Many would blame him and his wife for using their daughter to lure a boy from a wealthy family. She knew this would happen all along, yet she did very little to stop it. How could she have been so stupid?

In Vidvath's family courtyard, the two families had gathered after Rampa and his men escorted Radhika and Vidvath there. Following a tense exchange of words with Raghupathi Rao's men, Rampa and his entourage left, casting the courtyard into an ominous silence, save for the incoherent mumbling from Anasuya, Vidvath's grandmother. Radhika stood in one corner, a silent figure, while Vidvath positioned himself beside his father, who occupied the wooden swing. On the other side, Vidvath's mother stood with a stoic expression. At the entrance, Radhika's parents stood with bowed heads. Avinash, who had just arrived, was glaring at Vidvath.

"I never expected this from your family, Srinivas. Everyone in Jogibettu respects you for your honesty and self-respect. You are one of the most educated people here. I still can't believe your daughter would do something like this. If this is about money—"

"No," Srinivas Prasad spoke for the first time since their arrival. He stepped forward with joined palms. Radhika averted her eyes. "Please believe me, Rao *avre*[31]. I am as shocked by this incident as you are. This is a mistake, a grave one indeed. But they are children after all. Please forgive them."

"What do you mean by 'them'?" Anasuya, Vidvath's grandmother, inquired sharply. "Vidvath is innocent. Your daughter is the siren. She has used her dark magic to trap him. How else would someone like her find a wealthy and handsome boy like our Vidvath? She is a witch—" Vidvath's grandmother spoke in her high-pitched voice, hurling abuses at Radhika. Tears poured down Radhika's face as she looked at Vidvath, silently urging him to intervene. But Vidvath stood mum, his gaze fixed on the floor.

"Enough, Amma," Raghupathi Rao's quiet words silenced his mother.

"What is done is done. Now, we need to fix this with as little noise as

---

[31] : Suffix added to a name indicating respect

possible. We cannot change what has happened. Neither can we stop Jagannath and his goons from spreading this news throughout the village," sighed Vidvath's father.

"Srinivas, there is only one way to deal with this without jeopardizing my family's reputation and my son's future. I, along with my family, will come to your home next week and finalize Vidvath and Radhika's alliance. On the same day, our family Purohit will match their horoscopes and provide us with the engagement and wedding dates. The sooner, the better," Raghupathi Rao declared, then walked out of the house without waiting for Srinivas's reply.

It took a moment for Anasuya to register what her son had just said. The family she had disliked all her life, and the girl she had been abusing all this while, would become her grandson's wife!

"Why the long faces? Your dream has come true. Isn't this what you wanted all along? First, this Padmini befriends Vinaya and then Avinash befriends Vidvath and now this. For how many years were you plotting this, Padmini?" Anasuya spat, staring at Radhika's mother.

"Amma," Vinaya tried to calm her mother-in-law while looking apologetically at her friend Padmini. Srinivas shook his head and without another word walked out of the house. Avinash followed him. Padmini looked at her friend Vinaya for a moment before dragging Radhika out of the house.

"I don't know what my grandson saw in this crow. No money, no looks, no dignity," Anasuya's words reached Radhika's ears. Vidvath finally looked up, and his eyes met Radhika's bloodshot gaze. Radhika hoped to discern regret or guilt in Vidvath's eyes, but all she encountered was a familiar cowardice. It was the same demeanor he had exhibited at first when his sister's dignity was trampled in the streets, courtesy of her ruthless father.

In that moment, Radhika had a stark realization of her own blindness. She had believed that whatever she felt for him would be enough to change him, to alter the course society had groomed him to follow throughout his life. How naïve had she been.

After returning from Vidvath's house, Srinivas retired to his room. Radhika knew her father would spend the rest of the day in there like he always did when he was upset. The next morning, he would share his decision with the family. Until then, everyone in the house would tip-toe around, talk in whispers and make sure not to disturb him.

Padmini, on the other hand, chose to give Radhika the silent treatment and spent hours cleaning the kitchen. Radhika was thankful for that. She did not know what she would answer if her mother asked her how this had happened. Honestly, she did not know herself how it had happened. She had passed the last year in her own happy bubble, blissfully ignoring society's norms. She had experienced a myriad of emotions for the first time, each one a revelation that had all but consumed her. How was she to sense the whispers of reality when the fluttering of her heart had become a constant companion, and the mere thought of Vidvath had ignited a kaleidoscope of emotions within her each time?

Radhika locked herself in her room and cried for what felt like an eternity. Her tears were a torrent, a release for the profound humiliation her family had endured, the sting of Vidvath's refusal to stand by her, and the relentless abuses hurled at her by his grandmother. But, above all, she cried for her own perceived foolishness—the folly of falling in love. For which she would now have to pay with her future.

It was at this poignant moment that a stark realization dawned upon Radhika: the mere thought of marrying Vidvath elicited nothing but fear within her. What had seemed like the prospect of building a life together with Vidvath, akin to paradise only a day ago, now felt like a foreboding abyss. The thought of living with Raghupathi Rao and his mother under the same roof, alongside a husband who might stand as a mute witness to potential abuses, filled Radhika with an overwhelming sense of dread.

As hours passed by, the compulsive overthinker that she was, Radhika grew restless. The deafening silence in the house made her anxious. She needed someone to talk to, someone who could guide her in the right direction instead of judging her for what she had done. Wiping her face, Radhika got up from her bed and looked outside her window. It was pitch dark outside. She looked at the clock on her study desk. 8:30 PM.

Radhika knew she would only further anger her family if she left the house at this time. But she needed to talk to Suman before her father made a decision on her behalf. Radhika wanted to have the right ammunition if she needed to fight for herself the next morning.

Radhika wrapped a scarf around her head and speed-walked to Suman's house, making sure not to be seen by any passerby. She felt grateful that Jogibettu slept early. The roads were deserted, and the worn-out street lights flickered every now and then. It was in this quiet moment amidst the chaos that she realized it was the first time she had walked out of the house after sunset, unchaperoned. The sense of freedom, though born out of necessity, sparked a subtle rebellion within her, a defiance against the societal norms that sought to confine and control her.

Radhika paused in front of Suman's house and pondered whether it was right for her to burden Suman with her troubles. The fear lingered—what if Suman, too, blamed her for everything that had transpired? Where would she turn then? What seemed more haunting than confiding in Suman was the thought of returning home to the stifling silence once again. Without letting herself think for another second, Radhika rang the doorbell.

"Radhika! Thank God you came," Suman opened the door and, unlike her usual self, pulled Radhika into an embrace. Overwhelmed by Suman's warmth and understanding, despite the circumstances, Radhika felt fresh tears escape her eyes.

"I need to talk to you," Radhika whispered.

"Come in," Suman moved aside and closed the door behind them.

"Drink up. You'll feel better," Suman said, placing a cup of hot lemon tea in front of Radhika. The aroma soothed Radhika's nerves, but she still hated the taste the tea left behind in her mouth. Then Radhika began to narrate the happenings of the day. It occurred to Radhika that Suman already knew most of it. Jogibettu was a small town with big mouths. As she narrated the day's events, fresh tears poured down Radhika's face. Suman held her hand in a comforting gesture. After several minutes, Suman spoke.

"I'm sorry about what happened, Radhika. I know you didn't mean for it to happen," Suman's understanding words loosened the knot in Radhika's chest, and she began to sob like a child. Suman held her close, waiting patiently for Radhika to feel better.

When Radhika finally calmed down and finished her tea, Suman smiled at her. "What do you want, Radhika?" Suman asked. Radhika looked at her, confused.

"For a moment, forget that you live in Jogibettu. Forget about your family or society. Think about yourself. What is it that you want?"

"Do I really get a say in this?"

"Of course you do. No one can force you to do anything against your will," Suman replied. But Radhika was not convinced. Suman was a strong woman who held power to a certain level in the village, but would she be able to withstand Raghupathi Rao?

"Radhika, I will support you with everything I have. I will go against your parents or even the entire village again if it means your happiness will not be compromised. But first, you must make a decision. What is it that you want?" Again. With that one word, Suman was trying to tell Radhika that she knew what it was to be standing in the blazing limelight of society's cruel eye. She had experienced it, fought it, and come out of it to build a life for herself on her terms. It was a promise, that Radhika too would someday make it to the other side.

"I want to go back in time and undo everything. I want to finish my education, get a job, and travel the world. I wish I had never agreed to meet Vidvath. I wish I had never been so stupid to believe that he would go against his parents to protect me," Radhika replied. "Suman Akka, I don't want to get married."

"Radhika, do you love him?"

Radhika had asked herself this question many times over the last few weeks. Even when, under the blindfold of teenage emotions, Vidvath had seemed like the ideal life partner, Radhika had never felt entirely certain about what love truly meant. A handful of clandestine encounters, a sprinkle of tender words, and a collection of promises — did these truly capture the essence of love?

"I did," Radhika replied finally. Suman nodded in understanding. The duo sat in silence for several minutes before Radhika spoke again.

"I'm sorry, Suman Akka. For everything. I know I have let you down. Throughout my life, you tried to caution me about the consequences of such mistakes, but I went ahead and did it anyway."

"Attraction, this feeling of love is common at your age. In an ideal world, the elders in this situation would talk to you both about the things that mattered. Things like teen pregnancy, STDs, and heartbreak. But people here are more concerned about social status and caste. And here, the woman has much more to lose than the man," Suman replied, a faraway look on her face. "In my eyes, what you both did was natural. A mistake, yes, but not an unforgivable crime for which you have to sacrifice your future and remain bound to each other for the rest of your lives. I just wish you had come to me first and shared your feelings with me."

Radhika looked down at her fingers in her lap. She had no answer.

"Okay, here is what we are going to do," Suman said, her voice steady with a mixture of determination and concern. "Let's wait for your father's decision, though I already have a good idea of what it will be. When he announces it, don't argue with him. Just keep quiet. I will find a way to deal with this."

Radhika's eyes searched Suman's face, desperation etched across her features. "But..."

Suman reached out, placing a reassuring hand on Radhika's shoulder. "Trust me, Radhika. You will be fine."

A week had passed since Radhika had stepped out of the house. On that dreadful day, when she had returned from Suman's house at dinner time, her mother had just shaken her head in disappointment and let her in. Her father was still in his room, but her grandmother, Jayalakshmi, who had by then heard of the fiasco from her sources in the village, had started rambling. She cursed the stars under which Radhika was born, that had ultimately led to this day when her hard-working son had to face humiliation at the hands of a goon. She blamed Padmini and her friendship with Vinaya, Vidvath's mother, that had supposedly caused the closeness between Vidvath and Radhika.

Jayalakshmi had said everything that had been left unsaid by Vidvath's grandmother, Anasuya. The two old women spoke the same language of callousness, as though they were sisters from different mothers. At that moment, Radhika wondered what would happen if somehow it was identified that they were sisters indeed. It would automatically make Radhika and Vidvath cousins and hence the marriage would be called off. With that thought, Radhika realized how close she was to losing her mind.

Now, a week later, Radhika could not sit, stand, or sleep in one place for more than a few minutes as the jitters ran wild in her stomach. Today was the day Vidvath's father had set to visit Radhika's house with the ceremonial *Tambula*[32], making the alliance official between the two families. Today was the day the designated Purohit would suggest the auspicious day for the engagement and the wedding. However, Radhika knew that when the family's reputation was at stake, the engagement would not be held. Instead, the nearest wedding date would be fixed—unless there was a death in the family.

At this, another wild thought ran through Radhika's mind. What if Anasuya Ajji… She immediately slapped her cheeks and apologized to the Gods above for having such a cruel thought.

As one long hour passed after another, Radhika sat in front of the mirror

---

[32] : Ceremonial exchange of betel leaves, areca nuts, and auspicious items symbolizing goodwill and the start of a new relationship

while her mother did her hair and makeup. The tension between them was still palpable. Padmini was truly heartbroken. Every time Radhika looked into her mother's eyes, she saw disappointment. Every day since the incident, Radhika hoped for her mother to break down, launch at her, scream, slap, curse—anything was better than this silence.

Draped in her mother's best silk saree and jewelry, she saw the naïve fourteen-year-old who, not so long ago, had sat dressed similarly in front of the same crowd seeking blessings as she entered womanhood. People had smiled at her, blessed her, and teasingly hinted at how she would now be officially available should any family decide to ask for her hand. Today, the same people sat whispering about her, adding spice to what had happened and doing everything to rub her family's name in the dust. Radhika's mind drifted to another day when she too had naively gossiped about Yashodha. Suman's words rang in Radhika's ears: There is no such thing as harmless gossip, Radhika. You never know how your one casual comment can destroy a person.

The commotion of fake enthusiasm and forced greetings in the living room brought Radhika back to reality. She had always thought of this day and felt butterflies in her stomach imagining Vidavath's face in awe looking at her in semi-bridal attire. Today, all she felt were dread and regret. Every time she thought of him, his forlorn face on the day she was humiliated in his house appeared in her mind. It was as if that single image of Vidvath had washed away the thousand happy memories they had shared in the past.

When Radhika was called into the living room, she walked with her head bowed as instructed by her mother, who now spoke to her on a need basis in a nonchalant tone. Another thing she had not imagined to happen on this day.

"I think we can begin now, Purohitre," it was Raghupathi Rao's voice. The Purohit cleared his throat in response and began matching the horoscopes. The two families were seated facing each other on the floor laden with carpets that Padmini brought out only on special occasions. On Radhika's side, Suman was missing. She had not been invited to avoid any trouble that might arise because of her attitude in such matters. On Vidvath's side, Yashodha was missing as she was no longer 'family'. The Purohit was seated in the middle where the two carpets met, facing both parties.

Outside, the sky was clear and cloudless, unaware of the storm growing in Radhika's mind. Inside, the air was thick with tension, accentuated further by Radhika's grandmother furiously mumbling prayers for the horoscopes to match.

"Considering the position of planets in both the *Jathakas*[33], I propose the engagement be held on seventeenth of February, Tuesday . The wedding will be two months after that on Friday, the sixteenth of April. I think it will give both families enough time to make the necessary arrangements."

After the humiliating incident when Raghupathi Rao had announced to the world that his son was a useless, spoiled brat who could not even pass his exams without his father's influence, Vidvath decided to reclaim his dignity. He resolved to retake his twelfth board exams. This time, he would clear the exams on his own. This decision served two purposes – firstly, it would elevate his standing in the eyes of his family and grant him the strength to meet his father's eyes. Secondly, the plan involved graduating alongside Radhika, and together they would enroll in the same degree or engineering college. Vidvath knew he would have to work hard if he aspired to share the same academic space as Radhika.

Other than Radhika, only Avinash knew of Vidvath's secret endeavor. Avinash, who was pursuing his second year in BSc in Jogibettu's Government College had agreed to tutor Vidvath during the weekends. To the rest of his family, Vidvath was simply wasting another year, delaying his gradual entry into his father's business. For several months now, Vidvath had dreamed of the day he would announce to his father that he had graduated twelfth on his own merit and would soon leave home for higher studies. But now, it all

---

[33] : Horoscope

seemed futile. How naïve he had been to think it would all unfold as easily as he thought.

It had been days since Vidvath had last slept soundly for more than a few hours. Unlike Radhika, his days had not changed much. He still went out, spoke to his friends, played cricket, and returned home at whatever time pleased him. He had little interest in studying anymore. For the first few days, his friends looked at him with curiosity, hoping he would narrate the happenings of that evening. But without Radhika's presence, everyone soon lost interest in the story. Vidvath felt both relieved and guilty. At night, he replayed the past years in his mind. From the first time, he had felt something for the fifteen-year-old girl to when he had asked her out for the first time. From the time they spent alternate Thursdays near the pond to the times they stole glances at each other when he visited her house to meet Avinash. Every time, Vidvath had seen nothing but love in Radhika's eyes. And he had so easily let her down.

Your daughter is the siren. She has used her dark magic to trap him. How else would someone like her find a wealthy and handsome boy like our Vidvath? She is a witch— Vidvath had stood mum listening to his grandmother crush Radhika with her words.

Radhika had not looked at him once during the Tambula ceremony. No one had spoken to her the entire time either. Her face was pale, and the one time she lifted her head in surprise when the wedding date was announced, Vidvath had witnessed nothing but regret and pain in her eyes. The love was gone. In that moment, Vidvath realized the only way he could atone for his silence was to set Radhika free. She deserved better. She deserved to be happy. However, if he refused to marry her now, it would do more damage than good.

His father's voice booming from the living room, followed by his grandmother's incoherent mumbling, brought Vidvath out of his room.

"What has happened?" his mother asked, emerging from the kitchen.

"That family will never let us live in peace. This is a letter from the Nari Shakti, Women's Welfare Association. They have warned us against conducting a child marriage. Radhika is not eighteen yet. Vidvath too is not twenty-one. They say not only is it a punishable offense but it might also affect the elections. How dare they—" Raghupathi Rao roared.

"What nonsense is this? I got married at fourteen. I had you and your brother by the time I was eighteen. What is this legal age rubbish now? I'm sure Srinivas asked his niece, that sorcerer Suman, to help him with this so that they will get more time to arrange for dowry"

"I think so too," Raghupathi replied. "Your son has ruined everything. I swear to God, if I lose this election, I will make sure the girl and her family pay for it. I have been good to them until now for the sake of my reputation," he scowled at his wife.

"Let the marriage be over. Once she joins our family, we will teach her our ways. You leave it to me," Vidvath's grandmother replied. Vidvath winced at his grandmother's words. Vinaya walked back into the kitchen. It made Vidvath wonder what his mother must have faced when she had come to this house as a young bride.

"I will send word to the Purohit, asking for a revised date for the wedding. We will have it on the first auspicious day after Radhika turns eighteen. Vidvath will be a little over twenty by then. I can handle that."

For the first time in weeks, Vidvath slept better that night, knowing Radhika would be relieved hearing the news. Maybe she had smiled too or perhaps cried in relief. They had almost a year's time to think of the next step.

"I must admit, I'm both relieved and worried," Srinivas confessed to his wife, Padmini.

"At least we have enough time to arrange the dowry," Padmini sighed.

"I'll start searching for potential buyers for the east side of the farm."

Radhika, who had been eavesdropping into the conversations from her room since the Purohit's unannounced mid-morning visit, couldn't believe her ears. With an entire year before the impending marriage, she could complete her twelfth board exams and begin college. There was so much that could unfold in a year. Perhaps the elders would recognize that the incident had faded from the villagers' memories and such drastic measures were unnecessary. Maybe she would get a seat in a medical or engineering college far away, and her parents would forgive her, allowing her to pursue her dreams. It was the most hopeful Radhika had felt in weeks.

"Do we really have to sell? We have already sold so much to settle our previous debts," Padmini's voice quivered with a mix of concern and weariness. Radhika knew how much it killed her father to sell his inheritance piece by piece in exchange for his inability to meet his family's needs.

Srinivas's salary as a postmaster barely managed to make ends meet. Padmini's tailoring brought in some income, but it was inconsistent. With her worsening knee pain, Srinivas had insisted she refrain from taking additional orders. All their savings had been depleted in marrying off Srinivas's sisters. At Jayalakshmi's insistence, the weddings had been conducted with a lavishness that plunged the family into years of debt.

"How much has Vidvath's family demanded?" Padmini asked.

"They haven't said anything directly about the dowry but have asked for a grand wedding. The Purohit hinted at least 10 tolas of gold on Radhika and a chain for Vidvath in addition to the wedding ring."

"I had always hoped Avinash and Radhika's weddings would be around the same time so that we can give Radhika what we get from Avinash's bride's dowry. But now it appears more debt is on our way," Padmini replied. The living room drowned in silence as the gravity of their financial situation sunk in.

Later that evening, Radhika approached her brother when their parents and grandmother were away.

"What is it that you want, Radhika?" Avinash asked when he spotted her lingering at his room door. Avinash had all but stopped talking to Radhika during the initial days after the incident. Radhika did not blame him for that; she had deserved it. However, after the Tambula ceremony, Avinash had started to speak, albeit curtly, to Radhika. It was as if it had suddenly struck him that his little sister would leave their home soon and would only be a guest henceforth. He now asked Radhika if she wanted anything when he left home, knowing she was not allowed to. He would bring her notes from Tara and books from the library.

"I want to go back to college," Radhika said, mustering all the courage she had. Three weeks had passed since Radhika had last stepped into the college. Tara had promptly kept her posted with updates and brought her notes. Radhika had wondered if she would ever go back. They had two months before the final board exam. Initially, she had planned to finish as a private student, studying at home and going directly for the exam. But now that the wedding was far away, Radhika hoped things would go back to normal.

"Okay," Avinash replied, not looking up from his book. "I'll talk to Appa."

Radhika had been so apprehensive about her father's response to her request to attend college that she had overlooked preparing for what she would do if he agreed. Avinash must have tried really hard to persuade their father, Radhika thought. While the humiliation for Radhika had ceased once she was confined within the four walls of her house three weeks ago, the situation was very different for her father, who had to traverse from house to house delivering letters every day. Radhika was well aware of the villagers' cruelty in such matters. Every day leading up to the Tambula ceremony, Srinivas had returned home in a bad mood, exhausted and defeated. So, his agreement to her going back to college, being seen in public again and triggering the gossip mill, felt surreal.

Avinash had visited her room the next morning, informing Radhika that she could go to college. The only condition imposed was that she would be dropped off at college every day by Avinash, and in the evening, her mother or Srinivas himself would accompany her home. Under different circumstances, Radhika might have felt humiliated by this arrangement. However, at that moment, she was simply grateful that her father had agreed at all.

Standing at the college gate, Radhika struggled to recall the thoughts that had occupied her mind when she last walked out. It suddenly struck her that the last time she had left the college was the day her world had unexpectedly crumbled. Radhika had been filled with excitement, eagerly anticipating her meeting with Vidvath by the pond. Throughout that day, she had watched the clock intently, urging time to move faster.

Radhika blinked back the tears and steeled herself, well aware that she needed to be her strongest self today. Suddenly, she realized she had not informed Tara of her return. Initially, Radhika had wanted to surprise her best friend, but now it seemed like a bad idea. If Tara were by her side in this moment, Radhika wouldn't have felt so alone.

Entering her classroom, Radhika received the expected welcome of collective gasps, surreptitious side glances, and hushed whispers. It was their typical response when a teacher returned from maternity leave or a student came back after a family tragedy. Only now, Radhika was at the receiving end of it. Despite being categorized as Pre-University College, the students in the eleventh and twelfth grades were, for all intents and purposes, barely evolved high schoolers.

Radhika sighed and made her way to her usual place, disappointed to see the place next to hers empty. Curious about Tara's whereabouts, Radhika asked one of the girls in the row ahead of her. However, the girl pretended not to hear Radhika and continued writing in her notebook. Radhika noticed everyone staring at them, as though expecting some sort of drama to unfold.

For the rest of the day, Radhika felt like an outcast. No one spoke to her, and people made way when she passed by, as though her ignominy was contagious. Some mean-spirited girls from her class, who had always resented her for her academic prowess, openly called her names and giggled behind her back in the hallway. Some boys she barely knew teased her using Vidvath's name.

Radhika sat alone during lunch and sought solace in a quiet corner with her nose in a book in the library during her free period. When the last class for the day concluded, all the excitement Radhika had initially felt about returning to college had vanished. As Radhika hurried out of the class, hoping her father would be at the gate ready to pick her up, she was surprised to find herself ushered into the principal's room. Her father was already seated there.

"Radhika, please come in," the college principal, Mrs. Sharma, said, gesturing to a chair next to Srinivas. In the brightly lit room, Srinivas appeared small and downtrodden compared to the bright-eyed, astute-looking woman seated opposite him.

"Radhika, I understand how difficult it must have been for you to return to college today... after everything that has happened." Mrs. Sharma had always taken pride in Radhika's academic achievements and often chose her for college competitions. Seeing the sympathy and disappointment in her principal's eyes now only added to Radhika's disheartenment.

"It pains me to have to tell you this, but both parents and teachers believe it's best for you to finish the remainder of the year at home," Mrs. Sharma said, briefly turning towards Srinivas, silently urging him to view the situation through a parent's eyes. It was clear she meant that parents feared Radhika's presence might negatively influence their children in class. Radhika didn't argue. Nor did she attempt to defend herself. What could she say, after all? Did she really want to endure the humiliation she had felt today every day for the next two months? Would that even make things normal?

Radhika and her father left the principal's office and the college without another word. Both knew it was best if Radhika stayed home for the rest of the academic year. As Radhika passed the school playground, she smiled at the sight of children playing. It reminded her of simpler times when she too could have joined them without a care in the world.

Standing outside, Radhika watched as little kids chased each other, while older ones engaged in various ball games. A group of girls practiced Throwball. However, her attention was drawn to one of the older boys from her school. Instinctively, she looked around, hoping not to see the person she knew would be there. At the far end of the cricket pitch, Vidvath stood behind the wickets, yelling instructions, unaware of the resentment growing in Radhika's mind.

Radhika's father left her at the door of their house and walked away without a word. Radhika had grown used to this coldness from her family over the last few weeks. To her, her father's silence had always felt indifferent, but now there was an undertone of distrust and disappointment.

Inside, there was another unpleasant surprise waiting for Radhika. Seated in her father's chair, opposite her anxious mother, was Anasuya, Vidvath's grandmother. Seeing her there, Radhika's first thought was relief that he father had left.

"Good, you're here," Anasuya said trying her best to appear polite. But the transformation of her wizened face from tolerance to disgust was not lost on Radhika or her mother. "I was just telling your mother what a bad idea it was to let you go to college again."

"You're going to be the daughter-in-law of the Rao family," Anasuya continued, standing up with her weight on her weathered wooden cane. "You will be Vidvath's support system, his pillar in front of society. So, you must understand how incongruous it will look if people were to know that you are more educated than your husband, the man of the house."

In a different situation, Radhika would have laughed at Anasuya's ridiculous words, but today she knew these were not just dismissive remarks from a woman who had lived nearly three-quarters of a century in the patriarchal society. These were words of pronouncement from Vidvath's family—a decision, their claim in her life.

Forty days had passed since Anasuya's visit. Forty days since Radhika had last stepped out of the house. Forty days since she had spoken more than three words at a stretch to anyone in her family. Radhika's life had now become a repetition of the same day over and over again. Each morning, she woke either startled by a nightmare or with a pricking headache from a sleepless night. Absentmindedly eating breakfast, she spent the morning in her room reading books brought by either Tara or Avinash from the library.

On better days, Radhika revised her lessons and answered the preparatory question papers that Tara brought during her weekly visits. Despite everything, Radhika held onto hope that by some miracle, she would be able to write her exams. Ever since learning that Suman had managed to postpone the wedding with the help of Nari Shakti, Radhika felt a spark of hope. Perhaps her tenacious cousin would find another way to help her.

Radhika often pondered how different things might have been if her mother were more like Suman. Would this incident feel as grievous as it did now? After all, all that had occurred was a fleeting kiss in the heat of the moment. In the village's history, far more severe transgressions had taken place, many of them not even consensual. Was she being punished because Vidvath was the son of a powerful man? If he were a commoner's son, would the matter be discreetly handled, allowing her to resume her life after a reasonable punishment?

Along with the preparatory question papers, Tara also brought Radhika letters from Binya and Vidvath. Vidvath's letters directly went into the black shoebox under her bed, while Binya's letters served as her anchor—a tiny porthole in the vast expanse of darkness that enveloped her.

"Radhika?" Tara's chirpy voice at the door made Radhika smile weakly.

"How are you doing today? You look better. Did you sleep well?" Tara asked, sitting beside Radhika on her bed. Radhika nodded unconvincingly, noticing Tara's ever-changing nails, this time delicately painted with tiny flowers.

"The exam timetable is out. I brought you a copy," Tara handed over a sheet of paper. Radhika's smile dropped as she realized she had less than two weeks.

"Radhika, have you tried talking to Vid—"

"No"

"Radhika, I know you don't want to talk to Vidvath but he is the only person right now who can help you. He has a shot at convincing his father to let you attend the finals." Tara sighed, "I understand, what he did is unforgivable. But don't let your anger ruin your future. Fight for what is rightfully yours. He is grappling with guilt right now. This is your chance."

"Promise me you'll think about it," Tara added when Radhika did not reply. Radhika nodded in response.

"And these are some additional notes. Ramesh Sir says he misses your questions in class. Given that you were the only one who was genuinely interested in Social Science," Tara tried to make Radhika laugh.

A moment later, "I have something that will make you feel better," Tara grinned holding out Binya's letter. Radhika's face broke into a smile. She placed the letter on her desk to read later.

"Are you sure Binya is not a guy?"

"Tara…"

"No, seriously. What if it's a boy who has been writing to you for almost, what… two years now?"

"Binya is not a boy. I don't think a boy of her age can write so intimately and passionately about things like relationships and family."

"What if it is a grown man? Grown men are supposed to be good at all these, or at least good at pretending."

"Tara… stop messing with me."

"Sorry. I did not mean to get you worried. I just see how her letters make you happy and how much you look forward to writing to her. She is your kindred spirit. More than I am or will ever be."

"That's not—"

"No, it's alright. I'm not envious. What I mean is, in my most hopeful dreams, I wish for someone like her to come and rescue you from all this chaos you're going through. I want you to experience love and live happily, just like those girls in your novels." Tara's face crumpled as she spoke, and before Radhika could respond, Tara began to weep. With no tears left to shed, Radhika simply held her friend.

That night, Radhika pondered the possibility. If Binya had been a boy her age, and if they had fallen in love over letters as the fourteen-year-old her had imagined, would Radhika have run away to meet him in the snow-capped golden mountains? Could she see herself living a Pahari life and embracing their lifestyle? And if she did, would it really matter if Binya was a girl or a boy? Would the essence of their connection be altered, whether framed by love or friendship?

Two days later, after discarding a bin full of scribbled and crumpled papers, Radhika was finally content with her letter to Vidvath—a perfect balance of dignity, anger, and hope. If, for the sake of her future, she had to set aside the last ounces of her self-respect, then so be it. She handed the letter to Tara, who did not say anything in return, for which Radhika was grateful.

As each day passed and the exams loomed closer, Radhika felt her hope dwindle. Vidvath had not responded to her letter, nor did he offer any explanation when Tara confronted him. With less than four days remaining, Radhika recognized there was nothing more she could do. A cloud of helplessness and anxiety began to envelope her.

As Radhika sat in her room, grappling with a knot of frustration and disappointment in the pit of her stomach, she heard footsteps approaching. It was Avinash.

"We'll leave two hours early for the exam. I'll wait outside your exam hall, and then we'll return together. No one needs to know about it," Avinash said, placing Radhika's hall ticket and a brand new pen on her table. It took a moment for Radhika to fully grasp Avinash's words. Radhika's eyes welled in tears as she hugged her brother for the first time in years.

Over the next three days, Radhika studied diligently. Unlike the last few months, she studied without the shadow of uncertainty. Mentally, she thanked her best friend, Tara, for never letting her give up and for keeping her updated with lessons and assignments.

On the day of the exam, Radhika woke up early, reviewed everything she had noted as important, took a bath, prayed, and then met Avinash in the living room. Her grandmother was still asleep. Oblivious to their children's furtive actions, her parents had left the house early – her mother to the vegetable market, her father to the mechanic where Avinash had left their scooter the previous evening.

Feeling more hopeful and excited than she had in months, Radhika stepped out of the house and noticed a man in the shadows of the old tree across the road. There was something ominous about the mustached, red-eyed, grim-looking bald man. Avinash's drained face indicated he recognized the man.

Gesturing for Radhika to wait, Avinash crossed the road. Though Radhika couldn't hear the conversation, she sensed its tension. Her heart thumped in her chest. Then, as the man's hand reached her brother's collar, it became clear. Vidvath's father had sent him to ensure Radhika did not leave the house. And just like that, her house of cards came crashing down.

When does one begin to notice the subtle shifts in their thoughts? The intuition that something within is amiss, that they need help? The urge to let go, surrender, or perhaps... end it all?

That year, the summer in coastal South India appeared to have extended into the monsoon season. With June's arrival, instead of a cooling trend, the temperature seemed to have increased by several degrees overnight. Umbrellas became constant companions – shielding against the relentless sun and hopeful for rain. The water level in lakes and wells was dwindling at an alarming rate, prompting farmers and landowners to offer daily prayers to the rain gods.

In Udupi, a coastal town near Jogibettu, the locals had recently concluded Mandooka Parinaya – the frog wedding dedicated to appeasing the rain gods. The little bride and groom hailing from two different villages, wore custom-made outfits and received blessings from hundreds of guests before heading off to their honeymoon.

At Radhika's home, the air was still thick with tension for a different reason. It was as if all their problems had become intertwined with Radhika's impending wedding. Somehow marrying her off and sending her away would put an end to the rumor mill that was churning in and around Jogibettu. Like trapping the elusive house rat responsible for wreaking havoc in their lives and finally relocating it to a distant place.

Today, on account of Avinash's birthday, the family sat together for dinner. Radhika, who had wondered for the last several months if she would ever again sit with her family to eat, now wished she could enjoy her meal in the comfort of her room. Normally, when she sat in her room, she could still hear the occasional chatter in the living room—Avinash teasing his grandmother in a half-hearted attempt to revisit the carefree past, her grandmother mumbling about how the food was bland, and Padmini scolding Avinash for forgetting to get something from the market even after three reminders, and the like.

But now, in her presence, everyone was quiet. Even the slight creaking of the chair when she squirmed cut through the silence like a knife. Her presence now felt ominous even to herself, as though it had sucked happiness and life from everything.

Radhika's grandmother had stopped talking to her completely. Her father, who had always spoken little to his children, seemed indifferent. His anger had subsided, Radhika could tell, but disappointment and pain had made a permanent home in his eyes. Everything they had, Srinivas had created with honesty and integrity. Now, everyone accused him of using his daughter to trap a rich boy and make money. His reputation in the village was his pride, and Radhika had taken away that pride.

Padmini had started speaking to Radhika, but it was more about providing instructions on how to prepare herself to be a good wife and daughter-in-law. Radhika now spent more hours in the kitchen than ever before. She hated it, but it gave her something to keep her mind occupied when she ran out of books to read. She cooked delicacies whenever she could, hoping to bring a smile to her mother's face. However, she barely received a nod in acknowledgment of her efforts.

Vidvath had betrayed her once again, and this time, he had taken away something even more significant from her. Throughout the week of the board exams, Radhika wondered how she had allowed this to happen. One naive decision to follow her heart had turned her world upside down. Radhika would undoubtedly be an 'eleventh pass' for the rest of her life, only slightly better than most women of the previous generation.

Avinash now smiled at Radhika more often and went out of his way to get her books, magazines, and chocolates. He teased her occasionally, hoping to elicit a smile in return. He even stood up against their grandmother when she made hurtful comments to Radhika. The annoying elder brother, who once found ways to get his little sister in trouble, was replaced by a responsible young man who felt helpless in the face of his sister's unfortunate circumstances.

Avinash's friendship with Vidvath was long gone, and as a result, his connections with the rest of the group had also shattered. He now only spoke to a few of his classmates and dedicated most of his time to studying in his room. On the bright side, he was excelling in college. With just one more year, he would secure a decent job, alleviating their financial troubles. It seemed as if he had taken on Radhika's dreams for their family.

In the weeks following the board exams, Radhika had experienced an unexpected surge of boldness—the kind that comes when you've hit rock bottom and have nothing left to lose. She now realized there was only one way to salvage the last shred of self-respect she possessed. It made her sad that she was about to ruin her brother's birthday dinner.

"Appa," Radhika spoke to her father, who barely acknowledged her. It did not bother Radhika as much as it used to.

"I have something important to say."

"Radhika, please let your father eat in peace. We can talk about whatever it is later," her mother said.

Radhika ignored her mother's instinctive need to nip potential conflicts at the bud. Why were women so afraid of conflicts and confrontations?

"I will not marry Vidvath, Appa," Radhika said with new determination. She watched the *rasam*[34] silently trickle out from beneath the rice fort she had made.

"Radhika!" Padmini warned her.

---

[34] : Tangy South Indian soup served with rice

"Hey Ram… this girl will be the end of this family. What more…" Radhika's grandmother, Jayalakshmi moaned.

"Enough Amma," Srinivas silenced his mother "Radhika, I know you're upset. But you must understand…"

"Understand what Appa? What happened that day… is it really such a big mistake that I'm being asked to sacrifice my entire future? You always taught me education is the only true wealth we have. Then why are you taking it away from me?"

"What do you want to do then? Live like that Suman? A black mark on the family and society. Is that what you want for yourself?" Jayalakshmi yelled.

"What is so bad about Suman Akka's life, Ajji? She is living a happier life than most women in this village. Far better than the life the women in Vidvath's family are given. Did you know? Raghupathi Rao hits his wife with a belt? Have you seen how Yashodha Akka is treated there? Is that the life you want for your granddaughter as well? Is that how much you resent me, Ajji?" Radhika looked directly into her grandmother's eyes.

Jayalakshmi did not respond. Mumbling something under her breath, she continued to eat.

"I have decided, Appa. I will not marry Vidvath. I am a minor now, so marriage is out of the question. Once I am eighteen, I will have the legal rights to choose for myself. I will stand up against Vidvath's family if that is what it takes. If need be, I will do it alone." Saying this, Radhika touched her half-eaten dinner in a gesture of apology and walked back into her room.

That night, Radhika did not sleep a wink. She lay on her bed alert. Every few minutes, she got up and pressed her ear to the door. From the moment she had walked out of dinner, no one had spoken in the house. Even her grandmother, who rarely kept her mouth shut, had not uttered a word in the last few hours. It meant Radhika's words had made an impact.

What she had done must have devastated her father. Or had he even taken it seriously? A seventeen-year-old opposing the most powerful man in Jogibettu with no support from her family – Radhika realized how ridiculous it sounded even to her own ears. On the other hand, her family now knew that she regretted what had happened and that she had no intention of marrying Vidvath. The message was clear.

Radhika had been anxious the entire day, rehearsing the lines that she wished to deliver without hesitation or fear. She thought she had done it successfully. She had managed to silence her grandmother, hadn't she? When the clock struck midnight and there was no sign of any discussion outside, Radhika's exhaustion took over and before she knew it, she had fallen asleep.

"Radhika! That girl is pure evil."

Radhika woke up startled at the commotion. She squinted towards the wall clock, which was visible in the dull light from outside the window. It was a little past five in the morning.

"Radhika! Get up!"

It was Radhika's grandmother. Her grandmother much have just woken up and decided to punish her for what she had done last night. For a moment, Radhika wondered if she had dreamed about the dinner incident. But her grandmother's words said otherwise. Radhika decided to ignore it and go back to sleep. A moment later, Avinash knocked on her door and called out.

"What is it, Anna? Why are you up so early?" Radhika asked, opening the door. The look on his face jarred her into complete alertness.

"Appa has suffered a heart attack. We are waiting for the ambulance."

Six months later.

Since the day Radhika and her family were insulted and accused of being opportunistic by Vidvath's parents, Radhika had changed. Gone was the small-town girl who dared to dream big.

Today, Radhika was a faint shadow of the ambitious girl she once was. After her father's heart attack, her rebellion became the scapegoat, with everyone attributing her actions as the cause. It had taken Srinivas several months to recover. Vidvath's family had taken up the responsibility of the wedding, making it look like a charity project in the village. This boosted Raghupathi Rao's reputation and helped him win the Panchayat elections. Within the two families, the wedding expenses borne by the groom's family were treated as a loan that Srinivas and Avinash—now working part-time in a medical store—had to repay within two years.

With each incident—the heart attack, silent treatment by her family members, Vidvath's indifference, the rumors, and the labeling—Radhika had turned into a shell of a person. More than once, she had had suicidal thoughts, which she could not confide in anyone. She knew she needed help but was afraid of being tagged with another label—insane from guilt. Ending her life would have freed her from her troubles but not without adding more to her family's. On some level, Radhika too blamed herself for her father's heart attack. Her harsh words had caused it.

Tara still brought her letters from Binya—the only good thing that was left in Radhika's life. Radhika now poured her heart out into those letters, sometimes replying with two or three pages. It was like therapy that kept her sane. But on her darkest days, Radhika couldn't help but wonder if she would be forbidden from writing letters to strangers once she was married. Would Vidvath help her do it secretly? She laughed at the thought.

Vidvath's letters had ceased, and the ones sent earlier remained unopened in the black shoebox beneath her bed. Radhika refused to open them, knowing they would only offer false hope. She couldn't afford to subject herself to that again and lose her last shred of sanity. There was no point in persistently knocking on a wall, hoping it would one day transform into a door.

On better days, Radhika allowed herself to entertain Tara's words from months ago about Binya possibly being a man who would one day rescue her from her misery, akin to the heroes from the commercial movies she had grown up disliking. When she indulged in such thoughts, she laughed heartily, only for them to be followed by inconsolable tears. Not that there was anyone around to comfort her.

Today, the usual silence in the house was broken, replaced by happy commotion mainly from relatives and friends who had come to help Radhika's family. Everyone now wanted to associate with Radhika's family, soon to be related to Jogibettu's Sarpanch. Suman had been invited to the ceremony at Radhika's request, on the condition that she would not create a scene. Suman had politely declined the invitation. Radhika knew how disappointed Suman was with her for having admitted defeat so easily.

In a few hours, Radhika would be engaged to Vidvath. Four months later, fifteen days after Radhika's eighteenth birthday, they would be legally married. Once again, Radhika found herself dressed in one of her mother's sarees that, along with the right makeup, made her almost as fair-skinned as the groom-to-be. This time, she did not protest. It had been a long time since she had opposed anything. Sometimes, it made her wonder if she was still the same person.

During the engagement ceremony, Radhika kept her eyes down and examined her pink fingernails. She knew Vidvath was glancing in her direction every now and then, trying to talk to her, but she pretended to not notice. She heard the Purohit chanting mantras, blessing the couple and their families. Radhika did not look at Vidvath even when they exchanged rings. As the façade continued around them, she looked at the ring Vidvath had just placed on her finger. The ring was simple in design, but the size of the diamond in the middle told her it was a symbol of the power and affluence that radiated from Vidvath's influential family. The simple gold band she had placed on Vidvath's finger rightly reflected their humble condition.

Radhika's despair about the situation was misinterpreted by everyone as shyness. After the ceremony, she was sent back to the room with Tara. The elders would now finalize everything about the wedding – the venue, menu, expenses, guest list, etc.

"Radhika, I can't see you like this. This is supposed to be one of the happiest days of your life," said Tara, who had been dreaming of her marriage, particularly the wedding ceremony, since she was eight. Radhika did not reply to her best friend; instead, she began clearing her makeup and removing pins from her hair.

"I know what Vidvath did was wrong. But can you not try to give him another chance? May be he is as scared as you are. God knows how cruel his family can be," Tara's hollow words did nothing to change Radhika's mind. She had made peace with what had happened. From now on, she was a no one. Her life would be just like any other woman in the village— from being someone's daughter to someone's wife and someone's daughter-in-law. A life worse than that of a cattle with no identity of its own.

Padmini stood in front of the calendar, making a note of all the important events that would fall between now and the wedding. Now that the engagement was done, everyone in Radhika's house breathed a little freely, as though an invisible weight had been lifted off from their chests, even if it still hovered just a few inches above.

On the day of the engagement, Padmini and Vinaya, Vidvath's mother, had spoken freely for the first time ever since the incident. It was as if the engagement had given their friendship a new lease on life. As the duo stood in the kitchen, preparing tea for everyone, Vinaya held Padmini's hand and promised to look after Radhika like her own daughter. Since then, Padmini had taken it upon herself to mend the relationship between the two families. During the ceremony, Srinivas and Raghupathi Rao spoke sparingly but made an effort to not make their mutual disdain evident in front of the guests. Avinash refused to even look at Vidvath.

What bothered Padmini the most was seeing Radhika waste away day after day. Despite their estranged relationship following the incident, Padmini kept a close eye on her daughter. In the last few months, especially after Srinivas's heart attack, Radhika had completely retreated into her shell. Sometimes she went days without talking to anyone. She had stopped reading and barely ate or slept. The signs had begun to show.

Radhika's once plump cheeks were now almost hollow. Her skin had turned dull, and the twinkle in her eyes was long gone. Padmini knew she had to do something. The wedding was in four months, and at this rate, Radhika would appear like a ghost next to Vidvath, giving people more to talk about. Padmini had tried talking to Radhika about eating and sleeping better, about working on looking better for the wedding like most girls did, but her words fell on deaf ears.

"What is bothering you, Padmini?" Srinivas's voice brought Padmini back to the present.

"Nothing," Padmini composed herself and smiled. There was no point placing more burden on her husband's shoulders. He had enough to deal with. According to the doctor, Srinivas was now almost back to his old self. He was allowed to work like before, expect lifting heavy weights or riding his scooter for long distances. But Padmini knew he would never be the same person again.

"You have been staring at the calendar for more than ten minutes now. What has happened?"

"Radhika does not look like herself. She has lost too much weight and does not sleep or eat well. I'm worried for her."

"I have been observing that too. She is unhappy…"

"I think we should go visit Nagapattinam. It has been years since we last went there as a family. All these troubles might be God's way of reminding us that we have not been grateful to him," Jayalakshmi, Srinivas's mother, whom they had assumed to be fast asleep, suggested.

"Amma—" Srinivas started to argue.

"I think Amma is right. We should all go to Nagapattinam once and seek the blessings of Lord Murugan. We can also meet Nandini Patti and invite her family to the wedding. She is our oldest family member after all," Padmini added. Srinivas thought for a long moment. He was a person of faith but did not subscribe to the notion of a punitive God. Although he did not believe that everything their family had been through was a divine reminder, he knew they all needed a break and that it would probably be their last trip as a family.

"Okay, let me go see if the train tickets are available. Inform the children," saying so, Srinivas walked out of the house, realizing how in a few months he would have to replace 'children' with Avinash in addressing the young in his family.

175

CHAPTER 6

A fortnight after the engagement, Radhika found herself aboard the Mangaluru-Chennai Express with her entire family. Her mother had only informed her of the trip to Nagapattinam two days prior. Radhika couldn't help but smile upon hearing about the week-long break—it was her first time leaving Jogibettu in nearly a year. She had fond memories of visiting Nagapattinam during her childhood summers, where her grandmother Jayalakshmi's oldest sister, Nandini, lived. Though most memories were now hazy, Radhika vividly recalled the wizened old woman: big kohl-rimmed eyes, unruly hair, a coin-sized bindi, a conch shell necklace, and a perpetually knowing smile. As a child, Radhika had been reluctant to be left alone with her.

After finding their coach and stowing their luggage, Radhika climbed to the top berth and opened a book Tara had fetched from the library especially for this journey. Below her, Avinash sat by the window, lost in music from his new cellphone—a purchase made after saving every penny from his earnings, after what he contributed to household expenses. Her father, mother, and grandmother discussed places to visit and rituals to perform at the temple. Across from her, two young children, a boy and a girl no more than five or six years old, were engrossed in a board game.

Half an hour into the book, Radhika slammed it shut in frustration. It was difficult to concentrate, knowing this might be her last family trip. Sitting up, she glanced down the aisle. The bogey had settled into a steady rhythm, nothing particularly interesting happening. With a sigh, Radhika decided to try sleeping. Then, her gaze landed on a young couple on the side berth.

They looked to be in their early twenties—the girl in jeans and a checkered shirt, the boy in khaki shorts and a t-shirt. They animatedly discussed what seemed to be an itinerary from a brochure. The boy made a comment, the girl playfully punched his arm, and he pretended to be hurt. Radhika smiled at their antics. They appeared genuinely happy together. Below, Radhika's grandmother muttered something about the shamelessness of today's youth.

Upon reaching Nagapattinam, two middle-aged men emerged to welcome Radhika's family—Nandini Patti's sons, as Radhika recalled. They assisted with the luggage and chauffeured the family home in their jeep.

As they navigated through narrow lanes bordered by towering trees and adorned with beautiful traditional houses, Radhika couldn't help but notice the enchanting display of big stars and twinkling lights adorning the verandahs and front yards. Some houses even boasted elaborately decorated Christmas trees, casting a festive glow over the surroundings. It dawned on Radhika that they were traveling on Christmas day.

Nandini Patti's house was expansive, with a sprawling garden encircled by tall coconut trees and an open courtyard large enough to accommodate a hundred people. The traditional duplex featured clay-tiled roofs and brick walls. Upon entering, Radhika's family greeted Nandini, taking turns to touch her feet. When it was Radhika's turn, Nandini spoke softly, as if sharing a secret.

"May Lord Murugan grant you your wish," she smiled, her eyes piercing Radhika's soul. Later that night, Radhika replayed the scene in her mind. There was something peculiar about Nandini Patti's blessing. Radhika recalled what her mother had told her many years ago about Nandini Patti. During her first visit at the age of five or six, she had questioned why everyone called her Nandini Patti instead of Ajji—the way they addressed her grandmother, Jayalakshmi. Padmini, Radhika's mother, had explained that Ajji in Kannada was Patti in Tamil.

Nandini had defied her family's wishes by marrying a Tamil man and settling in Nagapattinam over seventy years ago. However, Jayalakshmi, who had been close to her older sister, ensured that their bond remained unbroken. Their sisterhood thrived through letters for many decades until one day, when Nandini asked her eldest son to visit Srinivas in an attempt to rekindle the relationship between the two families.

Then realization hit Radhika like a coconut dropping from the treetop. Nandini Patti had not blessed her with 'Akhanda Soubhagyavathi Bhava' as she had done with her mother—a typical blessing for a long, happy, and healthy married life. Instead, she had blessed Radhika that Lord Murugan make her wish come true.

Foolish hope bubbled in Radhika's mind as she tried to comprehend the cryptic blessing. During the train journey, Jayalakshmi had shared many stories about Nandini Patti and her psychic abilities—how, even as a young woman of merely eighteen, Nandini Patti had predicted people's futures using her knowledge of astrology, cowrie-shell reading, and palmistry.

Though the stories intrigued Radhika and occasionally sent shivers down her spine, she hadn't truly believed in them. But desperate times called for hope, even in the most hopeless places. The more she dwelled on Nandini Patti's blessing and the piercing look she had received, the more it unsettled her. *May Lord Murugan grant you your wish.*

The only thing Radhika yearned for at the moment was for the marriage to dissolve. Yet, that seemed nearly impossible. Even if, by some miracle, it did end, it would devastate her family. Her father wouldn't be able to endure it. As much as she desired it, she couldn't allow that to happen.

Two days later, at sunrise, Radhika accompanied her family to the famous Sikkal Singaravelan Temple to seek the blessings of Lord Murugan, also known as Karthikeyan, elder brother to Lord Ganesha.

Located five kilometers from Nagapattinam, the Sikkal Singaravelan Temple, a splendid testament to Tamil Nadu's rich cultural heritage, unfolded its majestic beauty as Radhika and her family entered the main entrance with bowed heads. Inside, the intricate Dravidian architecture, soaring gopuram, and captivating frescoes immersed them in a divine atmosphere. As they explored the hallowed halls and absorbed the spiritual energy, Radhika was filled with an inexplicable sense of assurance. For the first time in a while, she found herself fully present in the moment.

Outside, an old man dressed like a temple priest was narrating the story of the temple to two youngsters in English. "You see, it all began with the wise Sage Vasishta, who, with divine inspiration, crafted a Sivalinga from the heavenly butter of Kamadhenu, the wish-granting cow. A Sivalinga of unique origin, I must say. After a reverent puja, something miraculous happened—the Sivalinga refused to budge, firmly rooted in its place. And so, this hallowed ground earned the name 'Sikkal' in Tamil."

After visiting some of the holy water points around the temple, including Parkulam, the milk pond, Radhika's family was ready for their return to Nagapattinam, where they would stay for the week before returning to Jogibettu. Somehow, the prospect of returning to Jogibettu did not seem to perturb Radhika anymore.

"Our Padrappa has requested me to collect a parcel from Velankanni church. I will collect it and meet you back home. Nandini Periyamma's driver will come to pick you up in an hour," Srinivas informed his family. Padrappa, as the people of Jogibettu called Father Vincent of the church, was a good friend of Srinivas's father. They had been classmates throughout their schooling, and their friendship had remained intact until Srinivas's father's passing. Now, occasionally, Srinivas visited Jogibettu's church to meet the retired octogenarian priest and inquire about his health.

"I will accompany you," Avinash replied. Srinivas nodded, and the two walked towards the temple exit.

"I think everything is going to be okay," Padmini said to herself with a smile as she sat under a tree facing the temple.

Radhika smiled, seeing her mother's relaxed face. It was a rare sight these days. The cloudless sky above made Radhika feel light and at ease. In this unfamiliar place, surrounded by strangers who knew nothing about what she or her family had gone through this past year, she felt less anxious. There was no one here who would spot her and come over to inquire about her father, her impending marriage, or her discontinued education, feigning sympathy while avidly collecting morsels of gossip.

"Yes, once the wedding is done, let's start looking for a suitable bride for Avinash. Someone from a good family who can bring enough dowry so that we can recover from the debt we have built for Radhika's wedding," Jayalakshmi replied, shattering the serenity with her callous words. "I wish to see my great-grandson before the Lord sends for me," she continued. "Radhika, you need to work hard in your new home. Listen to everyone and learn to control your tongue. Don't give a heart attack to someone there as you did to your own father. Try to preserve what little good name is left of this family."

Jayalakshmi's harsh words stung like arrows in Radhika's mind, but she knew better than to argue with her grandmother. It would only make things worse. But with each comment her grandmother made, Radhika sensed her patience cracking. So, she did the only thing that came to her mind: she stood up and started walking out of the temple.

"Radhika… stop…" Padmini's voice echoed behind her. Radhika turned around momentarily, hoping her mother would come to her defense for once.

"It's okay. Let her go," Jayalakshmi held her daughter-in-law's arm firmly. "She needs to learn to control her anger. How is she going to survive in her husband's house if she cannot accept criticism? There she has to live not with only her mother-in-law and sister-in-law but her mother-in-law's mother-in-law. And we all know what Anasuya is…" Jayalakshmi's words turned into an incomprehensible buzz as Radhika continued to walk out of the temple, disappointed.

Once outside the temple, onto the bustling road, Radhika kept walking, retracing the path to the bus stop. In anger, she pulled out her engagement ring from her finger and shoved it into her purse. She did not know where she wished to go, but she knew she had to get away from her family, even if only for a few hours. Her father and brother would take at least three hours to return home from Velankanni. She had enough time to reach home before them. Her mother and grandmother would first think Radhika had taken the bus home to Nagapattinam, but once they reached and saw she wasn't there, they would worry. However, Nandini Patti would manage to console them that Radhika was safe, what with her psychic abilities and all.

Radhika smiled, wondering how even in her angry state, she was thinking about not worrying her family. Some ingrained mental patterns never change.

Radhika climbed the first bus she found at the stop without looking at the board, which was in Tamil—a language she had never learned to read. She opened her purse and was relieved to find enough money—part of Nandini Patti's blessing—for the two-way journey and lunch. It would be a nice little solo trip, she thought, even though she would have to bear the wrath of her family when she returned home. But it no longer worried her, for they already thought of her as a guest who would soon leave them to join a new family.

The rhythmic hum of the bus engine accompanied Radhika's contemplation as she gazed out of the window. The increasing crowd of devotees outside, on their way to the temple, painted a lively picture of the holiday season that had attracted people from far and near to this little village. With each passing moment, the cool December breeze gently caressed her face, cooling her agitated nerves.

It was an old woman's heart-breaking wail, followed by a commotion from everyone around, that startled Radhika from her dreamless sleep. Within seconds, she found herself alert with a sinking feeling that something terrible had happened.

"What has happened?" she asked the middle-aged church sister next to her in Tamil, stringing together the few words she knew of the language.

"The old woman's family, who were at the beach, were taken away by the ocean. The man who boarded the bus at the previous stop is saying he saw waves rise above the coconut trees. He says it felt like an earthquake. Everyone is trying to call their families who live closer to the beach, but no one is able to reach them," she replied sympathetically in English, and then closed her eyes in prayer.

Radhika heard someone say Velankanni. Someone else shrieked Nagapattinam. Another person, trying to reach their family over the phone, began to cry. Someone asked the bus driver to take the bus as far away from the beachside as possible. Everyone was talking at the same time, each louder than the other, hoping to be heard. The commotion was the same outside the bus. Panic rose from the pit of her stomach as Radhika thought of her family. She looked at her watch, which indicated that two hours had passed since she had left the temple. She looked outside, but there was no indication of where she was. Tears streamed down Radhika's face.

"It's going to be alright, my child," the sister said. "Are you traveling alone?" she asked hesitantly. Radhika nodded. The bus had started to move again and honked ferociously every few minutes, trying to maneuver safely through the chaos on the road.

"Where are we?" Radhika asked the sister, the only calm and composed person on the bus.

"We are headed towards Trichy. The conductor said he was able to contact the depot there. We will have more clarity once we reach," the sister replied, holding her rosary. "Till then, all we can do is pray for the safety of our loved ones." Radhika's mind spiraled at the thought of what might have happened to her family. Tears welled in her eyes as she attempted to piece together the fragments of information swirling around her. By the time she managed to grasp the essence of the events that transpired mere minutes after she left the temple, a sinking realization settled in—she knew the worst had unfolded.

The bus stopped at Trichy an hour later where things appeared to be less chaotic. The people around were anxious, and strangers grouped around televisions in hotels and stores to get the latest information.

"Don't worry, my child. God is watching over us." The sister smiled as the duo got down from the bus and followed the driver with the other passengers. They had become a family of sorts, looking out for each other, many of whom did not speak the local language, which added to the helplessness of the situation.

"What is your name, dear?" the sister asked as they sat down on a bench outside a hotel. She held two cups of tea in her hands and offered one to Radhika. "Radhika," Radhika's voice came out hoarse. They sat in silence, praying in the best way they knew.

By late afternoon, there was some clarity about the situation as news organizations worldwide began reporting the calamity. Hundreds, if not thousands, had lost their lives due to the earthquake that had originated under the ocean. Massive waves, exceeding 100 feet in height, had devastated entire regions in Indonesia, Sri Lanka, Thailand, and several countries across the Indian Ocean. Nagapattinam was among the hardest-hit places in India. They were calling it a tsunami—a term Radhika had never heard before.

As hours passed, the news of death and devastation flooded the surroundings. Radhika had borrowed a fellow passenger's cellphone and tried Avinash's number, then the landline at Nandini Patti's house. When the exact time the tsunami had struck coastal Tamil Nadu became clear, Radhika knew in her heart that her entire family was likely gone.

Shell-shocked, Radhika sat in her seat, the voices around her fading as the world fell into darkness. The last thing she heard before succumbing to the darkness was Nandini Patti's blessing. *May Lord Murugan grant you your wish.*

Radhika woke up in an unknown house, on a stranger's bed. She sat up and looked around. It was a homely place, well-ventilated and filled with soothing light. Outside the window, the sky was cloudless. Tall coconut trees swayed in the gentle breeze, and the weeds glistened in the bright light. There was no sign of the catastrophe that had occurred just hours ago. Or was it days? Had she dreamt about the tsunami? Where was she? Whose house was this? Radhika wondered. Just then, the sister walked into the room with a cup of coffee and some biscuits.

"Good morning, Radhika. Hope you had a good night's sleep," she smiled. The sister's face brought back all the events of the previous day.

"Where am I?"

"You're in Trichy. You can call this my family home. It belonged to my late aunt, Pressy, who passed it on to me," the sister replied as she made herself comfortable on a chair opposite Radhika. "I know you must be feeling confused, Radhika. But this is the only safe place I knew of that I could bring you to. What happened yesterday was devastating to say the least. Thousands have lost their lives, families are separated, children orphaned, and those who survived have lost everything." Radhika noticed the glint of tears in the sister's eyes, and before she knew it, tears rolled down Radhika's face. The sister walked to the bed and held her, letting her sob her heart out.

Radhika's hopeful mind pondered the possibilities that her family had managed to escape. Perhaps her father and brother had been delayed at the Church. Maybe her mother and grandmother had stayed back at the Temple. And perhaps the Gods had come together to save her family, which, if not for her, would not have come here. *May Lord Murugan grant you your wish.*

They sat there for what felt like hours before Radhika stopped crying. There were only so many tears of regret that one could shed at once. "Radhika, is there someone I can contact? Your parents or relatives?" the sister asked once Radhika stopped crying. Overwhelmed by the situation and believing she was now an orphan, Radhika confided in the sister. She shared everything – her impending wedding, the situation at home, her relatives in Nagapattinam, and her regret over leaving the temple.

"I have volunteers working in Nagapattinam. The locals might be able to guide us to your Patti's house. I don't have a cellphone, and the landline here is disconnected. But I'll ask the neighbors to call your brother's phone. Let's pray for them and stay strong, Radhika."

"Thank you… sister," Radhika's voice was hoarse as her eyes brimmed with unshed tears of gratitude. She knew there was no point in hoping that her family had somehow survived. In this moment, she felt completely and utterly alone. But she was grateful for this stranger's kindness. "You're most welcome, dear," the sister replied. "You can call me Sister Shamita if you like." Feeling a little better after crying for the first time in weeks, Radhika looked more closely at Sister Shamita. The sister appeared to be in her late thirties, dressed in a beige saree similar to those worn by Sisters in and around Jogibettu. She wore round spectacles, a simple metal-strapped watch, and a rosary around her neck. Her bright eyes and calm demeanor made Radhika feel comforted. "Sister Shamita," Radhika began, voicing her greatest fear, "If my family is d—" Her voice caught in her throat. "Without them, I don't know where to go."

"Are you ready to go back to Jogibettu?" Sister Shamita asked. Radhika did not reply. The thought of returning to Jogibettu without her family made her shudder. If she was indeed an orphan, there was no telling how Vidvath's family would treat her. If they kept their word and went ahead with the wedding, it would be worse than death. If they refused the wedding, she would be forever labeled as the bad omen of the village. A witch who first tarnished the reputation of her family, made her parents bow their heads in shame, trapped an innocent boy, and then, just before the wedding, destroyed her entire family. Even with Suman on her side, Radhika knew she would not survive the hatred thrown at her by the very people she had grown up around.

Sister Shamita looked at Radhika for a moment and then smiled. "You can stay here for as long as you like. I will be volunteering in the nearby relief camps, schools, and hospitals with my fellow sisters. I'll be here in the mornings and at night. There is enough food in the house to last about a week. We will take it from there."

"I know it is a lot to take in, Radhika. But at this moment, I want you to take things one at a time. Yesterday, I found a three-year-old lost in the camp. We don't know if her parents are alive. She is now living with another family who have lost both their kids," Sister Shamita explained. "In this time of grief, pieces of families are coming together, trying to make a whole. You are not alone in this, Radhika, and this is not the end of the world."

A week later.

Radhika cautiously navigated the debris-strewn landscape, her surroundings a chaotic scene of broken memories and scattered remnants. Splintered wood, shattered glass, and fragments of what were once cherished belongings crunched beneath her every step. The air was heavy with the scent of salt and despair, and the faraway sounds of a world torn apart hung in the air like eerie whispers.

Radhika was alone at the abandoned beach. Everyone, locals and rescuers, had left after spending days identifying, reporting, and burying the dead. Hundreds and thousands of rotten, swollen unidentified bodies had been buried, while the list of missing people steadily grew.

With each step, Radhika closely examined the remains, hoping she would find nothing that belonged to her family. She believed they had escaped, that they had assumed her to be dead and made peace with it. They had left for Jogibettu to restart their lives. She hoped that her family would be spared the past shame on account of her death. But it appeared too good to be true. The tugging void in her chest told her she was an orphan, with or without the evidence.

Then, as though on cue, she found something glistening stuck between the splintered wood of a scaffolding. It was a gold pendant—her brother's bear-claw pendant that had once belonged to their grandfather. Jayalakshmi, their grandmother, had given it to him on his eighteenth birthday as a protective talisman against evil. Radhika picked it up but felt nothing. No pain, no sadness, not even the relief of closure. Behind her, the ocean rumbled.

In the distance, the rhythmic sound of waves reached her ears, a haunting symphony that underscored the gravity of the scene. And then, as if the ocean itself had summoned the remnants of its fury, a colossal wave began to form on the horizon.

There should have been fear, panic, the instinct to flee, but an unexpected serenity washed over Radhika. The approaching wave, towering and powerful, seemed like a specter of both destruction and renewal. As it approached with a graceful inevitability, Radhika felt peace, a surrender to the forces beyond her control.

The wave crashed over her with a roar, enveloping everything in a translucent cascade. Instead of the anticipated chaos, a profound calm enveloped

Radhika. She was suspended in the embrace of the water, weightless and un-burdened. The debris, the remnants of her fears, and the haunting shadows were carried away by the tide.

Radhika woke up with a start. Her forehead was beaded with sweat, and her breath came in huffs. She sat up in her bed and tried to calm herself. The nightmare again. Only this time it was her brother's pendant instead of her mother's toe ring or her father's watch. Thankfully, she had not screamed in her sleep like the last two nights. The last thing she wanted was to disturb Sister Shamita's sleep after the long, tiring day she had at the camp.

The following evening, Sister Shamita came with some fresh news. "One of the volunteers just visited Nagapattinam. He met a fisherman there who knew Nandini Patti's family," Sister Shamita said softly as she held Radhika's hand. Radhika's throat went dry as she waited for Sister Shamita's next words.

"The fisherman claimed Nandini Patti's entire family was discovered life-less in the house. Her youngest son, who had been away, has returned upon hearing the news. The locals identified the bodies of her two sons, their respective families, and servants. Amidst the tragic scene, there lay a young man in his early twenties and an elderly woman, not Nandini Patti." Radhika squeezed her eyes, anticipating the surge of tears, but none came. She was merely hearing a confirmation of what she already knew. If Avinash and Jay-alakshmi were in Nagapattinam during the catastrophe, it meant her mother and father were gone too.

"Nandini Patti's body was not found. Someone spotted her walking along the beach early that morning, according to one of the survivors in the area. The authorities are speculating that the missing people might have passed into the ocean," Sister Shamita added. "I will keep you updated as we gather more information, Radhika. But you must brace yourself for the worst while holding onto hope. That is the reality we are facing now," Sister Shamita said before leaving the room.

Three weeks passed by with no further information about Radhika's par-ents. According to Sister Shamita's sources the rescue operation had all but stopped at Nagapattinam. "Do you want to visit the house?" Sister Shamita had asked for the last time a week ago, before closing the chapter. There were far too many people looking for lost kin and there was only so much time the volunteers could allot to each family. Radhika had politely declined the offer. She knew she would not be able to bear it if, like in her nightmares, she found evidence of her family's death. This way, she could continue living with the ounce of hope that they had escaped and were now living in peace, free from the shame that was their daughter.

Radhika now spent her days cleaning, cooking, and caring for Sister Shamita's home. Over the past few days, Sister Shamita had brought in numerous children and elders who had survived the catastrophe but were either physically injured or mentally despondent. It's peculiar how witnessing others in greater adversities can momentarily make one forget their own woes.

Radhika helped Sister Shamita take care of them during their short stay at the house before their distant relatives, orphanages, or old age homes from neighboring cities found place for them. Listening to the stories of these helpless people, Radhika felt gratitude each day for the roof over her head, the food in her plate, and someone to call her own. Sister Shamita treated her like a younger sister. But Radhika knew this too was only temporary.

Today, Radhika decided to clean the storeroom next to the living room to make space for more people in need when they came. As she sorted the items into trash and usable, she found a stack of novels. Intrigued, she sat down, skimming through each one. Amidst the well-loved, once-treasured books, a bygone past came back to her – another life where she was only a little girl, her only worry being unable to understand the big words that stalled the revelation of the story in her book. Radhika sat down, skimming through each one. Among the thick hardbound copies and weathered paperbacks was a thin book - Ruskin Bond's The Blue Umbrella. Radhika smiled for the first time in what felt like years. It had been years since she had last read it.

And then it occurred to her. Binya...

Radhika had nearly forgotten about her pen friend. The thought gave her renewed hope. a total stranger like Sister Shamita had helped her during the worst day of her life. Could she expect something like that from Binya, with whom she had shared all the small and big things of her life for over two years? Who knew her better than her own family? And yet, whose real name she did not know...

Radhika spent the rest of her afternoon drafting a letter to Binya. She poured her heart out in the letter, informing Binya about what had happened from the fateful day she and her family left Jogibettu until the present day. The next morning, Radhika asked Sister Shamita for directions to the nearest postbox and posted the letter.

Dear Radhika,

It pains me to hear about what you've been through. I wish I could be there with you right now. There's so much I want to say, yet I know words alone can't ease your loss and pain. I'm a little relieved knowing Sister Shamita is with you. In moments of distress, divinity often manifests in the guise of strangers.

I'm sharing my Chachu's address and contact number with this letter. He's fully aware of your situation and has kindly agreed to make all necessary arrangements for your journey. I've also informed my parents about you and our friendship. They are eagerly waiting for your arrival.

Radhika, please don't hesitate for another moment. Board the earliest train from Trichy to Dehradun. Chachu will be there to pick you up from the train station, and you can spend a day with his family (my grandmother). He will also arrange transportation from Dehradun to Ranachatti.

Hoping to see you here as soon as possible.

Love,

Amruta Rana (Your Binya)

PART 3

CHAPTER 1

Jogibettu, December, 2004.

After a sleepless night of tossing and turning, Vidvath had woken up early and decided to go for a walk. The crisp air did little to ease his inner turmoil as he wandered through the familiar paths of Jogibettu. Radhika's sullen, unhappy face on the day of their engagement seemed to have made a permanent place in Vidvath's mind.

It felt like the universe was against him. Whatever he did to help Radhika had backfired. When he received a letter from Radhika requesting him to talk to his father to let her write the twelfth board exam, it broke Vidvath's heart. The girl had worked hard and excelled in her studies throughout her life, and now at this crucial point, she had to beg people to not ruin her future. On the other hand, he, who had all the freedom and choices in the world, had wasted two years of his life doing nothing.

When he had finally mustered enough courage to talk to his father about Radhika's exams, he had been once again humiliated.

"Why is it that you worry about your wife's future—destined for nothing more than a housewife—when your own future is wasting away in neglect?" his father had asked.

It was only later that Vidvath had been informed by his mother that his grandmother had visited Radhika's home to caution them against allowing her to take her exams.

Upon returning from his walk, Vidvath was welcomed with a chilling silence that hung in the air like an ominous premonition. His mother, Vinaya, was seated at the dining table, a look of utter disbelief on her face. His father was shaking his head in disappointment. Even his grandmother was quiet at the moment. Yashodha was standing at the threshold of her room, tears flowing down her cheeks.

The focal point of the room was the television, where an impeccably dressed reporter delivered the gravest headline of the year. Behind her, muted images of colossal waves obliterated everything in their path, leaving devastation in their wake.

Approaching the television, Vidvath felt a sinking sensation in the pit of his stomach as he read the words on the screen—Tsunami, devastation, thousands dead, thousands missing. In the top right corner, the words Nagapattinam, Tamil Nadu served as a stark reminder that tragedy had struck close to home.

Present Day, Dinnala Base.

Vidvath stood there watching the woman walk towards them from the woods. She was waving at Amruta, who was looking between him and the woman with a concerned look. Even before the woman's gaze met his and she froze in her steps, Vidvath had recognized her. A fleeting moment of joy surged within him, only to be swiftly engulfed by a tide of anger and sorrow. It felt as though his fondest dream and deepest nightmare had collided head-on.

Seventeen years. It had taken him seventeen years to finally find something that, even if only for a few hours, could take away the excruciating pain and guilt that came to him in waves every day. He had thought that the mountains were his escape, and today, as though mocking his misery, the mountains had brought his past back to him.

As he approached the woman standing beside Amruta, Vidvath felt exhaustion wash over him. Suddenly, walking the few steps between them felt like traversing mountains. When he was finally face-to-face with her, he knew for sure that the woman was who he thought she was. Her face was fuller, healthier than the last time he had seen her. The light had returned to her big black eyes. Her once bushy hair had softened and fell in curls over her shoulders. But there was no doubt who she was. The once awkward, studious teenager he knew had grown into this beautiful woman whose face radiated peace and confidence. Vidvath waited for the moment of recognition on her face. Her eyes softened and turned watery, her button nose had a rosy hue. A smile almost escaped his lips as he looked at her nose.

"Vidvath…" Kshama spoke first. The voice warmed his heart and he fought the urge to touch her face and hold her close. She was alive and she remembered him, which only further confirmed his biggest fear. She had left him. By choice.

Vidvath squeezed his eyes shut as he crossed her and began walking away. For years he had yearned to hear his name from her lips one last time. Now, when the truth was in front of him, he felt like a fool who had mourned her death for seventeen years cursing his fate for having snatched the love of his life from him. In reality, she had chosen to leave him and let him live forever believing that she was dead. It was the cruelest thing one could do to a person they loved.

"Vidvath—" Kshama tried to follow him but Amruta held her hand. "Give him some time. He has been climbing the entire day. He must be exhausted," Amruta said. "Let's reach the summit before sunset. You can talk to him there once we set up the camp." Kshama nodded. She knew she had nothing to say to him. At least the few hours ahead would give her time to gather her thoughts.

Vidvath walked as fast as his legs could take him. His numb feet and palms were warm again, but the adrenaline had vanished. He was no longer excited to finish the trek or even reach the summit. All he wanted were answers, but he was afraid to ask the questions. Everything around him was a blur, and he no longer felt the need to take in the scenic views.

After about fifteen minutes of brisk walking, he met the others. Amruta arrived a few minutes later and introduced everyone to him briefly. Vidvath shook their hands and exchanged pleasantries reluctantly. When Vidvath turned around, he saw Kshama several steps away, walking in their direction. She looked at him and then averted her gaze towards the mountains.

"I know you are angry, Vidvath," Amruta whispered, stepping beside him. "But we need to reach the top before sunset and set up camp. It will be very cold and dangerous to stay out here after dark. Although rare, wild animals have been spotted in this area," she explained. "I've asked Kshama to meet you there."

"Kshama?" Vidvath asked. Amruta nodded in reply before walking ahead, leading the group, hoping to increase their pace. Amruta returned Trisha's phone that she had found at the base.

Around them, the scene was turning picturesque by the minute. The snowcapped mountains that appeared intangible from the base now seemed a stone's throw away. The streams of the Yamuna were frozen enough to walk over. Amruta asked the group to follow her footsteps exactly to avoid stepping on frozen surfaces and slipping. Above them, the sky was turning grey, and a light snowfall had once again begun.

The group reached the summit shortly after sunset. Fortunately, Gattu and Rakesh had arrived earlier and set up camps and lit a fire. Everyone settled comfortably around the fire and enjoyed leftover snacks and protein bars they had brought along. Kshama joined Gattu, assisting him with cooking, which allowed Vidvath space to mingle with the rest of the group and enjoy the evening. The group sang, danced, and played games before dinner was served. After dinner, Vidvath excused himself and retired to his tent. The rest of the group sat in silence, stargazing. The sky was clearer than the previous night, and the stars twinkled brightly. Eventually, exhaustion took over, and one by one, the group retreated to their tents for the night. As they entered their tents, Sushant signed to his wife, "Two days ago we were all strangers. Two days from now, we will be strangers once again."

Ensuring everyone had gone to their tents and fastened the zips, Kshama walked to Vidvath's tent. Amruta smiled encouragingly at Kshama as she resigned to her own tent after wrapping up the makeshift kitchen. Kshama called out softly for Vidvath. When he didn't respond, she unzipped the tent and crawled in.

Kshama didn't know what to say to Vidvath. Even in her wildest dreams, she had not imagined reopening this closed, forgotten chapter of her life. Seeing Vidvath had ignited a new spark of hope in her. Now, she wished to know about her loved ones back home, her school friends, her house, and about Suman and Tara, whom like Vidvath, she had led to believe she was dead.

As she stepped into the tent, Kshama found Vidvath fast asleep, exhausted from covering so much trail in such a short time. She sat there, watching him sleep. She could not help but reflect on the transformation evident in Vidvath's face. She compared the features of the man sleeping before her to the memory of the 19-year-old boy she had left behind. His boyish innocence was now replaced by a manly ruggedness. His soft, pointed chin was now broad and angular. Fine lines framed his eyes, and his face was thinner.

Lost in her reflections, Kshama heard a groan escape Vidvath's lips and instinctively she touched his face. His forehead was burning.

'Vidvath…" she shook him gently. Vidvath opened his eyes and looked drowsily at her. "Go away," he said softly.

"Vidvath you have a very high fever. Do you have the medicines?" Kshama enquired. Ex-fiancé or not, he was her responsibility until they reached Ranachatti. Vidvath did not respond. The stubbornness hasn't changed. Kshama thought. "Fine, I'll send Amruta over."

As Kshama tried to get up, Vidvath unzipped his sleeping bag and held her hand softly. "Why, Radhika?" he asked. Kshama looked at his glazed eyes, but what concerned Kshama even more was his shivering hands. She walked out of the tent and returned with her medicine purse. Vidvath was now in a fetal position, trembling.

Kshama helped Vidvath into a sitting position with the lower half of his body still in the sleeping bag. "Vidvath, take these. You'll feel better," Kshama said, holding out two tablets. Vidvath took them gratefully. They sat there, shoulders touching, inside the tent, listening to the whooshing wind slicing through the eerie silence of the forest.

Kshama prepared herself for Vidvath's questions, knowing they would come the moment he started feeling better. Instead, she felt the weight of his body on her side. A few minutes later, Vidvath had fallen asleep. Kshama helped him into his sleeping bag and zipped it up. She then walked out and brought her own sleeping bag into Vidvath's tent. She had to keep an eye on him.

Kshama spent a sleepless night, checking on Vidvath every few hours whenever he moaned in his sleep. At one point, he locked eyes with her, and they stayed that way for several minutes before he drifted off again. There was so much to say, but neither knew where to begin. How does one fill seventeen years of silence in one night?

Early the next morning, Vidvath's fever had still not come down. He had exhausted himself by trying to cover two days' worth of climb in a single day. Kshama knew she would have to take him back to Ranachatti through the shortcut while the rest, along with Amruta and Rakesh, would take a more scenic route to return to Ranachatti in the evening. Kshama told herself everything was under control. She would get Vidvath safely back home, call the doctor, and get him better. Once he was fine, she would talk to him, make him understand why she did what she did, and get some closure. Then he would return to his life, and she to hers.

For a moment, her mind went back to Jogibettu. What must have happened there after the news of her death reached Vidvath's house? Did they find another bride and get him married? It was the most probable possibility considering it often happened in small villages like Jogibettu. A suitable substitute bride would be found in the case of the death or absconding of the original one. This was done to reduce the damage to the groom's family reputation. Or had he waited a few years for her to come back? Kshama laughed at the thought—a thought the naïve seventeen-year-old her would have hoped to be true.

CHAPTER 2

When the first rays of sunlight appeared, Kshama walked out of the tent and asked Gattu to start a fire and boil some water. Fortunately, there had been only a light snowfall at night but the ground was still covered in ankle deep snow. Kshama then helped Vidvath out of the tent and asked him to sit in front of the fire. Gattu offered him a cup of hot water. Vidvath made a face as the strong stench of charcoal hit his nose. But he continued to sip the water and let the warmth seep into his body. Rakesh dismantled Vidvath's tent, rolled the sleeping bag and attached it to his gear. Rakesh, Kshama and Vidvath would leave for the base where the mules would be awaiting them. It was an arrangement made anticipating something like this might happen. City-dwellers, even if seasoned trekkers, were not accustomed to such weather.

"Are you sure you want to go with him?" Amruta asked. "I could take him. You can go with the group, and by the time you return, he might get better and leave."

"No, Amruta. I have left this chapter open for a really long time. Maybe this is my chance to get closure," Kshama replied.

Kshama sat next to Vidvath and asked, "Will you be able to walk?" Considering the amount of accumulated snow, it would take the mules longer to reach the summit than it would take them to reach the base. But Kshama wondered if Vidvath would be able to cover the three kilometers, which was

199

the shortest path to the base.

"Do I have a choice?" asked Vidvath as he popped another paracetamol and stood up. Kshama carried his backpack.

The trio walked slowly in silence, Rakesh leading the way. Kshama watched Vidvath carefully as he forced himself to place one foot in front of the other. They took short breaks every thirty minutes, but no one spoke. Vidvath stopped in his tracks and shuddered every time the cold wind whooshed past them. The sun was out, but it did very little to keep them warm. Finally, after what seemed like days, they reached Ranachatti. Kshama helped Vidvath settle down in one of the rooms they had arranged for the trekkers. She then went to the kitchen to inform Gitanjali of what had happened. Gitanjali began preparing her homemade *kadha*[35] while Kshama called the doctor. When she returned, Vidvath had fallen fast asleep.

---

[35] : Traditional herbal decoction

CHAPTER 3

Vidvath woke with a start and found himself drenched in perspiration. The room was dark and vacant, with all the windows and the door closed. He sat up in bed and reached for his phone; it was a little past 6 PM. He had slept the entire day. Beside him, on a small table, were his thermos, medicines, and a thermometer. His throat felt parched, and he sipped warm water from the bottle, ignoring the smell of charcoal.

As he sat there, taking in his surroundings, he started to feel better. His fever had come down, and his body was warm. He was still dressed in the four layers of clothes he had worn during the trek, with his hands covered in gloves and socks. Someone had removed his shoes and placed them by the door.

Vidvath had a vague memory of Gitanjali placing a damp cloth on his forehead and the doctor giving him an injection. After that, he had drifted into a dreamless sleep. A few minutes later, the door squeaked open, and light from a bulb outside seeped in. It was Radhika.

Vidvath watched as Radhika pulled a chair in front of him and sat down. She placed a plate of what looked like piping hot *khichdi*[36] in front of him.

Unaware of the anger bubbling in his mind, Vidvath's stomach grumbled. He saw Radhika avert her eyes and suppress a smile. Momentarily, the tension in the air was broken.

---

[36] : A comforting Indian dish made from rice and lentils, and seasoned with spices.

"Eat," Radhika said softly. "You haven't eaten anything since yesterday."

Vidvath picked up the plate and began eating as Radhika busied herself sorting out the medicines. She placed three tablets in a small cup.

"Thanks," Vidvath said, gulping down the tablets.

"Vidvath, I know you're angry—" Radhika began but was cut off.

"I'm not angry, Radhika. I'm hurt," Vidvath replied, trying hard to keep his voice low as he heard Gitanjali and Amruta talking to the others in the verandah. "I knew you hated me. I knew how badly you wanted to call off the wedding. And trust me, I too realized it was for the best. You deserved better. I was a coward who let you get hurt again and again. You were better off without me." Vidvath swallowed the lump lodged in his throat. "But it is equally true that I loved you, Radhika. I did not deserve you but I deserved to know that you were alive. I spent all these years waking every day with nothing but guilt and regret. Wishing to go back and tell you that I was with you. That I would find a way to make it all better. I lived each day thinking you were dead because of me." Vidvath no longer had control over the tears that flowed down his face. "Radhika, did you hate me so much that you wished for me to live in pain for the rest of my life?"

Vidvath locked gazes with Radhika, searching for answers, for sympathy, and perhaps... love. But all he saw was disappointment.

"That's the thing, Vidvath. Even now your focus is on how you suffered and what you endured." Radhika's voice remained calm. "Did it ever occur to you what I must have gone through after losing my entire family overnight? Did it ever cross your mind how much I wanted to escape, that I chose to run away thousands of kilometers and start life afresh among strangers rather than coming back to you? I was so scared of what your family would do to me that I chose to let not just you, but everyone I ever knew, believe that I was dead." Vidvath noticed the quiver in Radhika's voice.

"But you could have let me know you were alive. If not immediately, later. A message, a hint, anything would have been better than living so many years in agonizing pain. I deserved at least that much."

"Trust me, Vidvath. I thought about it several times. But there was no telling what your father would do if he knew I was alive," Radhika replied softly. "I became an orphan overnight, Vidvath. I had no one to protect me."

"I would have protected you, Radhika," the words slipped out of Vidvath's mouth.

Radhika smiled gently. "I thought so too," Radhika continued. "During those initial days after the disaster, I kept telling myself that you would change. Knowing that I was alone, you would stand up for me if it came to that. I even convinced myself that on the day your family called me a siren, a witch, and a gold-digger among many other things, you were just scared. That given a chance to go back, you would take equal accountability for what had happened rather than just standing there like a victim," Vidvath winced. "The pain of losing everyone I loved in a matter of hours was so raw and excruciating that I told myself I was not alone. That I had you. All I had to do was call you." Radhika smiled through the tears. "Then Yashodha's face flashed in front of my eyes. The truth was as clear as day."

Silence enveloped them as Radhika's words sank in. After what felt like hours, Radhika stood up. There was nothing more to say.

"I love you, Radhika. I really do," Vidvath said desperately, reaching for her hand. He wanted to express how sorry he was and how much he had changed over the years. He knew every word Radhika had spoken was true. The Vidvath she once knew was a spineless coward who feared his father's wrath. He had since grown and found his voice, becoming a better man. But it was also true that the weight of guilt over Radhika's assumed death had spurred him towards that change.

"The truth is, Vidvath, you never understood love," Radhika said softly as she gently withdrew her hand and turned towards the door. "And until many years later, neither did I."

———— ○ ◈ ○ ————

2004.

Binya's letter provided Radhika with much-needed solace, reassuring her that she was not alone in the world. Yet, Radhika couldn't find the courage to travel thousands of kilometers to an unknown place based solely on the assurance of a teenage girl she had never met.

In reality, Radhika had no proof to convince herself that her pen friend was truly a teenager, or even a girl. It could all be a trap. Even Binya revealing her real name in the last letter offered little comfort. In this moment, Radhika deeply missed Tara. She knew Tara would be devastated by the news of her supposed death. The talk of the town would undoubtedly revolve around the Prasad Family's tragedy in the tsunami. The rumour mill would be running in full speed at school and her dear friend Tara would be fighting alone on her behalf.

With Binya's letter in her hand, Radhika pondered her options. In a sudden realization, she understood that for the first time, she held the reins of her destiny without someone else deciding for her. A bittersweet freedom embraced her—a world of possibilities tinged with stark loneliness. She stood at the crossroads, grappling with the weight of choice and the absence of guidance.

Just then, a series of knocks on the door brought Radhika back to the present. She walked to the front door and peeped through the hole. Sister Shamita was in the kitchen packing her lunch. Looking at Radhika from the other side of the door was Asokan *Maama*[37], Nandini Paati's youngest son. Radhika stood shocked for a moment, then rushed inside to inform Sister Shamita. With a sense of urgency, Radhika pleaded with Sister Shamita to conceal her whereabouts if Asokan Maama was indeed inquiring about her. Sister Shamita agreed.

Sister Shamita opened the door with her signature smile. Radhika stood in the adjacent room where she could hear the conversation without being seen.

"Vanakkam," Asokan greeted her with joined palms. She returned the gesture.

"I am Asokan from Nagapattinam. Like most people from my village, I

---

[37] : Maternal Uncle

too have lost my family in the tsunami," Asokan said softly. Sister Shamita sympathetically made the sign of the Cross.

"Unfortunately, I was in Bengaluru when this happened. It took me several weeks to come to terms with reality. I have lost my brothers, my mother, my wife, and my children. Call it an ugly twist of fate, my cousin's family had come home only a day before the tsunami. The rescuers have found bodies and evidence to prove that they were in the house when the killer waves struck. Except for their daughter Radhika," Asokan explained. Radhika's breath caught in her throat as she realized he had indeed come looking for her.

"The elders of my family now want me to perform the final rites for those who have passed on," Asokan added.

"One of my farm workers, who was on his way to Trichy that day, claims he saw Radhika on the same bus he had boarded," Asokan continued. "It could be a mistake, I understand, considering the chaos that erupted that day. But the man is known for his sharp memory in the village. I could not overlook his claim, as it would be a great sin if I performed her last rites while she was alive. So I decided to probe further. I was able to track down the conductor, who told me from his vague memory that a kind Sister had cared for the child."

"Accidentally, I overheard someone outside the relief camp mention that a Sister was fostering helpless orphans and senior citizens at her home here in Trichy. I knew it was a long shot, but I had to try. This is what brings me to your doorstep, Sister. By any chance, was Radhika with you at any point in the last few weeks? She is seventeen years old, dusky, with big eyes and bushy hair. She is not fluent in Tamil but speaks English very well." Radhika felt guilt creep into her mind as she listened to Asokan's desperate words. He was looking for closure, and the uncertainty of her death was delaying it. Sister Shamita's silence made Radhika anxious.

"I understand, Sir. I've spent the last few weeks trying to reunite families, find new homes for orphans, and help elders find a home. We are trying to piece together whatever little is left of the families. But I must apologize; I do not recall any teenager named Radhika taking shelter here. Perhaps, it was someone else from our sisterhood who took her in," Sister Shamita replied as she once again held the rosary and gestured the sign of the cross, this time in apology.

"Either way, Sir, I think you should believe your man's words and refrain from performing her last rites. In times of uncertainty, a flicker of hope becomes our greatest strength," Sister Shamita added. "I'm sure she will come back to you when she is ready." Asokan nodded with a soft smile and left.

In that moment, the gravity of Asokan's visit sank in. If Vidvath's family or Suman contacted Nandini Patti's family, they would eventually reach Asokan, who would reiterate his farm worker's claim and the visit to Trichy. Vidvath's father, for the sake of his family's reputation, would start looking for Radhika, and it would be much more difficult to hide then. The more she thought about it, the more Radhika was convinced that she had to leave Trichy as soon as she could.

The next day, Radhika explained her fears to Sister Shamita, who, after initial hesitance, agreed that it was best she left Trichy sooner rather than later. In a few weeks, Sister Shamita too would have to return to her convent and unfortunately could not let Radhika live by herself in the house.

Radhika spent the rest of the day packing her meager belongings into a bag she had found in the storeroom. Inside, she placed her clothes, toothbrush, towels, a few books from the storeroom, and a blanket, all of which Sister Shamita had been kind enough to lend her. Learning about the extreme winters in North India, Sister Shamita had purchased a winter jacket for Radhika.

Radhika knew there was a good chance she would never see Sister Shamita again and might never be able to repay her kindness. The least she could do was to help Sister Shamita take care of others in need like her. It was then that Radhika realized she still had her engagement ring in her purse. It was an expensive piece of jewelry, but to Radhika, it was nothing but a reminder of her painful past. Getting rid of it would be akin to snapping the last thread that connected her to her past. Radhika took out the ring from her purse and placed it on her table with a thank you note.

In the evening, on Radhika's request, Sister Shamita returned with a one-way train ticket from Trichy to Dehradun. Radhika was too afraid to go out of the house to buy the ticket herself. She often daydreamed of Asokan or someone from Vidvath's family waiting around the corner of the street to catch her red-handed. It was out of this fear that Radhika requested Sister Shamita to buy the ticket under a different name.

"Kshama?" Radhika asked as she looked at the ticket. It was a pleasant name, but Radhika wondered why Sister Shamita had chosen it.

"God has given you a second chance, Radhika. To be able to move forward, you must let go of the past. You must forgive those who have wronged you, wounded you, and above all, you must forgive yourself," Sister Shamita replied. "Your name will be a reminder of that," Sister Shamita explained. Radhika smiled, knowing it would be a long time before she forgave herself.

"I know you are a very mature girl, Radhika. You seem to know what you're doing, and I want you to know that you will always be in my prayers," Sister Shamita said as Radhika boarded the train later that day. "But in case you find yourself in trouble, I want you to call me. I will do whatever I can to help you," she added, placing an envelope in Radhika's hand.

As the train began to move, Radhika saw tears welling in Sister Shamita's eyes, mirroring their shared emotion. The silence between them now held an unspoken vow that, despite the miles that separated them, the bond forged in adversity would endure.

Sitting in the Bolero with eleven other passengers enroute to Ranach-atti from Dehradun, Radhika's exhausted mind began to wander. She had spent two days traveling by train, and upon reaching Dehradun, she prompt-ly called Amruta's uncle, Prajwal, as instructed in Amruta's letter. Prajwal had arranged for her stay at his home, where his mother—Amruta's grandmother—had warmly welcomed her. The kind woman had served Radhika a fresh, home-cooked meal and shared stories about the local area, hoping to help Radhika feel more at ease. That night, neither Prajwal nor his mother had pressed Radhika about her family, past, or the tragedy she had endured. For this, Radhika felt grateful.

After the train departed from Trichy, Radhika opened the envelope given by Sister Shamita. Inside, she found a small bundle of cash along with a piece of paper containing Sister Shamita's contact information and a small laminated photo of Lord Murugan. Tears welled up in Radhika's eyes at the gesture. During the journey, her co-passengers, a family of four, shared their food with her while she also purchased some from the vendors who passed by occasionally. Suddenly, Radhika felt overwhelmed by the kindness that absolute strangers had shown her in the last few days.

Radhika looked at her watch, which indicated it was 12 PM. The driver, who spoke Hindi, had informed her that they would reach Ranachatti by 5:30 PM. It gave Radhika enough time to gather her thoughts. As she watched the sparkling Yamuna curving around the snow-topped mountains, Radhika realized how far she had come from home. "Home" — the word made her stomach churn. There was no home anymore.

As the jeep ascended several thousand feet above sea level, Radhika began to feel nauseous. Never before had she travelled like this alone, surrounded by strangers whose language sounded familiar yet incomprehensible. It was a little bit like Hindi but braided with words from another language she did not recognize.

The fellow passengers were villagers mostly returning after a brief stint in Dehradun city. They all seemed to know each other well. As Radhika studied their faces, she tried to imagine how Amruta looked. Despite never receiving a photograph, Radhika knew Amruta adorned a nose ring, had brown eyes, and sported a visible scar on her chin earned from childhood mischief.

As hours passed by, Radhika's anxiety returned, but now it was tinged with excitement and pride. The old Radhika would never have believed she was capable of making such a bold decision on her own. She chose to start afresh far away from everything she had ever known instead of taking the safe, easy path that awaited her in Jogibettu.

Returning to Jogibettu meant accepting her fate and joining Vidvath's family, where she would now be a charity project, if not worse—an orphan they took under their wings to provide a new life. Radhika did not want that. Suman would definitely stand by her no matter what her decision. But was she really strong enough to resist Raghupathi Rao? Suman had fought battles all her life. Radhika did not want to put her through that again.

Weighing all the options repeatedly, Radhika tried to convince herself that she was making the right choice, praying that Amruta's family would accept her and that she could start anew in the little mountain village of Ranachatti.

At four in the evening, when the sun had almost set for the day, the jeep made a quick stop at Barkot. The driver informed Radhika that this was the only market around where one could buy everything. People from Hanuman-chatti, Ranachatti, all the way to Yamunotri depended on Barkot for winter wear, tents, festive wear, school supplies, and basically everything that could not be grown or made in the mountains.

Looking around, Radhika felt nostalgic. Barkot reminded her of Jogibettu's central market where she and her friends went shopping during weekends and holidays. Pictures of Tara and her skimming through books at the only bookstore in Jogibettu flashed before Radhika's eyes. She recalled Tara's impatience at Radhika's desire to read the back cover blurb of each book, followed by Radhika's reluctant visit to the fancy store where Tara leafed through packets of decorative Bindis and bangles.

An hour after leaving Barkot, Radhika was dropped at Ranachatti in front of a school that was closed for the day. The road was deserted, shops were closed, and except for a few furry, bear-like stray dogs, there was no one around. The temperature seemed to drop by the minute, and Radhika's winter jacket could not do much to keep her warm. She stuffed her hands into her pockets and wriggled her toes inside her shoes, desperately trying to prevent them from going numb. Her breath came out in mists, and her eyes pricked with cold.

Ranachatti was exactly how Amruta had described it in her letters. From Radhika's vantage point, she could see a huge mountain on the other side of the road, with several flattened surfaces and terrace fields. Among the fields were colorful wooden houses, some in the open, others tucked behind bare apple trees. At the top, above the hamlet, the mountain, covered in thick forest, rose to the sky. A few silhouettes appeared here and there, carrying hay or firewood on their backs. In front of a house at the bottom, a group of men and a dog were crouched in front of a small fire.

From the narrow path leading to the road, two figures emerged. In the dusky light, Radhika squinted, wondering if they were coming towards her. One was a thin, tall man, and the other was a teenage girl. As they got closer, Radhika noticed the girl's bright smile and twinkling eyes, which instantly made her feel at home.

"Amruta," Radhika felt relief wash over her face. After months of speculation, ever since Tara had put the thought in her head, Radhika now knew for sure that Amruta was indeed what she claimed to be in her letters. Radhika wished Tara were by her side now.

"Radhika! We finally meet," Amruta squealed, embracing Radhika. Radhika instinctively squirmed a little, not accustomed to being hugged. Amruta didn't seem to notice and began leading Radhika towards the mountain.

"Namaste, shall I take your bag?" the man spoke. Amruta introduced him as her father, Rakesh Rana.

"Actually, my name is Kshama. Radhika was my pen name," Radhika replied as she handed over her bag to Amruta's father, who led the way.

"What? You lied to me!" Amruta feigned being hurt.

"Sorry," Radhika replied with nothing more to offer.

"That's okay. I like Kshama better. There is a spirit to it that is missing in Radhika, don't you think?"

"Yes, Radhika did not have any spirit left in her."

"Other than the name, you're exactly like I imagined you would be," Amruta smiled. It was evident she was trying hard to make Radhika feel welcomed.

"How was the journey? I hope it was not very tiring. My uncle says it is hard for people from the south to take this journey, especially in this season. Don't worry, I have enough warm clothes and blankets for you. Ma has set your room as well," Amruta's excitement was evident in her voice, her twinkling eyes, and the skip in her steps. Under different circumstances, Radhika would have found Amruta's excitement contagious. But today, it did nothing to cheer her up.

Amruta, in an odd way, reminded Radhika of Jogibettu. She was the only one who knew Radhika's world in the little coastal village, and now that Radhika had lost everyone from her hometown, it felt like Amruta was the only reminder she had of her past life. It was a strange, irrational feeling considering Amruta had never even been to Jogibettu. Tears pooled in Radhika's eyes as she recalled the day she had first received a letter from Amruta. How happy she had been as she discussed it with Suman. And how, for all the years, Radhika had managed to hide the letters from her mother, who would now never know Amruta.

"By the way—" Amruta turned around to start another topic. Her excitement seemed to increase by the minute. Amruta's smile faded as she noticed Radhika's teary eyes.

"Radhika… I'm sorry. I was so excited that I didn't realize… I'm so sorry," Amruta apologized profusely, her face draining of color. Radhika tried to smile through the tears. Amruta held Radhika's hand and continued to walk up the mountain path silently, knowing no amount of words could heal Radhika's pain.

After a steep climb of less than two hundred meters, Radhika found herself gasping for breath. She sat down on one of the steps and held her head, waiting for the nausea to pass. She had not eaten or slept well in the last three days, except for the meal at Prajwal's home the previous night. The cold air hurt her lungs, and her knees began to wobble a little. Amruta waited for her while Rakesh climbed a flight of steps carved into the mountain to reach a flat surface where two mules stood, looking at Amruta and Radhika.

"Raja and Rani?" Radhika enquired once her breath returned to normal. Amruta nodded with a smile.

Finally, when Radhika felt better, they climbed the stairs and reached Amruta's house. Amruta's mother, Gitanjali, welcomed Radhika and, realizing she was shivering, wrapped her in a shawl and offered her sweet, piping hot tea, which Radhika accepted gratefully. In that moment, Radhika did not know that for many years she would drink this sweet, jaggery-based, milkless tea every day.

A few minutes later, the sun had gone down completely, and the clear night sky twinkled with bright stars. Radhika sat on a chair in the open space in front of the house, wrapped in three layers of warm clothes, a scarf over her head, gloves, socks, and a neck warmer. At her feet, Rakesh was busy making a fire from small pieces of firewood.

"The ones that are moving fast are satellites," Amruta pointed towards the sky and smiled at Radhika. Radhika nodded and continued to gaze at the sky, trying to identify constellations. A few neighboring women, Gitanjali's friends, dropped by to see who the 'Madrasi' guest was. Radhika smiled at them politely but did not have the energy to start a conversation. After a few curious looks, the women left.

An hour later, Gitanjali called everyone into the little kitchen where she had made hot wheat rotis on a chullah that was similar to the 'olle' many houses still used in Jogibettu. Radhika learned that in the mountains, families ate together in the kitchen where the wooden floor made a comfortable seating and the food stayed warm longer. Also, the fire made in the chullah using firewood from the forest above doubled as a heater to keep them warm. She also learned that things like dairy, especially milk, certain vegetables that did not grow in cold places, and many of the grains like millet and jowar were rarely available in the mountains or even in the Barkot market. People here mostly survived on what they grew in their fields or what the forests provided them with.

After dinner, Amruta showed Radhika her room, which they would share. Whether it was from the sub-zero temperature or the relief that Radhika now had someone to rely on, she felt her pain turn numb as she lay down under thick blankets. For the first time since the fateful day, Radhika slept through the night.

The next morning, Radhika woke up to the view of the majestic mountain over which the sun dropped its veil of light at a dramatically slow pace. With each passing hour, the mountain shone, bringing into light the women descending it with huge bundles of hay on their backs. Ranachatti looked full of life in the morning, unlike the previous evening. People here followed the sun, rising with it and retiring to their homes at sundown. Though seeing the sunlight made Radhika feel warm, it did not help with the chill she felt in her palms and feet. Her eyes and nose were watering constantly, and her lips had chapped. She remembered Amruta's description of the winter sun in these parts: "You can only see the sun, not feel it."

"Do you see my mother?" It was Amruta.

"Good morning," Radhika greeted her, squinting as she tried to locate Gitanjali.

"There, the one with the red scarf in the front," Amruta pointed out. Gitanjali was moving down at a fast pace with hay, thrice her size, tied to her back.

"Women here leave for the mountains well before sunrise and return with hay before noon, after which they cook for the family and go about other chores," Amruta explained.

"Oh, and the men?" Radhika was surprised at her own question to which she already knew the answer.

"Men here mostly do nothing during this season. Father gets firewood from the mountains and occasionally helps with the hay. But it's mostly the women who do the hard labor," Amruta's irritation with the practice was evident in her tone. Radhika realized not everything was different in Ranachatti from where she had come.

"I have prepared *puris*[38] for breakfast and made hot water for you to wash up. Go to the bathroom quickly before it cools down. I'll fry the puris once you're back," Amruta said, pulling her sweater closer to her body as she walked into the kitchen.

The warm water felt heavenly as Radhika splashed it on her face, though she immediately regretted it when the neck of her sweater got wet, soon turning icy cold. She could no longer feel her toes, which had just been washed. Walking out of the bathroom, Radhika hurried into the kitchen and sat as close to the chullah as possible without risking a burn. Amruta chuckled as she handed Radhika her breakfast of puris with a simple sabji made of tomatoes, onion, and capsicum, ingredients available in the grocery store below.

Radhika moaned with pleasure as she savored the hot puris in the warmth of the small, poorly ventilated kitchen. Unlike kitchens in Jogibettu and other coastal villages, which were large and airy with a backdoor for cross ventilation, this kitchen retained its warmth against the cold mountain air.

"Today, I'll take you to our Yamuna temple where you can get a closer look at the river. But only if you're up for it," Amruta said as she handed Radhika a cup of piping hot tea. Radhika contemplated for a moment. Sitting in the house, she had nothing to do but dwell on everything she had lost or might have had under different circumstances. It wouldn't help, and she didn't want to worry Gitanjali with her unhappiness.

"Or we could sit here and talk. I know you've got a lot going on, and I'm willing to listen if you want to share," Amruta offered.

"Let's go to the temple," Radhika responded a bit too quickly. Talking about what happened wouldn't change anything.

---

[38] : Deep-fried Indian breads

A year later.

A month after arriving in Ranachatti, Radhika had regained her strength, even if only physically. The fresh mountain air and wholesome local food contributed to her recovery. Initially, she took slow walks along the steep village paths several times a day to strengthen her legs. On weekends, Amruta and other local girls took Radhika on hikes to the forest above. These excursions, routine for mountain dwellers since childhood, proved challenging for Radhika, often leaving her with fevers and cramps the following day.

As winter yielded to warmer days, Radhika's health improved further. The sun's warmth reminded her of Jogibettu. She began tackling longer and more difficult trails, gradually forming a bond with the mountains.

During the Yamunotri season in May, Amruta's house was filled with guests. Rakesh's brothers, cousins, and uncles worked as guides, leading devotees and tourists on the six-kilometer steep and somewhat challenging trek to Yamunotri—the birthplace of the river Yamuna. They often carried elderly tourists in seats on their backs, in *Palkis*[39], or on mules. Raja, Rani, and all the mules from Ranachatti worked tirelessly during these months, bringing substantial income to their owners.

When the yatra season ended in September, the Yamunotri temple closed, and everyone from the area migrated down to lower altitudes where winters were milder. Relatives returned to their respective villages, and once again, Ranachatti transformed into the quaint little village that Radhika had grown to love.

By the next winter, Radhika found herself completing three or more days-long snow treks in sub-zero temperatures. She was accompanied by Amruta, her father Rakesh, and a young man from the village named Gattu. According to Amruta, Gattu was the strongest man in the village. He appeared to be anywhere between twenty-five and forty-five years old and rarely spoke more than a few words. With a lean, muscular body, he could carry three sets of tents and sleeping bags along with his own gear on his back and still walk upright. He climbed the mountains briskly and rarely took breaks.

---

[39] : Palanquin

The villagers, envious of his strength, teased him as a Khacchar in human form. Gitanjali had once playfully warned the girls to be cautious around him, joking that his strength was supposedly fueled by Raksi—the local millet-based elixir of power. But Radhika found Gattu to be a gentle soul, oblivious to his own strength.

During warmer days, several times a week, Radhika joined Gitanjali and other women on their morning hike up the mountain to collect hay. Initially, she struggled, barely managing the round trip while carrying her own weight. However, with time, she progressed to shouldering small bundles of hay on her back, eventually carrying loads as substantial as the others'. She even pitched in to care for Raja and Rani. Radhika often felt guilty for being a freeloader in Amruta's home, but the family never perceived her that way.

The Pahari people were not only welcoming but also known for keeping their homes open to those in need. Amruta had once told Radhika about a Nepali hiker who stayed at one of the houses at the top for six months. Despite the language barrier, the hosts had given him a room and shared their meals with him. Eventually, he repaid their kindness by making Raksi, which became popular among men from all the surrounding villages.

"I don't think I'm skilled enough to become a Raksi maker," Radhika pouted upon hearing the Nepali man's story, prompting Amruta to double over laughing.

"All I'm saying is, you need to stop feeling guilty. You can stay here for as long as you like. The longer the better," Amruta replied. "Or if you want to make your own home, we could look for a good-looking Pahari man," she teased, earning a playful punch on her arm.

Sometimes, Radhika accompanied Rakesh and Gattu to the forest above leading to Dinnala Bugiyal, where they collected lichens called Jhula Ghas from the barks of trees. These delicate lichens had to be hand-picked, and an additional hand meant more income. This made Radhika feel more at home. During the winter break, Radhika taught English and Mathematics to the neighborhood children for a small fee, which she insisted on paying to Gitanjali as rent, despite her protests.

The treks made Radhika feel alive, and with each passing day, she began to love the mountains even more. It felt like an addiction that only made her stronger and better, both physically and mentally. But on some days, when the weather was really bad, she was forced to stay at home where there was no escape from her thoughts.

On such nights when her body was not tired enough, Radhika found it hard to sleep. She spent the night staring at the ceiling, reminiscing about her days in Jogibettu and wondering how Suman, Tara, and a few others who genuinely cared for her were doing. She did not let herself think about Vidvath or her deceased family. Whenever she found her mind drifting from Jogibettu's pleasant memories to the dark side, she immediately snapped out of it and occupied herself with something mundane, like cleaning her room.

Many times, Radhika had contemplated visiting the PCO booth outside the medical store below and contacting Suman. Once, she even mustered enough courage to dial the number but dropped the receiver immediately upon hearing Suman's voice. Instead, she called Sister Shamita and learned that she had been transferred to South Africa for a year. After that, Radhika decided not to reach out again; it was best to avoid any connection between her present and past.

CHAPTER 4

Present day, Ranachatti.

Two days after their return to Ranachatti, Vidvath found himself sitting alone on the verandah, replaying the events of the past few days in his mind for the hundredth time. By now, he knew he had lost Radhika forever. Everything she had said was true, and there was nothing he could say or do to change that.

The group had departed for Dehradun early that morning, while Vidvath, on the doctor's advice, had chosen to stay one more day. He was scheduled to leave Ranachatti the following morning. Radhika had not returned after their last conversation. Gitanjali had informed him that Kshama's house was at the top of the village. Amruta had just dropped by to inform him that the jeep to Dehradun was booked for the next morning.

Vidvath noticed a change in Amruta's demeanor towards him since his encounter with Radhika. Over the past two days, the typically talkative woman had grown quiet. She only spoke when necessary and avoided discussing Radhika whenever he brought her up. Her politeness and hospitality persisted, but there was a noticeable furrow on her forehead, conveying an unspoken resentment. It made Vidvath wonder if Radhika had told her about him— the self-centered version of himself who had foolishly lost such an amazing girl.

Now that he was here, the realization struck Vidvath hard. He wondered how Radhika, at seventeen, had arrived here alone and begun anew. He contemplated the challenges she must have faced adapting to the mountain weather and lifestyle, while learning the ways of the community. Vidvath pondered how scared she must have been to live among strangers and admired her boldness in doing so.

In that moment, Vidvath knew he had to see Radhika one last time. He needed to apologize once more and try to alleviate at least a little of the pain he had caused her before leaving.

That evening, Vidvath mustered his courage and walked up to Radhika's house. The blue wooden cottage, adorned with icicles hanging like crystal ornaments, nestled cozily amid thick blankets of snow. On one side, a bare apple tree stood stoically, while a picturesque backdrop of tall, snow-laden trees framed the scene, casting a serene charm over the surroundings.

As he opened the gate, Vidvath was welcomed by the booming sound of a dog's bark. The dog appeared at the door, frowning. He was huge, shaggy, and old. Vidvath smiled at the thought of Radhika having a furry companion.

A moment later, Radhika appeared at the door, looking surprised. Vidvath stood there, unable to find his words as a cold wind whooshed past him, making him shiver. Radhika opened the door wide and welcomed him in. She gestured for him to sit down on the couch in the living room before disappearing into the kitchen to prepare tea. The warmth from the fireplace instantly enveloped Vidvath, easing his discomfort.

"I'm sorry to drop in unannounced, Radhika," Vidvath fumbled with his words, unsure of how Radhika might perceive his sudden visit. "But I had to see you before I leave. It would kill me if I left without—"

"I'm glad you came here, Vidvath," Radhika said with an assuring smile. "A kind woman once told me that to embrace this new life completely, I must let go of the past and forgive myself. Despite everything I did over the years, I was never able to do that. But now might be my chance."

"I'm sorry, Radhika. I really am," Vidvath replied solemnly. "I know no matter how many times I say this, I will never be able to take away the pain I caused you and your family. I never forgave myself or my father for it. Even when I was standing in front of his funeral pyre, I could only think of all the evil things he did and all the people he hurt. I realized I did not want to live like that."

"Radhika, I know it is not easy for you to forgive me. But you must not consider yourself responsible for your family's unfortunate demise. If anything, I should be the one repenting for my deeds. You were a daughter every parent wished for. You were kind, compassionate, and hardworking. You made them proud at school every year. Miss Suman still talks about you at school," Vidvath said, his voice filled with remorse.

As Vidvath spoke these words, Radhika began to cry. It was as if she had waited all her life to hear such understanding and acknowledgment.

"Radhika, I now understand why you did what you did. It was incredibly bold of you to take this step," Vidvath continued. "I was a fool to let you go. You have nothing to forgive yourself for."

As the words left his lips, Vidvath felt a sense of peace settle within him. He took a handkerchief out of his pocket and offered it to Radhika. They sat in silence, unsure of what to say next.

"Do you want to know what happened after…" Vidvath began, knowing well that Radhika must be dying to hear about the events in Jogibettu after she left.

"Yes, please…" Radhika replied, managing to smile a little.

"Where do I begin?" Vidvath wondered aloud, scratching his stubble. "After you left, besides me, I think Tara was the most affected. She became this quiet girl who kept to herself. It was around this time at Gundmi's degree college that she became good friends with Amit."

"Nerdy Amit?"

"More like scientist Amit now, but yes, the same one. He took your place in her life," Vidvath smiled at the memory. It had been the only good thing that happened around when all he could feel was darkness.

"How is she now? Is she still in Jogibettu?" Radhika asked eagerly.

"Amit managed to bring back the bossy, energetic Tara that we knew.

They got married a few years later and moved to Bengaluru where Amit works. They have a daughter, Sia. Tara is a makeup artist now. I've met them a few times. They are happy together," Vidvath replied, his heart warming as he looked at Radhika's bright smile.

"Jogibettu now has changed for good in the hands of women leaders. Miss Suman is the headmistress of our school and is working closely with the Panchayat to improve the educational sector. My sister, Yashodha completed her post-graduation and teaches there," Vidvath said, observing as Radhika blinked back tears. He gently placed his hand over hers, and surprisingly, Radhika didn't withdraw her hand.

"Little Radhi is now in tenth grade. She is a little spoiled but is a good kid," Vidvath continued, picturing their little village and all the people he loved there. Now that he knew Radhika was alive and happy, remembering Jogibettu was becoming easier.

"Little Radhi?" Radhika asked.

"Oh," Vidvath realized he had left out an important part. "Yashodha adopted a baby girl. We named her Radhika. Me being the maternal uncle and all," Vidvath tried to make it seem casual.

"You named her after me?"

"Yes, that was my feeble attempt to keep you close," he finally admitted. "But I could not call out your name. Every time I tried, the gaping hole in my chest hurt. So I started calling her little Radhi."

Tears now freely streamed down Radhika's face as she made no attempt to hide them. Vidvath ached to touch her face and wipe them off. Instead, he continued.

"I must say little Radhi is nothing like how you were. She is stubborn and feisty. When I leave the house, I swear, it's like a scene from a teenage romance movie – boys on bikes loitering, hoping for a glimpse of Radhi. It drives me up the wall!"

"Hmmm... reminiscent of the days when you used to casually stroll past my house, isn't it?"

"You knew that?" Vidvath blushed. Radhika burst out laughing, and the sound made Vidvath's heart fill with warmth.

"Vidvath, you have no idea how much happiness you have brought to me today. Knowing that my loved ones are happy and safe back home…" Radhika paused, realizing she had referred to Jogibettu as her home.

"What about my house?" she asked tentatively, almost wanting to retract the question out of fear of hearing something unpleasant.

"One of your father's cousins sold it. A family stays there now. They have two boys who play in the front yard. Every time I pass by, it reminds me of Avinash. My childhood practically passed in that house," Vidvath replied.

He continued narrating the small and big happenings of Jogibettu while Radhika listened with rapt attention. It was as if she was trying to absorb as much of her beloved little village as she could while she had the chance.

"What about you, Vidvath? What did you do after…"

"Well, once the marriage was called off, my father tried to rope me into his politics. He wanted me to follow in his footsteps. I probably would have agreed, but my mother talked sense into me at the right time. I moved to Bengaluru, enrolled in BCA, and landed a job in an IT company," Vidvath explained, recounting his college experiences—weekend adventures, cooking experiments, and friendships—while omitting the sleepless nights he spent thinking about Radhika.

"Cooking? You?" Radhika mocked with disbelief, causing Vidvath to purse his lips.

"Okay, let me show you what a wonderful cook I am. Where's your kitchen?"

Laughing and joking, they moved into the kitchen where Vidvath took off his gloves. It took him a moment to realize why Radhika had suddenly gone silent—she was looking at the ring on his hand, their engagement ring. Vidvath quickly averted his eyes, pretending not to notice, and placed the pan on the stove.

An hour later, a modified version of *Avial*[40] was ready. Vidvath took a spoonful and blew on it a few times before touching it to Radhika's lips. Radhika's eyes widened momentarily at the intimacy before she smiled and sipped at the curry.

"This is good," Radhika sighed as she helped herself to some more.

It was in that moment, standing in that house, watching Radhika savor the curry, looking impressed as she reminisced her childhood in Jogibettu, that Vidvath realized a part of him would always continue to love her.

Radhika and Vidvath spoke into the night, attempting to bridge the seventeen years of silence that lingered between them. For that night, the weight of the past seemed to dissipate and an unspoken understanding enveloped them.

As the night unfolded, they filled each other in on the details of what they had missed during those long years apart. Radhika spoke of her journey to the mountains, the challenges she faced, and the resilient spirit that carried her through. Vidvath, in turn, shared the twists and turns of his life, the lessons learned, and the growth that came once he started living independently in Bengaluru.

In the early hours of the next morning, Vidvath woke up to find himself on the couch, covered in a thick blanket. He freshened up and, realizing Radhika must be asleep in her room, decided to wait for her before leaving. He wished to see her one last time before he left Ranachatti. He had four hours before the jeep to Dehradun would arrive.

Making a cup of tea for himself, Vidvath walked around the living room. Now that all his attention was not on Radhika, he noticed how tastefully she had decorated the house. It reminded him of her room that he had entered

---

[40] : A South Indian dish made with mixed vegetables, coconut, yogurt, and seasoned with curry leaves and coconut oil.

only once in his life before it had become someone else's room. There were traces of that seventeen-year-old girl's taste here as well.

Vidvath walked to the bookshelf in the living room and was surprised to find a collection of old and new Kannada novels. There was also a sketchbook that piqued his curiosity, considering Radhika had never shown much interest in art before. Opening it, Vidvath smiled at the incomplete sketches, clearly the work of an amateur yet determined hand. As he flipped through the first few pages, he noticed the sketches improving in detail and skill. There was a tile-roofed school, a village carnival, a modest home—scenes from Jogibettu that stirred memories he could never forget. Other sketches seemed more personal, as if capturing fleeting memories—a brown stuffed bear, a pair of bangles. Each sketch echoed parts of their childhood and life together in Jogibettu. Vidvath felt a strange mix of nostalgia and longing as he gazed at the last sketch in the book.

Surrounded by wilderness, a boy and a girl sat on the lush green carpet of grass under a blue sky speckled with white clouds. Tall trees and overgrown bushes enclosed them on three sides, while a small pond with guppies and frogs shimmered to their right. Across the pond stood an old, dilapidated church with a cross atop, overseeing the serene scene. In the distance, an old tea stall, Ramanna's tea stall, completed the backdrop. This was the place where Vidvath and Radhika had met privately for the first time, where he had confessed his feelings for her, where they had shared their first and only kiss.

"A few years after settling down here, a strange fear began creeping up in my mind." Radhika's voice broke the silence. Vidvath turned around, wiping his eyes. "I couldn't recall details of some incidents and places in Jogibettu. Some faces in school and our neighborhood were a blur, and I realized I didn't have any photographs or mementos to remember my past life by. That's when I decided to preserve my memories through sketches. As you can see, I'm not very good at it." Vidvath nodded but did not reply.

He walked towards the wall covered in framed photographs. Among them was a picture of Radhika with Amruta and her family, smiling at the camera, over a decade ago. There was one with little Harper. Other photos captured scenes from around the world—Radhika had realized her dreams of seeing the world. Vidvath's heart swelled with pride. Many pictures featured strangers and locals alongside Radhika, but in most, there was one face consistently beside her, and in those, Radhika's face beamed with happiness.

It was then that Vidvath realized Radhika, unlike him, may have found someone. Instead of the pang of jealousy he expected, he felt warmth in his chest. He was genuinely happy for her. Yet, somewhere deep down, there was a spark of regret—that he was not the reason behind her smile.

Vidvath wanted to know who the man in the photographs was, not just out of curiosity but to ensure Radhika's happiness. He needed reassurance that her past, tainted by him, hadn't followed her here, and that she still believed in love enough to give herself another chance. It was the only way Vidvath could find peace upon his return.

As if reading his thoughts, Radhika said, "That's Abhay. My fiancé," and began setting up the table for breakfast.

"Congratulations," Vidvath smiled. "Where—"

"What time is the jeep coming for you?" Radhika quickly changed the topic. Vidvath realized she didn't want to discuss Abhay. Perhaps she feared Abhay learning about Vidvath and Radhika's past. It made sense to Vidvath, as he too often revealed very little when his colleagues asked about his family or relationships.

"In two hours. I need to stop by Amruta's place to collect my bag before leaving," Vidvath replied. Unlike last night, they ate in silence. A subtle hangover lingered in the air, not from excessive revelry, but from the depth of their rediscovered connection. After breakfast, Vidvath helped Radhika clear the table and then bid her goodbye.

"Have a great life, Radhika," Vidvath said, fumbling to find the right words, realizing the finality of the moment. To his surprise, Radhika's face contorted, not with sadness, but with a complex array of emotions. Without a word, she embraced him, the warmth of the hug conveying more than any words could. They stayed that way for a long moment before pulling apart.

"Do you mind if I take a photo with you?" Vidvath asked as he reached for the front door. Radhika pursed her lips in response.

"Vidvath, Jogibettu's Radhika died seventeen years ago. I feel it is better we keep it that way," Radhika replied. Vidvath nodded understandingly and walked out of the house, feeling at peace more than he had ever felt before..

CHAPTER 5

Two hours after leaving Radhika's house, Vidvath found himself below the mountain, standing by the side of the road, waiting for the Bolero. Amruta's father, Rakesh, had come to see him off. From his vantage point, the entirety of Ranachatti sprawled out before him. Somehow, the mountain now seemed smaller, more accessible than when he had arrived.

As the moments passed, Vidvath felt his heart swell with gratitude. He had come to these mountains with a heart full of pain and a mind heavy with regret. The mountains had heard his desperate cry for help and led him to Radhika. Now, for the first time in years, he felt light, as if the mountains themselves had lifted his sorrow. As Vidvath gazed reverentially at the mountain, the jeep arrived, and he stepped in. Once again, he expressed his gratitude to Rakesh for the hospitality.

Glancing out of the window, Vidvath was taken aback to see Radhika descending from the mountain in hurried steps, with Amruta following closely. For a moment, his heart leaped in his chest with anticipation.

As Radhika came closer, Vidvath was shocked to see her bloodshot eyes and pink face. She was in her night suit with only a shawl wrapped around her to protect her from the biting cold. She got into the jeep beside him, and a moment later, Amruta sat next to her. Amruta informed her father where they were going in the local language. Vidvath caught the words "Abhay" and "Dehra."

Suddenly, Radhika began to sob, shaking. Vidvath was about to take his jacket off when Rakesh handed Amruta his jacket and dashed for his home in the mountains, clutching his arms around his body. Amruta looked at Vidvath and said softly, "Our friend is in the hospital." Her expression told Vidvath that she was not at liberty to say more.

Radhika's pain made Vidvath's heart ache. He wished to hold her close, console her, and tell her that Abhay would be okay, even though he wasn't sure what had happened to him. But he didn't know if it was the right time. There were five other people in the van staring at her, and the driver was trying his best to traverse the treacherous path as fast as he could.

An hour passed, and Radhika fell asleep out of exhaustion. Amruta was on her phone, enquiring about Abhay's wellbeing. Something about Amruta's demeanor told Vidvath that she had done this before. Vidvath wondered if Radhika's reluctance to talk more about Abhay had something to do with it. Maybe, Radhika wasn't okay after all. Vidvath knew from experience how easy it was to create a façade of contentment for the world to see while inside, you silently cried for help.

Several hours later, the three of them were dropped at the City Hospital in Dehradun. Amruta got the details of Abhay's room from the reception and filled out the visitor details. As soon as she heard the room number, Radhika rushed up the stairs. Vidvath ran behind her.

On reaching Abhay's room, Radhika walked in while Vidvath sat outside, hoping for Radhika's sake that Abhay was alright. The smell of antiseptic and disinfectants was heavy in the air. The corridor was silent except for the muffled sound of Radhika speaking to Abhay. Abhay's voice was not heard. Vidvath wondered if Radhika was talking to him in his unconscious state. A moment later, Amruta arrived and took a seat beside him.

"Did Kshama tell you about…" Amruta asked.

"She told me he is her fiancé," Vidvath replied.

"Was it an accident? Abhay?" Vidvath asked.

"No," Amruta replied softly. Before she could say anything else, something shattered inside the room.

"Leave me alone, Kshama!" Abhay was shouting at Radhika. "Why can't you understand? I don't want you here."

The hospital staff rushed to the room upon hearing the commotion. A few moments later, Radhika came out sobbing, her face drained of color. Amruta hugged her and helped her into a seat. Vidvath offered her some water.

A few minutes later, an older woman approached Abhay's room carrying dinner. She stopped to look at Radhika, a flash of sympathy crossing her face before shaking her head in disappointment. By this point, Vidvath was totally confused. It was clear something was amiss between Radhika and Abhay. Vidvath excused himself as he saw Radhika approach the older woman, who he guessed was Abhay's mother. Vidvath then approached one of the nurses who had gone into Abhay's room earlier.

"Is Abhay doing okay?" Vidvath asked the nurse.

"He is okay now. We have given him a mild sedative."

"What happened?"

"He attempted suicide," the nurse replied without looking up from the file. "It is not his first time."

Seeing Vidvath's shocked expression, the nurse continued, "I don't blame him for it. In fact, I would do the same if I were in his place." Before Vidvath could ask any further, the nurse was called by the doctor to see another patient. Vidvath returned to his seat, feeling a deep sense of unease. Sitting in the hospital made him anxious. The last time he had been in a hospital was when his father was breathing his last.

"You should go home, Vidvath. We are here with Radhika," Amruta said. "What time is your flight?"

"In about ten minutes," Vidvath replied, looking at his watch. He had missed two flights in a week. He was sure he had lost his job too, but he couldn't care less. "I can't leave her like this. I can't leave without knowing that she is going to be okay."

"Okay," Amruta replied. "The doctor said Abhay needs to be here for a few more days. Knowing Kshama, she will not move from here until he is discharged. You may want to get a room in a hotel nearby. I'll go get things for her from Prajwal Chachu's home."

On Amruta's advice, Vidvath secured a room nearby. That night, a new spark of hope flickered in his mind. Did he still have a chance with Radhika? Before he could fully absorb the thought, guilt crept in. It saddened him that Radhika had faced misfortune in love for the second time. Yet, it was evident that she loved Abhay more than she had ever loved him. The realization left Vidvath grappling with complex emotions, questioning the nature of love and wondering if what he had felt for her was truly love.

The next morning, Vidvath found Radhika in Abhay's room again. The door was slightly ajar, and in the silence of the corridor, Vidvath could hear their conversation. He knew it was wrong to eavesdrop, but he had to know what was going on. Why was Abhay refusing to even talk to Radhika properly while Radhika was crying so desperately for him? Was Radhika the cause of his suicide attempt? It seemed unlikely, knowing Radhika would never intentionally hurt anyone, let alone her fiancé.

"Kshama, I don't love you anymore. It's the truth you have to accept," Abhay's voice was soft but firm.

"Don't say that, Abhay," Radhika's voice trembled with anxiety, as though she hung by a delicate thread and Abhay was on the verge of severing it. "Please, I'm sure we can find a way. Don't give up on us, Abhay. Not so easily."

"Easily?" Abhay's voice was low, spoken through gritted teeth. "Do you think any of this is easy?" Vidvath felt a surge of anger towards Abhay. Yesterday, Vidvath had sympathized with Abhay's reaction given what he had just been through. Recovering from a near-death experience, whether self-inflicted or not, was no small feat. He had learned that from Yashodha. Today, however, Abhay seemed nothing but cruel to Radhika.

"That's not what I meant, Abhay," Radhika said, her tone echoing the earnestness of the seventeen-year-old girl she once was.

"I know. But the truth remains. No matter what you do, you cannot understand me. We are not the same anymore. Things have changed, and by not accepting that, you're only making it harder for me."

"Abhay—" Radhika's voice was now a whisper.

"I wish I had never met you, Kshama. I wish I had never fallen for you. I was so stupid to think of a happily ever after with you. It was all a big mistake," Abhay said, his words carrying finality as if a thread had finally snapped.

Silence.

Radhika dashed out of the room, tears flowing down her cheeks. She glanced at Vidvath for a moment before walking away. Anger bubbled in Vidvath's mind, and without a second thought, he swung Abhay's door open. He needed to give Abhay a piece of his mind. How could he say such things to Radhika?

Inside was what Vidvath could only describe as the haunting image of someone who had once been a good-looking man. Abhay appeared to be about Vidvath's age but looked older and fragile. His limbs and arms, exposed as two male nurses carried him from a wheelchair onto the bed, were immobile and showed signs of muscle atrophy. Taking a deep breath, Vidvath walked into the room. Abhay smiled at him and then gestured for the nurses to leave. He thanked them as they exited and closed the door.

"I'm Vidvath," Vidvath introduced himself instinctively, offering his hand, but immediately put it down and apologized. In that single glance, Vidvath's anger had dissolved, replaced by sympathy and sadness. He silently cursed the hand that seemed to be writing Radhika's fate.

"Don't worry about it," Abhay chuckled.

Vidvath saw a flash of sadness in Abhay's eyes when he heard his name.

"You know, if I had met you a couple of years ago, I would be punching your face right now," Abhay said, laughing softly. It confirmed that Radhika had told Abhay about Vidvath.

"I know," Vidvath managed to smile.

"But today, I'm glad you are here," Abhay said with a genuine smile. Vidvath frowned in confusion.

"You were her first love, Vidvath," Abhay continued, and Vidvath pursed his lips as he heard the words. "And when she left you and your village, she left behind a part of her there. No matter what I did or said, there was always something amiss. A void I just could not fill," Abhay said softly as he tried to adjust his position on the bed. Vidvath moved to his side and adjusted the pillow.

"Now that you're here, I hope she will finally get closure, and maybe I can finally be at peace knowing she is not alone," Abhay added, looking at Vidvath with hopeful eyes. It amazed Vidvath to see this man—wheelchair-bound, in unthinkable pain, who had just tried to kill himself—worrying about Radhika's happiness instead of his own misery. Suddenly, Radhika's words rang in Vidvath's ears: *The truth is, Vidvath. You never understood love. And until many years later, neither did I.*

If what Abhay was doing right now was not the definition of true love, Vidvath did not know what was.

"What has Radhika told you about me?" Vidvath asked, sitting down on a chair by Abhay's side.

"Everything," Abhay replied. "Don't worry. I'm no longer angry at you. The fact that you have stayed with her for the last three days in the hospital while she prayed for me shows you're a changed man." Vidvath wondered if the nurse or Abhay's mother had told Abhay about his presence.

On Abhay's request, Vidvath narrated the happenings of the last few days. Abhay was amused at Vidvath's chance encounter with Kshama. He beamed when Vidvath told him about his love for the trek, the snow, and sleeping in the forest at sub-zero temperatures. Vidvath sensed how much the adventurous man, judging from the dozens of travel pictures on Radhika's walls, might be yearning to experience it all one more time. Vidvath quickly switched the topic to how he fell sick from the cold weather, narrating his dislike for the charcoal-infused water that turned ice-cold within minutes, the watery eyes and nose, and the cracked lips. Abhay laughed heartily at Vidvath's attempt to lighten the mood, instantly reducing the tension in the air.

"Why won't you talk to Radhi—Kshama?" Vidvath finally asked. It had been three days since Radhika had gone home. Amruta brought her meals and change of clothes every day. She slept on the bench outside Abhay's room and woke up startled whenever he rang for the nurse. But Abhay refused to even look at her. Even now, she was in the canteen talking to Abhay's mother.

"I know it might sound unfair, what I am doing to her," Abhay said, looking outside the window. "But it is the only way I can set her free."

January, 2015.

Two weeks after their secret engagement in Jibhi, Abhay and Kshama excitedly shared the news with their families, marking the beginning of wedding preparations. A date was finalized, and they decided on a modest ceremony at Brij Vatika, attended by close family and friends. However, Gitanjali and Sumitra, not quite understanding the concept of a 'simple ceremony,' were going all out with the preparations. Amruta, ever the enthusiastic and hands-on presence, had self-appointed herself as the host, bridesmaid, decorator, and coordinator.

Abhay had not seen Kshama for over a week now as Amruta had whisked her into countless shopping sprees, spa sessions, and makeup trials. Despite the physical distance, their phone calls and messages had increased, sharing live updates about the happenings in their respective houses. With each passing minute, the anticipation heightened, making it increasingly challenging for the two to patiently wait for the days to unfold.

Now, with only a week left until the big day, Abhay found himself strolling along Paltan Bazaar on a sunny afternoon, a smile adorning his face. He had spent the past two weeks planning a surprise honeymoon in New Zealand—a destination from their bucket list yet to be explored.

Even amidst the bustling chaos of the bazaar with Abhay's car having broken down, he couldn't help but smile at the anticipation of the upcoming joy in their lives. As he walked amidst the dust, heat and bustling crowd, his thoughts were filled with the excitement of revealing the surprise to Kshama.

When the traffic light signaled pedestrians to cross, Abhay stepped into the crosswalk that led to his home. Unbeknownst to him, a distracted driver ran a red light, colliding with another vehicle and careening into Abhay's path.

In the chaos of screeching tires and alarmed shouts, Abhay was struck by the oncoming vehicle. What followed next was a mix of disorienting sounds as Abhay's heart drummed in his chest. He had hit his head, and blood trickled from the side of his face. Someone from the shop beside was trying to drag him to safety on the pavement while a woman who had been standing by his side before was sprinkling water on his face. His body was a pulsating mix of pain and numbness. Then, gradually, his heart began to calm, each beat echoing in the stillness, and his eyes drooped in a slow descent before everything turned to an enveloping darkness.

The thing about tragedies is that they befall you when you least expect it. They come as a shock because often you are too happy in life to even consider something so terrible coming your way.

When Abhay regained consciousness, it took a few seconds for him to realize he was in a hospital. Images of the accident flashed before his eyes: the roaring of the speeding bike, the impact, the excruciating pain, the blood-curdling scream of a woman on the footpath, the frantic murmurs of people who had gathered, and then darkness.

Abhay smiled weakly when his mother came into view. Sumitra looked like she had been crying for many hours. It reminded Abhay of the time his father had left for work and never returned. Sumitra had been in shock for days, and then one night she had woken up in the middle of the night, crying inconsolably as the truth had finally settled in. He realized how scared his mother might have been when the news of his accident reached her.

"I'm okay, Ma. I'm not going anywhere," Abhay said, trying to hold his mother's hand. Sumitra lovingly touched his face and then clasped his hand tightly. Overcome by emotion, Abhay didn't realize something was amiss.

"Kshama," he called out to his fiancée, who stood beside his mother, still in shock.

"I'm sorry. I should have been more careful," Abhay said. Hearing Abhay's words, Kshama began to sob. Instinctively, Abhay tried to sit up and pull her into a hug for comfort. But he couldn't budge. He attempted to raise his hand and grasp the bed railing for support, but his arms refused to move even a little. Abhay glanced at his mother, whom he had always known to be calm and composed. Now, she was sobbing, barely able to hold herself together.

"What has happened to me?" Abhay asked softly. Just then, Abhay's neurosurgeon, Dr. Bhat, entered the room with the most devastating news of Abhay's life.

Abhay had suffered a spinal cord injury that had left him paralyzed in all four limbs for the rest of his life—a condition for which there was no known cure.

For the entirety of his life, Abhay had never placed much emphasis on his wealth. The significance of money had eluded him, especially considering that it had been unable to rescue his father from a tragic fate or restore the joy that had vanished from his mother's life. But the accident had changed his perspective towards wealth. In the days following the accident, Abhay found himself experiencing a newfound gratitude for the financial resources he possessed. It gave him access to the finest medical treatments available worldwide for his condition. It became the lifeline that could potentially pave the way for his recovery.

During the first two years, guided by Dr. Bhat, Kshama and Abhay travelled to many countries, staying for months at a time to explore and pursue cutting-edge therapies and interventions. Sumitra stayed behind to manage their businesses, ensuring they had the financial resources needed for Abhay's ongoing care.

Following the failure of each treatment, Kshama immediately began researching the next best option. She tirelessly read, surfed the internet, assessed risks, and connected with patients worldwide who shared similar conditions. A young boy named Shyam was appointed as a helper, assisting Abhay with bathing, using the toilet, and repositioning in bed to prevent cramps and sores. Kshama insisted on personally feeding Abhay his meals and administering his many medications.

Abhay, who had been on his own since the age of twenty-one, found it difficult to rely on Shyam even for the simplest tasks. At times, his frustration got the best of him, and he yelled at the boy for not doing things his way. Hours later, Abhay would apologize for his outbursts. Soon, he realized that his condition was taking a toll on his mental health. He began therapy with Dr. Roy, a psychiatrist specialized in treating quadriplegic and paraplegic patients. While the sessions with Dr. Roy helped keep suicidal thoughts at bay, they did little to alleviate his mood swings.

At the end of the second year, miraculously, Abhay regained sensation in the fingers of his right hand. This development boosted his confidence and reinforced his trust in experimental treatments. Against Kshama's and Dr. Bhat's advice, Abhay took bigger risks and prayed harder. With the use of his fingers restored, Abhay could now surf the internet, operate his state-of-the-art wheelchair, and perform tasks that were otherwise impossible without functional fingers.

Two more years passed, with lakhs of money spent and three additional hospital stays, but there was no improvement in Abhay's condition. Dr. Bhat and his colleagues had all but given up on Abhay, and Dr. Roy's sessions now felt more like hospice care.

After four years of painful treatments, a dozen hospital stays, innumerable medicines, and therapies, Abhay had slowly begun to accept his condition. During this time, he immersed himself in reading books and listening to talks by people with similar conditions who had found their calling, such as renowned artists, motivational speakers, and successful entrepreneurs who, despite their challenges, had achieved remarkable feats and made significant contributions to society. Stephen Hawking's "My Brief History," published a few years ago, became a profound inspiration for him and helped him realize that there were far worse things that could happen to a person.

Abhay's quiet acceptance starkly contrasted with Kshama's persistent efforts to instill hope. While her words were well-intentioned, they often felt hollow—a desperate plea from someone who loved him more than herself. Abhay's reluctance to try new things frequently led to heated arguments, causing Kshama to leave his room for hours, only to return later as if nothing had happened.

It was during his exploration of Stephen Hawking's life that Abhay discovered the story of Hawking's devoted wife, Jane, who stood by him for thirty years despite his debilitating condition. Learning that Hawking, out of consideration for Jane, had asked her to leave, Abhay began to reflect on the fairness of his own situation. With his focus shifted away from himself, Abhay realized the toll these past years had taken on Kshama.

Kshama was now a mere shadow of her former self. Dark circles marred her eyes, and worry lines etched her temples. She had lost weight, and a sense of fear seemed to have taken up residence in her eyes. Abhay couldn't recall the last time he had seen her laugh wholeheartedly.

Abhay recalled the incident that had occurred months ago. One morning, Abhay was woken up by someone turning him in bed. Initially assuming it was Shyam, he was shocked to see Kshama instead. It took him a moment to realize that he had soiled himself, and Kshama was helping him change.

Frustrated and embarrassed, Abhay had yelled at her, causing her to move away in shock. He had then dismissed Shyam and replaced him. Kshama had left the room, and Abhay had spent hours gripped with fear that she might not return. But she had returned, as always, a few hours later, with his favorite breakfast, pretending nothing had happened. Abhay had apologized profusely but was grateful that she had returned. He had not once considered the situation from her perspective.

Unlike the rest of the world, 2019 proved to be a silver lining in Abhay's life. While the world grappled with the sudden halt the pandemic had brought, Abhay found an unexpected opportunity to confront a difficult truth – it was time to let Kshama go. Due to his fragile condition, he asked his mother, Sumitra, to close Brij Vatika completely, barring any outsiders from entering. He conveyed the same to Kshama, who, after much persuasion, reluctantly agreed that it was best for them to stay apart for a few weeks to avoid any infections that could be fatal to Abhay's fragile immune system.

As weeks turned into months, Abhay devised new ways to maintain distance from Kshama. The daily calls dwindled to once or twice a week, with Abhay frequently offering excuses of having fallen asleep or missed the call. When the pandemic situation relaxed and people resumed their normal activities, Abhay was dismayed to find Kshama persistently visiting his home every week, even staying overnight. His attempts to create distance seemed to be failing.

Then, one day, Abhay discovered that Kshama had turned down Prajwal's offer to rejoin Apna Travels. She had prioritized being his caretaker as her primary goal in life. All her dreams of exploring the world, writing travel articles, and leading a memorable life had taken a back seat. This revelation was a sharp knife, demanding Abhay to cut through the tangled threads of their relationship swiftly before it suffocated Kshama and her dreams completely.

Fully aware of the pain it would cause Kshama, Abhay blocked her number and severed all social media contacts with her. Then he ensured she no longer had access to his room without his permission. When Sumitra initially hesitated to implement these measures, Abhay convinced her that it was the right thing to do.

As the intervals between Kshama's visits stretched, Abhay felt a bitter-sweet sense of victory. The idea of losing her became more unbearable than his physical disability. From behind the curtains of his room, Abhay watched Kshama sitting in his living room every week, weeping and pleading, while Sumitra steadfastly denied her access to him. Witnessing Kshama's pain was a heavy burden for Abhay; he had promised her all the happiness in the world, and if this was the only way he could give it to her, then so be it.

When Prajwal informed Abhay about Kshama rejoining Apna Travels, primarily to support Amruta's family that had suffered losses during the pandemic, Abhay felt a mixture of pride and joy. He read her blog every week and bought every magazine where her articles were published. He even became a patron who secretly promoted her writing. Then, one day, he learned about Apna Travels' new venture in Ranachatti that Kshama had agreed to lead. Abhay felt a sense of satisfaction and accomplishment tinged with sadness that he would not be a part of this new phase in her life.

Present day, Dehradun.

That night as Vidvath lay on his bed in the hotel room, Abhay's words echoed in his ears. Abhay and Kshama's story, which began as an attraction between two seemingly different people, had matured and transformed into an all-consuming love that Vidvath could not begin to fathom.

Abhay, who was a prisoner of his own body, wanted nothing more than Kshama to be happy, even if it meant he had to tear his own heart apart from hers. Even if it meant she would never be his and they would never be able to build a life they had dreamed of together.

Kshama, who had a long life in front of her with all the options and resources at her disposal was ready to give it all up if it meant she could spend a few more years with Abhay, even if it was just to be his caretaker.

Vidvath knew this was the kind of selfless love Radhika deserved, a love he could never offer her. Vidvath had stayed back in Dehradun to ensure Radhika was truly happy. The thought of carrying the burden of her unhappiness home with him was unbearable. He had also held on to a flicker of selfish hope that perhaps they could reunite, but now, he understood there was no place for him in her life anymore. His role in her life had been that of a catalyst, propelling her towards a better, happier future.

With that, Vidvath knew there was no point in staying any longer. It was time to leave Dehradun and step away from Radhika's life for good. The next morning, as Vidvath left for the airport, there was a smile on his lips and a prayer in his heart.

EPILOGUE

It has been two months since Abhay's discharge from the hospital and Kshama's return to Ranachatti. The snow has melted, and the mountains are making way for spring. Ranachatti, wrapped in its cocoon of white silence during the frigid months, stirs awake with the promise of warmer days. Little buds of wildflowers appear in nooks and crannies. Streams of Yamuna, frozen during the winter months, now flow freely, and new leaves make their presence known on treetops. Soon, the people of the quaint little village will begin their preparations for the yatra season.

This morning, Kshama stands at her bedroom window with a warm cup of Ghur Chai, recalling the events of the past winter. It was an eventful season, to say the least. Abhay has finally accepted that he will never be able to rid himself of her, no matter what he says or does. Reluctantly, he has agreed to give one more shot to his treatment and is currently in Germany undergoing an experimental neurostimulation technique. Kshama prays for a miracle every single day. The chances are slim, but there is hope as long as Abhay does not give up. In return, Abhay has asked Kshama to break up with him.

I cannot do this if I know that your whole life is halted, hinging on the success of my treatment. It's too much pressure and it's unfair.

Kshama is not allowed to contact him by any means, and Abhay has instructed his mother to do the same. Kshama hasn't spoken to Abhay in more than a month, the longest duration the two have gone without contact since Abhay's discharge from the hospital. Abhay's demand has only further confirmed Kshama's suspicion that he still loves her. And it is this love that gives them both hope of a future together.

Kshama has not heard from Vidvath after his departure from Dehradun. He didn't even stop to say goodbye before leaving. Amruta said the last person he spoke to was Abhay. Abhay refuses to tell Kshama what they spoke about.

Just then, Kshama spots Gattu entering the front gate and leaving a package at her doorstep. He looks at her window and smiles. He must have collected it from Barkot courier place last evening. Placing her tea cup on the table, Kshama walks to the front door. It's been a while since she received a parcel. It makes her wonder who it is from. As she bends down to pick it up, she's surprised to see Vidvath's name on it, from Jogibettu. Sitting down on the porch, her heart thumps with excitement as she opens the parcel. Harper, who was sunbathing in the garden, walks over and plops at her feet.

As Kshama opens the box, the smell of nostalgia hits her, taking her back to Jogibettu's embrace. Inside, there is a bundle of her novels that she had devoured during her high school days, her stationery, her stamp collection, and below it, a photograph of her family. She holds the photograph close to her and lets the tears stream down. Vidvath must have visited the house before it was sold and managed to save some of her precious things. It makes Kshama smile gratefully. The sight of the brown stuffed bear that Vidvath had won at the village fair makes her chuckle. A nudging pain pulsates in her chest as she remembers her brother, whom they had slyly diverted at the fair and slipped away to steal a precious few minutes alone.

Vidvath has added some things to the box: school photographs, Jogibettu's special jaggery candies, a few shells from the beach, among many other things. There is a framed photograph of their favorite spot by the pond. At the bottom is a decorated shoebox. It takes a moment for Kshama to realize that it is her box. She quickly opens the lid and beams at the sight of all the maps, travel articles, and photographs she had collected as a young girl—the beginning of a dream she never thought would come true.

Tears well in Kshama's eyes as she holds each item in her hand, inhaling the familiar scents and reminiscing about her childhood and teenage years. She no longer needs to fear forgetting her loved ones as she now has the essence of Jogibettu to remind her of what she once was. As she stands up, carrying the box, Kshama smiles at the golden mountains shimmering in the first light of the day, touched by the gentle caress of the morning sun.

ACKNOWLEDGEMENTS

First and foremost, I would like to express my deepest gratitude to Harish Kamath, whose keen eye and invaluable constructive feedback were instrumental in shaping this novel.

To Aditya Hiremath and the wonderful Rana family at Ranachatti, I am immensely grateful for your warmth, kindness, and unparalleled hospitality during our stay. The serene surroundings and the welcoming atmosphere you provided were a true inspiration and played a significant role in the creation of this book.

A heartfelt thank you to Mr. Prasant of Holistic Publishing, my publisher, whose belief in this project and unwavering support made this journey smoother and more fulfilling.

I would also like to extend my sincere thanks to Bibin Kumar for the stunning cover layout. Your artistic vision and attention to detail perfectly captured the essence of this novel and brought the story to life visually.

To my beloved parents, Rekha and Ramachandra Shenoy, your unwavering support, love, and encouragement have been my anchor.

To my dearest husband, Karthik, who not only encouraged me to embark on the trek that inspired this book but also stood by me every step of the way. Thank you for being my rock and my inspiration.

Lastly, to you, my dear Reader, for your support. Without you, there would not be a book.

ALSO BY ASHWINI SHENOY

SHIKHANDINI –

WARRIOR PRINCESS OF THE MAHABHARATA

Centuries have passed since the Great War of Kurukshetra, yet the name still evokes conflicting emotions. Neither man nor woman, was this all there was to Shikhandini, Princess of Panchala? Trained to be a warrior from early childhood, she was a fearsome fighter, an Athirathi. Her one ambition was to slay the Maharathi of Hasthinapur, in a transgenerational act of vengeance. In this retelling of epochal events, Shikhandini's transformation from woman to man, based on ancient medical science, is told with riveting intensity, as real as it is tragic in its final denouement. Now, in this new age, when the third gender is finally gaining acceptance and identity, it is perhaps time Shikhandini's story was retold in all its tragic glory

GIFT OF LIFE

Gift of Life is Shyamala's story. A seventy-year-old women, living alone in the small coastal town of Perdur. She is simple and relatable. Yet there is something bold and impressive about the way she lives her life alone, refusing to depend on anyone.

Carrying the burden of a tragic past, Shyamala believes that the only way she can survive is to follow a routine that allows her to spend most of her time outside the house that is a constant reminder of the past. For years this routine is her anchor. But what happens when the whole world is confronted by a challenge that halts normal life and Shyamala is confined to the house that screams of everything she has lost? Does she surrender to her fate, or does she fight back and rediscover herself? This beautifully narrated, deeply felt story is told with an innate understanding of both the frailty and the strength of human experience. Based on the nationwide lockdown of 2020, Gift of Life is a story of acceptance, hope and healing in times of great uncertainty.

www.ingramcontent.com/pod-product-compliance
Lightning Source LLC
Chambersburg PA
CBHW020322160726
47992CB00004B/1657

* 9 7 8 9 3 9 3 2 6 2 9 2 9 *